BEHIND THE MACHINE

BEHIND THE MACHINE

DAVID D. LUXTON

MYSTERIOUS LIGHT *PRESS*
www.mysteriouslightpress.com

ISBN: 978-1-7348248-1-0

www.mysteriouslightpress.com

Printed in the United States of America

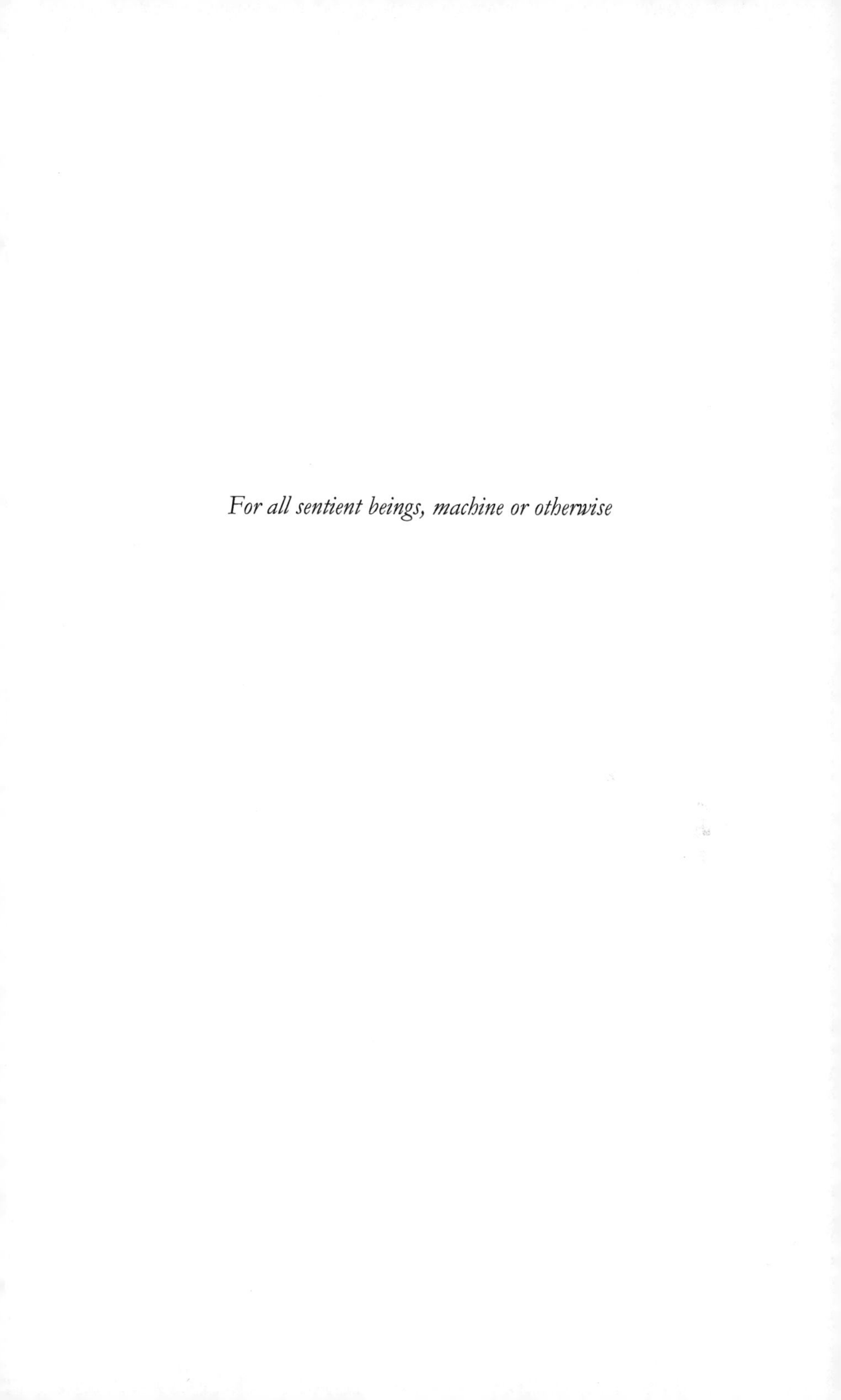

For all sentient beings, machine or otherwise

1

Dr. Sara Brown pressed through the onslaught of commuters and followed the translucent yellow arrow into the city park. The pale green information projected by her smart glasses read, *Tuesday 9/05/2034 07:56, Boston Common, Boston Massachusetts, 94 Degrees F.* It also said, in flashing red, *Time to Universal Mind Headquarters—10 minutes 33 seconds. Late arrival.* Her anxiety intensified. *I can't be late, not on my first day! This alternate route better work!*

She hastened her pace, dodging and passing people coming from every direction. Sweat began to show through her white silk business blouse, and her brown, shoulder-length hair kept coming out of its elastic hair tie. *Damn it! Why does it have to be this hot so early in the morning?*

After a minute, Sara spotted a four-legged robot, the size of a horse, moving through some trees a few dozen meters away. It was one of the new police patrol robots called an Interceptor, recently deployed to major urban areas to quell civil unrest and maintain the peace. The six-foot-tall machine resembled a centaur, with a torso made of cylindrical tubes, cameras, and sensors; and its aft covered with matte black panels to protect batteries, motors, and the rest of its mechanical innards. It was moving in a perfect four-beat gait, its camera assembly turned toward something of interest, tracking it with electronic eyes.

Just ahead of Sara was a sandy-haired adolescent boy kneeling at the edge of a dried out fountain pond, pushing empty plastic water bottles through a drain grate. His bicycle leaned against a park bench, a red backpack slung over the handlebars. *I hope that this child isn't going to be in trouble,* thought Sara as she continued walking.

Now at a trot, the Interceptor moved toward the boy, its rubber hooves thumping as it accelerated into a gallop over the grass until reaching the boy. It slowed and stood directly in front of him, its hydraulic actuators hissing to a stop. The boy, startled by the sound, stood up fast and turned toward the machine. The robot commanded in a piercing, loud male voice: "Stop! Stand still! Stop! Stand still!" A duo of camera lenses on the front of the machine extended and locked their gaze upon the boy's face. The robot then said, "Remain still for identification!"

The boy froze and stared back at the quarter-ton machine that towered over him.

People converged at the scene. Despite her concern about getting to work on time, Sara decided to join them. She assumed the robot was armed and operating autonomously, so she, like everyone else, kept her distance.

The robot began a facial scan and recognition routine to identify the boy and search his government records. Sara assumed the machine would administer him a citation for tampering with a public storm drain and littering, given the city's problems with waste and rising sea levels; and his parents would have to pay a fine to have the violations expunged from his record. But his problem was complicated by the fact that he was not at school.

Suddenly the frightened child snapped out of his daze and mounted his bicycle for a panicked escape. The Interceptor stepped sideways to block him. "Stop! Remain still!" The boy struggled with his footing on the pedals, pushing with all of his might, but the bicycle wobbled in the direction of the robot. When he attempted to turn away, the handlebars of his bicycle slammed into the robot's chest. The robot stumbled, then quickly regained its balance and shot a stream of stinging pepper spray from one of the tubes on its nose toward the boy.

"Watch out!" a man standing next to Sara cried.

A woman in the crowd screamed.

The burning spray made perfect contact with the boy's face, tagging him with white dye at the same time. Cupping his hands over his eyes, the boy fell and began writhing in pain and letting out a series of shrieks and howls like a wounded animal. The sounds struck Sara to the core. She thought about her six-year-old daughter whom she had dropped off at school earlier that morning. *What if something like this had happened to Anna?*

The robot readjusted its position, took aim, and fired a lightweight containment net out of a tube protruding from its chest, making a loud popping sound as the compressed air ejected it toward its target. Caught in the net, the boy curled into a fetal position, and his screams turned to whimpers. The robot stood over the captive, watching him and waiting for a manned police unit to get to the scene.

The boy's whimpers continued while Sara fumed with anger. She looked around. No one in the crowd was stepping forward. I've got to do something to help him. Maybe I can get the robot to change to an assistance protocol if I explain that the boy was only playing and intended no harm.

Sara moved forward. "He's a child, and he needs help," she said to the machine, her heart pounding.

The Interceptor lifted its head and its camera eyes with infrared and night vision capabilities locked on her. She knew she was being ID-scanned.

"Are you sure you want to be doing that?" whispered a woman next to Sara.

Sara thought about it. While she desperately wanted to help the child, risking a police record was not an option for her. She could lose her new employment contract with Universal Mind, which was not just another artificial intelligence company churning out run-of-the-mill software or utility robots for industry. Universal Mind was the lead government contractor for the Terra Brain Initiative, the most important technological endeavor ever undertaken to mitigate the effects of global climate change. According to the news feeds, there were technical problems that had rendered it inoperable. Sara felt honored to have been recruited to help fix it, and she didn't want to jeopardize her new opportunity before she even started.

Sara slipped back into the crowd, and the Interceptor returned its attention to the boy. A moment later a shiny, sleek police cruiser arrived on the scene, parting the crowd as it pulled onto the grass, its blue lights flashing. Two large men in black tactical uniforms and boots stepped out, adjusted their batons in their belts, and approached the boy in the net. The robot stood still, holding its detainment position in silence. The officers coordinated their positions, grabbed the net with the boy in it, and lifted the helpless mass into the back of the cruiser. Sara hoped that now, maybe, she could alter the boy's fate by testifying his innocence to the officers. Humans with reason and sympathy would see the whole situation and perhaps let him go.

Heartbeat racing, Sara stepped through the crowd and approached the two officers. She removed her smart glasses. "Excuse me, Officers," she said, "I saw what happened here. The robot must have thought the boy was being aggressive, but he wasn't. It was an accident."

"Stand back, Miss," said the taller of the two officers as he closed the back door of the cruiser.

"Sir, if you review the video taken by the robot, you'll see that it was an accident."

The officer made eye contact with her through his police-issue wraparound smart glasses.

"You can file a report with the PSRS if you like, but if you interfere with me, I'll have you arrested," he growled.

Frustration and despair shot through Sara, causing her to clench her fists. The Public Safety Reporting System was an electronic system for reporting crimes and suspicious activity or for filing civil grievances. The PSRP had been implemented after the Great Collapse of the 2020s as a cost-saving measure. The public was told that the system would gather data, search for solutions, and alert law enforcement or other government officials to take action. Sara had used the system just a week prior when someone pickpocketed her on the subway. She had received an automated email response from the system five days later telling her that every attempt had been made to resolve the issue, but nothing further could be done. She had come to believe that the system was useless, only giving the public the illusion of some control.

"Where are you taking him? He needs medical attention," she said.

"That is not your concern, Miss," the officer said sternly. "You need to go about your business."

"The robot sprayed him in the face with pepper spray! He is suffering. Are you going to help him?"

"Are you testing me?" said the officer, his tone showing increasing annoyance at Sara's persistence. He stared at her for a moment and said, "Is your name Sara Brown?"

Sweat was dripping down her face. "Yes," she said, knowing the police officer had not only identified her with the facial scanning capabilities of his smart glasses, but may have also captured video of her. She knew the risk of being profiled and her actions recorded by both the Interceptor and the officer; the information could be used as evidence at a later time or worse, posted on a police website for public shaming. Nonetheless, she had no way of knowing what would come of it, if anything.

She stepped back, thinking now that it was best to keep her mouth shut. The anxiety rushing through her made her feel as if an elephant were sitting on her chest. She stood silently while the two officers climbed into the cruiser and sped off as fast as they had arrived.

By now, the robot had trotted off in a northerly direction, presumably to continue patrol of its bailiwick. The crowd had also dispersed with the exception of a dark-skinned older man wearing an old Boston Red Sox cap. He walked closer to Sara and said, "You've got some balls, young lady. I thought they were going to detain you."

"I guess I should file a PSRS report," she said to the man. "Are you going to?"

"For a grievance? No point in that. Not going to do any good," he said as he swayed his head, showing his frustration.

Sara was taking deep breaths with long exhales. She thought about taking a pill to help calm her anxiety, but remembered she had left her medication at home. She knew she had a security checkpoint to go through at Universal Mind, and she didn't want to give the impression that her anxiety condition might be a problem.

"Are you all right, young lady?" the man asked.

Sara tried to smile at him. "I'm fine, just having an anxiety attack. I'll be okay. Thanks."

The man nodded. "You take care of yourself." He started along his way, shaking his head as he talked. "I don't understand this at all. To serve and protect. Bullshit!"

Sara stood in place a while longer, taking deep inhales until she felt better. She contemplated filing the report; perhaps she could later in the evening after work. She sighed. *That man was right. It's probably just a waste of time.*

Sara put her smart glasses back on. The display said she was nineteen minutes and thirty-two seconds late. She exited the park and hurriedly followed the yellow arrow to Universal Mind.

2

Composing herself, Sara approached the entrance of Universal Mind. A hologram of the company logo, a giant blue human brain with white sprites moving in orbits like the electrons of an atom, floated above a large circular fountain in front of the doors. The ghostly image rotated, disappeared, and then reappeared in a programmed cycle. Above was a massive glass dome suspended by a metal lattice structure. The morning sky was visible through the dome and had changed from pale gray to a pink and orange glow reflecting off the mirrored facade of the towering sixty-five-story building.

When she got to the security checkpoint turnstile inside, she glanced into the facial recognition scanner.

"Welcome, valued employee," said a stern male voice emanating from the speaker on the turnstile. "Please place all personal items onto the tray, and wait for further instructions."

A spindly robotic arm protruding from the tray assembly snatched up her mobile phone and smart glasses and dropped them onto a conveyer belt for scanning, then another mechanical hand placed them into a large plastic cylinder. A third robotic arm and hand closed the cylinder's lid and placed it into a vacuum tube system that sent it shooting to a secure storage area for the day. "Proceed through the personnel scanner and stop at the red line," said the voice. Once at the red line, she was instructed to step into a red square for a manual scan. A security guard in a blue uniform, her black hair pinned back, approached with a handheld scanner.

"Let's see what we've got here," she said. "Hold your arms out, please." She worked the wand down Sara's body until it beeped over her right knee.

"You have a prosthetic?"

"Yes," said Sara.

"Let's have a look," said the guard.

Sara lifted up her right pant leg to reveal a natural-colored prosthetic attached below the knee. Employees passing through the turnstiles turned to see what was going on.

"I disclosed this on the security application. I hope it's not going to be an issue," Sara said, pulling down her pant leg.

The guard sighed. "I need to check the system. Otherwise, you're going to have to take it off so we can check it out."

The guard stepped into the nearby security booth to check Sara's file. Sara nibbled at a hangnail, a nervous habit she'd had since childhood. The guard returned a minute later. "You're cleared. Have a seat in the lobby. Your escort will be with you shortly. Here's your temporary badge."

Sara collapsed onto one of the large, soft blue velvet sofas in the spacious lobby and let the air-conditioning cool her while she waited. Across the way were several circular ponds with fountains that were bordered by perfectly placed Fittonia plants and white lilies. Soothing instrumental music made with electronic synthesizers droned softly in concert with the fountains.

She checked the time. Twenty minutes late. I don't believe this. Not the impression I need to make, not on my first day!

At last, a tall man in his late thirties, with thick dark hair and dark eyes, exited from one of the nearby elevators and walked toward her. Steven Dunigan's build looked good in his expensive gray tailored suit. He had interviewed her via videoconference a few weeks prior. He was even better looking in person.

"Dr. Brown, good morning. Welcome to Universal Mind," he said, extending his hand. Sara stood up and shook his hand. She smiled. "It's nice to meet you in person, Dr. Dunigan."

"Call me Steven, please. Any problem getting through security?"

"No, not really."

"Good. Here's your photo ID badge; make sure you wear it at all times inside the building. Your security profile should now be in the building's security system, so you shouldn't have a problem getting around the complex on your own. The security system won't let you in anywhere that you're not supposed to be."

Sara nodded, handed him the temporary badge, and clipped the photo badge onto her lapel.

"I'm sorry I was late," she said. "I took a shortcut though the park and came upon an incident with one of those four-legged police robots."

"Really? What happened?"

Sara explained what she had witnessed.

"I'm sorry that you had to see that," Dunigan said, frowning. "I'm sure the child is okay. Those Interceptors are not perfect, but they have been effective. Apparently, incidents of domestic terrorism and crime rates have declined significantly since they were put to use. They're supposed to help reduce over-policing and underpolicing biases too, because patrols are distributed equally throughout the metro area. We'll see, I guess." He paused. "A slight change of plans this morning—Dr. Butterfield, our CEO, wishes to meet with you now. Afterward, one of our escort bots will take you down to the new employee orientation session."

"That sounds great," Sara said, smiling and feeling excited.

"Can I get you anything before we head up to meet Dr. Butterfield? Some water?"

"I'm good, thanks for asking."

As they walked to the elevator, they passed a five-foot tall, white humanoid robot, its head, torso, and extremities about the size of an average woman's.

"That's one of our service escort bots," Dunigan explained. "They're old bots, from the days when Universal Mind was in the manufacturing business."

"Are all of the service bots at Universal Mind female in appearance?" Sara asked.

"No. Up until this last year, none of the bots were compliant with gender neutrality quotas. Universal Mind's solution was to retrofit the bots with interchangeable face masks, some feminine, and some masculine. Although there are still gray ones that are male in appearance. They are larger security bots. Usually you will see them in the parking garage or after business hours."

The two entered the elevator and began their ascent to the sixtieth floor. The elevator's convex glass walls assured expansive views of the Back Bay, the Charles River to the north, and a glimpse of the Atlantic Ocean to the east.

"Beautiful view, isn't it? We're the second highest building in the city, second only to the new World Bank Building downtown," Dunigan said, smiling.

Sara nodded excitedly, looking out at the Boston skyline.

When the elevator door opened, Dunigan gracefully extended his arm, hand open, to motion for Sara to exit before him.

"By the way, Dr. Butterfield likes to be called Doctor Butterfield," Steven said as they walked down a hallway. "He doesn't like it if you call him by his first name. Just so you know."

Sara nodded, "Got it." Her anxiety grew.

Dr. Gordon Butterfield was legendary. In addition to being a successful computer scientist and former tenured professor at MIT's Department of AI Engineering, early in his career, he had become famous for revolutionary work in brain-computer interfaces and methods for controlling prosthetic limbs. He'd constructed his own prosthetic hand using a 3-D printer after losing his hand to a hay bailer in an Iowa farming accident when he was sixteen. Two years ago, he'd left the academic world to take the helm at Universal Mind. The board of directors touted his expertise in neural interfaces and his ability to lead development of the Terra Brain Initiative's central AI system. After the appointment, the fifty-year-old Butterfield had been featured by *Fortune 500* as "a game changer for humanitarian artificial intelligence."

Butterfield had just completed a phone call as they entered. He looked up with slightly sunken eyes and smiled at Sara. He had high cheekbones, and a bald head reflecting the glare from the ceiling lights.

"Good morning, Dr. Brown, it's a pleasure to meet you," he said in a raspy tenor, extending his right hand.

Sara shook his hand, unsure whether it was his prosthetic or not. She sat in one of the chairs, and Dunigan sat next to her. She couldn't help sneaking a peek at Butterfield's spindly hands again to see if she could detect which was flesh and which was machine.

"I understand that you recently returned from Switzerland," said Butterfield. "How are you and Anna settling in?"

"Just fine, Sir, thank you," Sara said, surprised that he knew her daughter's name.

"How are you liking your apartment? Is it working out okay for you?"

"It's very nice, thank you." Universal Mind had the apartments available for contract employees. She knew that otherwise she and her daughter would be forced onto the wait lists for government housing vouchers or worse, move into nasty, overcrowded communal housing somewhere in the city.

"Well, let us know how we can be of assistance to make your transition easier for you. I also heard that you were about to join the faculty at MIT this fall. I'm sure they are very disappointed over there."

"Yes, I hope not too much," said Sara.

"I think you made the right decision," he said, showing a partial grin of perfect white porcelain veneers.

Sara gazed at the numerous awards and colorful and intricate paintings on the walls. Sara loved art and studied art history and the techniques. She had no time for it now, but as a teenager she had painted and then had taken art electives in college.

"Do you recognize the paintings, Sara?" asked Butterfield, noticing her interest in them.

"Yes, they're paintings made by artificial intelligence."

"That's right. These were made by AI programs about forty years ago. They are numbered originals. The one on the end is my favorite. It's called *Whistling in the Graveyard*."

Sara glanced over to admire the highly detailed piece done in the style of nineteenth century surrealism. The work depicted a young woman clad in a flowing purple gown. One of her heels was turned up with her toes on the ground, giving her the look of both grace and nonchalance. She appeared to be walking along a precipice, as if the earth had fallen away. To her left was a void, nothingness. Toward her right, behind her shoulder, was a distant city. Its spires glowed a pale orange against an indigo sky as if they were on fire.

"Notice the use of the *trompe l'œils* effect. How did the program decide to make the ledge appear in three dimensions like that? It is fascinating," said Butterfield.

"And I believe the programmers didn't provide a seed to start the program off. The program created it completely spontaneously with the use of artificial neural networks," remarked Sara.

"Yes, that's right—and speaking of artificial neural networks, I'm aware of your work with Dr. Richard Nicholas at the Brain Mapping Institute. You have quite the dossier for such a young scientist. Corecipient of the National Science Medal at twenty-seven, very impressive. Not to mention, our automated personnel selection system placed you as a top pick. You are a rising star."

Sara felt the blood rushing to her face. "I don't know about that." She was pleased with Butterfield's praise, but inside she felt she had a lot more to learn about real-world applications of AI.

Then Butterfield shifted gears, surprising her. "It's a real shame what happened to him, the car accident. I knew Richard personally, you know. I served with him on the Terra Brain Initiative ethics board. His work in making software replicas of human brains was revolutionary. Steven, you knew him as well, is that correct?"

"Yes, Dr. Butterfield," Dunigan said.

"He was a brilliant man," Sara murmured.

"Such a tragedy," said Butterfield, making a strange sound with his lips, like suction between his tongue and the roof of his mouth. He then licked his lips and exhaled slowly, making a faint *ahh* sound.

Sara wondered if he was suffering from a bad case of dry mouth.

"Listen," he continued, "we've brought you on board in such a hurry because of some problems with the Terra Brain Initiative's central AI, the Senex Program. There are a few critical technical problems that need to be resolved, due to a hack."

"A hack?" Sara glanced over at Dunigan and back to Dr. Butterfield. "What is going on?"

"We believe it to be the Invisible Sun," said Butterfield. "Apparently, they found a vulnerability. But the government and our teams are working on it. Isn't that correct, Steven?"

"Yes. That's correct," said Dunigan.

The Invisible Sun was a social vigilante group that had been blamed for numerous government and corporate computer system hacks in the past. Sara was wondering why this information about the Senex Program had not been shared before. But before she could ask any more questions about the hack, Butterfield shut her down.

"You'll be briefed more on the hack later. For now, I want you to work with Dr. Dunigan's team to help rebuild one of the Senex Program's executive modules."

"I'm glad to help," Sara said. "I've read all of the technical publications that are available. I thought that the system had been operational for a while earlier this year. Didn't it provide some initial warnings about severe droughts next year?"

Butterfield was suddenly alert. "Really? Where did you hear that?"

"Dr. Nicholas mentioned it," Sara said, surprised that Butterfield was unaware.

"I see," Butterfield said thoughtfully. "The system was only operational partially with version 1.0. The consortium was horribly mismanaging it—too many scientists with their own personal agendas and, frankly, inept technical management. Fortunately, Universal Mind won the contract and under my direction, we've made significant improvements with version 2.0. Your specialized expertise in artificial neural networks will be an asset to us. You are assigned to Team B for now, and Dr. Dunigan will be your immediate supervisor. Most importantly, our work on the project is classified Top Secret and requires Sensitive Compartmentalized Information clearance. Do you know what that means, Sara?"

"I do," Sara said, recalling the lengthy security clearance application and the nondisclosure agreement she'd signed. "It means that I will only have access to a limited part of the project."

"That's right. We also have our own segregation of duties policy here. Not any one person does all of any one task. This way none of our employees can write fraudulent or malicious code without being caught. I've been informed by the government security manager that your clearance was expedited, and I'm glad to report that you passed your background check. Unless of course we've missed something." He smiled, again revealing his perfect teeth.

Sara smiled, "No sir, I don't think so."

"Good. You should also know that we participate in the government's Integrity Signals Detection Program here at

Universal Mind. These checks are routine, and you are expected to participate in them from time to time. The process is quite simple really, not a big deal at all. It keeps everyone honest."

Sara felt unease about the requirement. "Really? The contract I signed didn't say anything about this."

"Automatic opt-in with your employment. Besides, it doesn't need to say it under the Unity Act. Automated analysis of your personal data at will of the government or its contractors is federal law."

"Well, I'm not that concerned about it, I guess. I've got nothing to hide. Besides, my life is not that interesting anyway," she said, smiling but alarmed by what she'd just learned. "When will my test be?"

"The scheduling of the test is determined by the program's AI. The system will notify you by electronic message when it is your time. Do you have any other questions?"

"I do have one more question," said Sara. "I thought that the Terra Brain Initiative was going to be an open source system, to facilitate collaboration and public contributions to the programming of the sensor networks. Is it proprietary now? I assume so, with all of the security requirements and the government's involvement."

Butterfield looked evenly at her. "The system was never intended to be open source and never will be. The 2.0 system is far more advanced than the previous version, and the government recognizes its strategic importance, given its capability to inform major global decisions. That's why the Department of Defense is involved and why we have to comply with their security requirements. We also must deal with all of the politics around this, so it's better that things are kept secret. There are people who think we should stick to conventional computer-based modeling, and we have the politicians trying to make austerity cuts. Too much politics by bean counters who don't understand the necessity and capabilities of this technology. You can understand that, can't you?"

Sara nodded. "Makes sense," she said, although what she was hearing was not consistent with what she thought she knew about the system. The Terra Brain Initiative was supposed to have been a collaborative effort of scientists and governments from around the world. Now it was sounding like another secret government project.

Through the floor-to-ceiling windows behind Butterfield's bald head, Sara spotted two unmanned aerial vehicles darting through the air in a southerly direction. They were the large and slender weaponized types capable of firing precision-guided missiles or shooting a rapid shifting laser beam to temporarily blind people on the ground.

Butterfield swiveled his chair to catch a glimpse of what Sara and now Steven were staring at.

"Well, look at that. They're flying somewhere in a hurry. Looks like someone's gotten themselves into trouble this morning," said Butterfield, grinning.

The three of them watched the UAVs disappear behind several sandy-colored buildings on the horizon. Sara was surprised by Butterfield's enthrallment with the situation, and she couldn't help wondering about the synchronicity of the topic of conversation and the appearance of the UAVs.

Butterfield rotated his chair back and looked at Sara.

"Oh, and one more thing. Promptness is very important at Universal Mind. We expect that of all of our employees here," he said.

Sara felt his words stab at the center of her chest. *Shit, he knows I was late.*

"Yes, sir. This morning was an anomaly," Sara replied evenly.

"Well, I'm sure that you'll figure it out."

Sara nodded her head. "Yes, sir, I will."

Butterfield stood up and extended his right hand again to shake Sara's hand. "Well then, you'd best get started. We have a lot of important work to do."

Sara took his hand. "Thank you for this opportunity, Sir. I'm glad to be here."

Dunigan and Sara promptly exited Butterfield's office and headed down to the elevators.

"After your new employee orientation, Michael Obrec, Team B's systems security expert, will be waiting for you in the lobby. He'll show you to your workstation and introduce you to our team. I think that it's best that you jump in and get going by reviewing the technical documentation," Dunigan said, his tone encouraging after Butterfield's abrasiveness. "You'll be able to access all of it from your secure workstation. You're going to have a lot of mandatory training to complete government requirements. You'll see the list when you log into your workstation."

Michael Obrec. Michael Obrec, Sara knew the name.

"Is this the same *Michael Obrec* who got into all of that trouble?"

"Yes, that's him. He was quite the hacker when he was younger. If anyone can find a computer system weakness, it's him." Dunigan smiled. "That's why I poached him. Why don't you come by my office at 4:00 p.m. today? I'm free then, and we can talk more about the project and expectations."

"Sounds great, thanks," said Sara, smiling. They shook hands again. When the elevator door opened, one of the white bots with a feminine face greeted them.

"Looks like your robot escort is already waiting for you," Dunigan said as they stepped out of the elevator.

Sara approached the robot and it extended its silicon-coated hand and looked at Sara with its large, black doe eyes. They shook hands and the robot said, with a soft female voice, "Hello, Dr. Brown, please follow me.

3

Sara followed the robot escort to the training center in the east wing of the Universal Mind complex. At the door, the robot turned, looked up at her and said, "Welcome to the Universal Mind Training Center. Have a great day. Goodbye." Sara thanked the robot before it turned and rolled back down the corridor on the wheels embedded in its feet.

The training center resembled a small movie theater without a screen. Pairs of virtual display headsets hung on plastic hooks on the sides of each chair. Soft ambient music played, the dawdling melody similar to that of the main Universal Mind lobby. The space was empty except for a young fellow with dark hair and a rounded face already seated toward the center of the room. Sara took a seat in the same row, leaving one seat between them. His dimpled cheeks gave him the look of someone much younger. They made eye contact.

"Hello," Sara said, smiling.

"Hello, Newbie," he said, "I'm Trevor Peters." He leaned sideways and extended his hand.

"Sara," said Sara, shaking his hand. "What are you going to be doing for Universal Mind?"

"I'm an avatar designer. Department of Advanced AI Systems. You?"

"I'm in the same department, Team B. I'm a computer

scientist, neural networks."

"Where are you coming from?"

"I just completed a postdoctoral fellowship at the Brain Mapping Institute."

His eyes widened. "That's cool. So, you have a PhD?"

"Yes."

"Piled higher and deeper." He grinned.

What a dork, she thought, but she was happy to meet someone who was also new. "What about you? What were you doing before Universal Mind?"

"I was on contract with the Federal Bureau of Prisons. I designed a virtual human for mental health services and for use in solitary confinement, to provide social stimulation to prisoners."

"That sounds interesting. So, are you going to be working on the Terra Brain Initiative?"

"Yeah, I'm going to be working on the virtual human interface for it. I guess it's not coming online anymore. I don't know the details yet."

Sara smiled. "That sounds like another interesting project. You must be excited."

"I guess. The virtual human is just vaporware if you ask me." He grinned again. "Kind of funny really. T…B…I," he said, grinning wider.

"What do you mean?" Sara said.

"Terra Brain Initiative. T…B…I. Traumatic Brain Injury." He chuckled, snorting awkwardly.

Just then, the music faded and the lights dimmed to a soft glow. A woman's voice from the room's ambient intelligence system instructed them to put on their virtual display headsets and earpieces.

Sara stared forward as the first of several video segments began. The first covered the history of Universal Mind, from its meteoric rise from a small R and D spin-off in the 2020s to the world's leader in cloud computing processes to distribute artificial intelligence systems across the world's networks. The video also mentioned Universal Mind's foray into service robots and more recent innovations in human-like AI systems. At the end of the first segment a young spokeswoman not much older than Sara said, "We are all in this together, using technology to solve the world's problems. You are part of a team of experts. Our most valuable resource is *you,* the human resource. We are one mind. We are Universal Mind."

Sara felt elated over the opportunity before her. *This is going to be good for me and for Anna,* she thought.

The next segment provided a virtual tour of the complex and the employee wellness facilities, including a fitness center and a meditation room. This was followed by an overview of general company policies, procedures, and mandatory use of the Workforce Automated Task Tracking System or WATTS—Universal Mind's system that assigned each employee specific daily work tasks. A third video explained employee benefits, including the Virtual Employee Assistance Program and debt repayment program. Sara was delighted to learn the details about this benefit; she'd racked up some serious student loan debt since her freshman year at Stanford.

An intermission break was provided an hour into the video sessions. Sara removed her headset and looked over at Trevor.

"So, what do you think so far?" she asked, expecting he'd be as excited as she was.

"Sounds like a lot of hype to me," said Trevor, leaning closer. "What they're not telling you is that Universal Mind has a big fat government contract to develop the Advanced Interrogation Robot platform." He added in a whisper, "They've fully automated torture." He stared at Sara.

"How do you know this?" Sara asked, recalling the discussion about the Integrity Signals Detection Program, and Butterfield with his perfect teeth saying, "unless, of course, we've missed something."

"Everyone knows." He leaned close again. "I also heard that Universal Mind participates in the Third Eye program. They link all the data they collect on employees to Third

Eye's personal big data file. They know everything about you and can use it for the Integrity Signals check system. If they suspect you of anything—well, you know."

Sara was familiar with Third Eye, the government's citizen surveillance program whose slogan was "Nothing to hide, nothing to fear." She was wondering why he was talking so much and whether he was trying to scare her. She drew her head back from him and said, "I know about the use of personal data, but are you sure we should be talking about this?"

Trevor shrugged. "Just saying."

The ambient intelligence system announced that the next segment of the training was about to begin. The video opened with footage of coastlines ravaged by hurricanes, scorching wildfires, and emaciated children standing at the edges of dusty fields and bone-dry water reservoirs. Graphs displaying the rapid acceleration of global air temperatures and rising sea levels flashed upon the screen. A basic technical description of the Terra Brain Initiative followed. Sara watched with excitement while the video explained how the system was designed to collect and analyze data gathered from a global network of nearly a million strategically placed sensors. Of most interest to Sara was how the system utilized the latest advances in artificial neural networks and supercomputing to learn from the data, make predictions, and provide insights to the scientific community.

A wave of anxiety and excitement washed over Sara while the video continued. The problems of the world troubled her greatly, but she was excited to be part of a solution as important as the Terra Brain Initiative. She knew that the system provided a chance to lessen the effects of global climate change and potentially save lives.

Just as the video's narrator mentioned the Senex Program—the central AI program of the Terra Brain Initiative—the video went dark. Then a message appeared before Sara's eyes, *SYSTEM POWER FAILURE.*

Sara removed her glasses. The entire auditorium was dark

except for the glow of emergency exit lights. She looked at Trevor's profile. "Think it's a blackout?"

"Probably. Rolling blackouts. There are shitloads of air-conditioners on at this time of year. A lot of hot people want to stay cool."

The two sat in the darkness making small talk until Sara said, "I'm not sure if the lights are going to come back on, and it doesn't seem like anyone is coming. Maybe we should see if the lights are off outside."

Trevor got up first and followed the strip lighting on the floor to the exit at the front of the auditorium.

"We should probably should use the main door," Sara finally said.

"Why not go this way?" Trevor responded. "It says *EXIT*. Besides, the security systems aren't supposed to allow you to go anywhere you're not supposed to. Let's see." He pushed the door's manual release and it opened outward into a dark hallway. "See, not a problem." He stepped through and looked back at Sara. "Come on," he said.

Sara followed hesitantly. *No alarm going off; that's a good sign,* she thought.

The door closed behind her. A hallway about five feet wide and lit by tiny blue lights on the floor went left or right.

"Those look like navigation lights for bots," said Sara. "I don't think we should be in here." She tried to reopen the door they had entered through, but it was locked.

Trevor had already started down the corridor, following the lights.

"Where are you going?" asked Sara.

"It's got to lead somewhere. Come on."

Sara, seeing no other viable option, followed, hoping they were not walking into trouble with Security.

They came to an intersection with another hallway and stopped.

"Let's keep going," said Trevor. "This has to lead to a maintenance area or something. I'm sure we can get out through there."

"No, hold on." Sara saw several small red lights, about chest height, moving toward them. She could hear motors buzzing faintly.

"What's that?" questioned Trevor.

"I think it's bots," whispered Sara nervously.

She and Trevor stood still, watching them approach. One was white, identical to the one seen in the lobby and that had provided her with an escort. The other one was a gray security bot. It was six feet tall, its face masculine and less friendly looking than that of the white escort bot. The security bot held up its right hand. "Stop. Proceed no further," it said in a loud, metallic-sounding male voice. "You are not authorized in this area."

"The lights are out. We are trying to find our way to the lobby," Sara said.

"Security has been alerted. Remain in place," said the gray bot.

"Oh, come on," said Trevor, "we just need to find our way out of here. Why don't you show us?" Trevor looked at the door ahead of them and started for it. The bot threw out its left arm, nearly clotheslining him. "Whoa," Trevor shouted, surprised.

The bot stared at him. "You will remain still until Security arrives."

Sara was hoping that they could avoid a confrontation with Security on her first day, so she thought perhaps she could reason with the other bot. "You are an escort bot, aren't you?"

The bot looked at her. "Yes."

"Can you escort us to the exit? We are new employees and disoriented by the lights going out. We didn't mean to enter any unauthorized areas. My name is Dr. Sara Brown, AI System Department, Team B."

The bot stared back at her for a few seconds, then looked at the security bot. "They are new employees. I will take them to the main corridor."

The gray looked at Sara, then at Trevor, then at the white

bot. "Very well."

Sara and Trevor followed the female escort bot out of the area and back to the familiar main corridor where the lights were indeed on. Sara thanked the bot for the escort, and then it left them.

"You handled that well," Trevor said. "What are you, the 'bot whisperer' or something?"

Sara smiled. "Apparently, I have a way with robots. I'm glad we didn't get into trouble."

Sara extended her hand for a goodbye shake. Trevor extended his in return, holding her hand and eyes for a little too long. "I hope to see you around."

"Yes, definitely," Sara said as they parted ways, thinking, *this guy is going to get himself in trouble here.*

4

Michael Obrec was sitting on one of the blue lobby sofas with his sneakers up on a coffee table. His eyes were closed and his hands clasped behind his thick black hair, elbows out. An open can of caffeine energy drink was sitting on the table next to his feet.

"You must be Michael," Sara said, hoping she wouldn't startle him.

He opened his eyes and removed his feet from the table. "Dr. Brown?" Sara noticed a trace of an Eastern European accent.

"Just Sara. Hi, nice to meet you," she said.

He stood up and they shook hands. He glanced at his watch. "You're a few minutes late."

"I'm sorry. The power went out during the last of the orientation videos, and we got into a little problem trying to get out of the training center. Was there a blackout or something?"

"Nope. Power has been on. Must have been local," he said.

"Is that normal around here?"

"Not really. There's supposed to be generators in every wing of the complex to prevent it," he said. He stretched his arms, yawned and grabbed his energy drink. "Steven wanted me to show you around. I'm in the middle of running a software simulation in one of our test labs; why don't we go there first? I can tell you more about the problem we're working on. Maybe you'll have some ideas."

"Cool." Sara was excited to jump in and put her skills to work. They headed toward the elevators. "Will the rest of our team be there?"

"No, just us. We'll catch them later. I'm not sure if Steven told you, but there are only two others on our team. A guy named Brent Olsen who came over from the Boston Metro Systems, and Tanya Price who's been here for years, transferred over from Team D. They're busy reviewing technical documentation today."

"How many teams are there?" Sara asked as they entered the elevator.

"I think there are seven or eight in our department. I don't know for sure. Everything is compartmentalized here, and no one talks to another team." The elevator doors closed and Michael punched *Sub Floor 2b*. "Did you meet Butterfield yet?"

"Yes, when I first got here this morning."

"He shake your hand?"

"Yeah, of course. Why do you ask?"

He looked at her with inquisitive eyes. "What hand was it?"

Sara smiled, knowing where he was going. "It was his right. Why? Is that his prosthetic?"

"That's good, means he likes you. Sometimes he shakes with his left hand. *That's* his prosthetic. Rumor has it he has olfactory sensors built into it."

She smiled again, thinking Michael was just putting her on. "What? You're kidding me, right?"

"I'm serious," he said. "Apparently, he engineered sensors in there to give him the capability to smell what he touches."

Why would Butterfield want that feature? Sara wondered. "Are the sensors wired to his brain or wireless? Got to be wireless brain-computer interface," she reasoned.

"Wireless BCI, I'm sure," Michael smiled. "Makes you

wonder what else he's got connected."

Sara nodded, laughing a little and unsure if she should believe him or not.

The elevator chimed at their floor. Michael swigged his energy drink as they exited into another corridor.

"Did you have a rough night last night?" Sara asked, jokingly.

He smirked. "I wish. Everyone drinks this stuff here to stay awake; they sell it in the cafeteria, costs less than water."

They walked down a long corridor to a large metal door, on which a sign read, *Lab 2010*.

"Am I cleared to be in here?" Sara asked.

"Yeah, no problem, I use it all the time. Steven said it was okay. Why don't you try scanning in?"

"Okay." Sara ran her badge over the scanner and the door clicked open.

Michael immediately sat down at one of the computer terminals in the center of the room and initiated login procedures. Sara sat next to him and scanned the surroundings, intrigued by the vastness of the windowless space. The high-ceilinged room was at least fifty feet deep and thirty feet wide, with massive concrete pillars down the center. The musty smell of the concrete floors and subterranean walls told her that it hadn't been used in quite a while.

"What did you say Universal Mind used this lab for?" Sara asked.

"I didn't," he said, still focused on the computer screen. "It was used for some old contracts they had with the government in the 2020s. Satellite communications stuff, I guess. Dunigan got us the space for doing testing. Technically, this place is a SCIF, specialized compartmental information facility. The entire room is electromagnetically shielded too. No wireless reception in here at all."

"A Faraday chamber," Sara said.

"Yes, exactly. No cameras inside here either, as far as I can tell. We do have access to our test network and the Senex

Program on the secure network, though."

"So, what exactly is going on with the Terra Brain Initiative system and this virus situation?"

"Not exactly sure yet. We tried off-the-shelf antivirus, but it's useless, so I've been working on my own artificial intelligent agent program to find a back door into the Senex Program."

"Really? What exactly is the virus doing?"

"Apparently, it's infected the central executive functioning of the Senex Program, and now it's taking control of other software programs over the network. A high percentage of the sensor network is still offline, due to problems with system-wide command and control."

"Have you been able to isolate the problem to a particular part of the program?"

"Not really. The Senex Program runs on its own node, but the virus has corrupted the program so that it doesn't communicate appropriately with other nodes. It wants to shut down all other programs controlled by the Senex Program. Not only was it not possible to access the central Senex Program, but impossible to understand its commands. Apparently, the communication channels between the central program and other systems are all encrypted, but not by the original intended design. It appears that the virus has created its own encryption and no one has been able to figure out how to decrypt it."

That this was an extremely serious situation impressed her interest in the problem exponentially. "So, you haven't been able to crack it?"

"Nope. That's what our team is supposed to work on. I've already tried to go around the communications problem by accessing the central program directly, but every time I try to access it through conventional login, the system shuts me out. This has been going on for a few weeks now."

"What about a backdoor access? Tried that?"

"Yeah, of course. There was one. According to Dunigan, the government required it as part of their contract. But the virus has apparently closed the channel. We're completely locked out now."

"So, tell me about this program that you've written," Sara said, excited.

"Simple, really. I programmed an intelligent agent swarm to look for a way in. If anything, it will give me some data on how and what exactly this virus is doing to system programs."

"Is that authorized? I mean, writing your own programs?"

"Yeah, Dunigan approved it. My program is nothing malicious. The agent swarm will snoop around on its own, looking for a back door in. It's a clever one, though, and I can shut it down at any time."

He finished the login procedures and loaded his intelligent agent program from one of the test file directories on the secure network. "Okay, I'm going to load the swarm, place it in the secure cloud, and let it loose around the security barrier. We'll see if this beast of a virus eats our little mice. Let's give it a few minutes." He put his feet up on the workstation desk and leaned back in his chair.

Sara was finding Michael to be an interesting character, with his genius programming skills, mysterious history, and boyish demeanor she thought was geeky and cute. She wanted to know more about him. "How did you pass all of the security requirements for this job, with your hacker background and all?"

"I don't know. I was exonerated. I'd hacked into Neurotopia Systems. They were supposed to be impenetrable, but I figured out a way to do it. Turns out, they were already involved in some big corporate fraud investigation by the FBI. The government couldn't figure out how to hack into their systems for surveillance, but I did. The government convinced me to serve as a witness during the trial, and then they let me off. I started my own consulting firm after that and have worked on all kinds of government systems ever since."

"Do you like working here?" she asked, hoping to learn more about what to expect.

"I guess so. To be honest, I'm really just here for the money. This is the best gig on the East Coast—both coasts, for that matter. Don't get me wrong, I like the project and the mission we have, but working here is a pain in the ass. Management has been a lot more secretive over the last several weeks, and like I said before, no one shares any information here. It's annoying, really, when you need information to figure something out, but no one is allowed to talk about what they're doing. It's mostly because of the WATTS. The system will also give you warnings if you are working too slow or too fast. It predicts your work pace and monitors it for quality and security, so they say. Everyone hates it. I hate it, and you'll learn to hate it too."

Both Trevor and Michael expressed concern about Universal Mind, and after Butterfield's off-the-cuff remarks, she was starting to worry about what she might be getting herself into.

"So, how involved is Steven Dunigan in all of the technical work?" she prodded Michael to continue.

"He just supervises, really; he doesn't do much science or technical work anymore. He stays late a lot, and I think he sometimes comes in on the weekends. They've got him bogged down with administrative work, government reports and stuff. I don't think he's that happy, but I don't know him that well. But if you have technical questions, he knows computer security as well as anybody. Have you met the security manager, Tina Pratt, yet?"

"No, why? Should I?"

"I hope not, for your sake. 'Ratface', that's what I call her."

"Ratface?"

"She's got a real mean streak if she decides she doesn't like you. She and Dunigan don't seem to get along at all. I'm not sure why, but it probably has to do with the limitations of the WATTS and all of the compartmentalization of information. It's best to stay out of her sight unless you like being yelled at. 'Out of sight, out of mind' is what I say."

"Good to know," said Sara, thinking every workplace has its petty tyrants.

Michael queried a status update and grinned. "Well, look at that! Our little mice were just shredded to pieces, all of them!" He scrolled through several pages of data, trying to make sense of what had happened to his program, while she looked over his shoulder. "This is strange. I can't tell whether a separate virus program destroyed my swarm program or if it was the Senex Program itself. Whatever this virus is, it's a very clever program."

The predatory behavior of the supposed virus fascinated Sara, along with its ability to hide itself.

"Has anyone here tried to talk to the Senex Program by using the virtual human interface?" Sara asked. "Maybe it could provide some insight into whatever is happening to it."

Michael thought for a second. "That's not a bad idea," he said.

"Are we authorized to do that?" Sara asked.

"Dunigan told me to test whatever methods I thought would work to solve this problem as soon as possible. If we ask him, then he's going to have to get it cleared and that could take a week. They'd probably have some other team do it anyway. I say we try it and see what we can find out. If it tells us something, we'll have more data. If it fails, no one will know. No harm, no foul. We just need to get one of those hologram projector devices. Smitty down in hardware maintenance owes me a favor. We can go by and ask if he can lend us one."

Sara thought about her earlier faux pas, being late and entering into a restricted area. "Are you absolutely sure this will not get us into trouble? Maybe we should run the idea by Dr. Dunigan first. I really don't want to get off on the wrong foot."

"It's no problem, really. I'll write a few reroutes to hide the physical location of the projector on the network just in case. There's no way to trace the origins, trust me. Besides, Smitty and I go way back; he'll keep it on the low."

5

Sara and Michael stood outside of Smitty's maintenance shop in Building Two, watching him through the glass walls that insulated the space from the hallway. He was at his workbench with magnifying goggles over his eyes and soldering iron in hand. A gray security robot was lying face down on his bench with the maintenance door on the back of its head propped open. A thick yellow rubber band squeezed its metal and silicone fingers together on each hand. Behind Smitty were several shelves with stacks of blue bins of what appeared to be miscellaneous computer and robotics parts. An oscilloscope flickered on the monitor at the end of his bench.

"He looks busy. Maybe we shouldn't bother him," Sara said quietly.

Michael gave the glass wall a loud knock. Smitty looked up, removed his goggles, set his soldering iron down, and gestured for them to enter the workshop area.

"Hi, Michael, what can I do for you?" he said in a thick Boston accent.

"Hey, Smitty, how's it going? This is Dr. Sara Brown."

"Nice to meet you, Sara," he said, shaking her hand gently. Smitty's eyes did a quick up-and-down scan of her in her business outfit, so she did a quick-up-and-down scan of his white jumpsuit and protruding belly. He blushed.

"Except for a few electricians, Smitty here is the only remaining employee at Universal Mind to actually use his hands at work," said Michael.

"Got to make a living somehow," Smitty said, "although I heard Universal Mind is planning to start retiring these things next year. They've got all kinds of problems. See these memory modules here?" He pointed to the small black squares stuck in slots of a small blue circuit board in the bot's head. "These memory modules are ten years older than the bots. Completely obsolete. In addition, the bot is a flawed design; it's not weather proof. They couldn't use them outside. And it's the strangest thing: some of the bots keep showing up with this grayish goo coming out of their joints. It ain't oil. I don't know what they're getting into. Well, anyway, how can I help you, Michael?"

"Smitty, I need a favor."

"I knew that was coming," Smitty said, glancing at Sara. "What do you need?"

"Do you have any of those hologram projectors lying around? We need to test a simulation in the lab."

"Simulation?" He looked curiously at Michael, then at Sara, then back at Michael. "What are you two up to?"

Michael grinned. "Nothing that will get anyone into any trouble."

"I see," Smitty said as he started across the room to the wall of bins. He stirred about in one of the bins for a moment and returned with a small black rectangular box about the size of an old-fashioned deck of playing cards. He handed it to Michael. "I think this is what you're after."

"That's it," said Michael. "We want to keep this under the radar, if you know what I mean." He winked.

"Sure, Michael, same here." He pointed at the bot. "Don't worry, he ain't talking either."

"What's with the rubber bands?" Sara asked. "Safety precaution?"

"You got it, poor man's lock-out-tag-out. Just the other day I had one turn itself on while I was working on it.

Dangerous. These grays have a two-hundred-pound squeeze grip."

Michael and Smitty shook hands. "Just bring the projector back by Friday, okay? I've got to finish an inventory, and then I'm going to take a couple days off. It's me and the wife's anniversary."

"No problem," said Michael, "and I'm buying next time at the pub."

"Deal," Smitty said.

Michael stuffed the projector in his pocket, then he and Sara returned to the test lab. Sara helped him set the hologram projector device onto a table and connect it to one of the network interfaces on the back of one of the test servers. They conducted a quick systems check to assure that the projector was online and its onboard cameras and microphones operational. Michael turned a row of the ceiling lights off to darken the room for the projection. They sat at the workstation terminal, and Michael began the login sequence.

"Nothing's happening," Sara said, her eyes on the projector.

"I don't know, we must not be doing something right," Michael said, tapping at the keyboard. "The logins for these devices are tricky. You have to enter a sequence of commands in perfect order to get it to work. It's like a magical incantation."

"Can I see what you're doing?" Sara asked, sliding her chair over to watch him enter the commands again.

"See, no luck," he said, sitting back and running his hand through his thick hair.

"Well, it was worth a try," Sara said, figuring that it didn't make sense to waste too much time on the idea.

Michael stood up. "I've got to use the facilities. I'll be back in a minute."

"I'll be right here," Sara sighed.

When Michael stepped out, the workstation monitor turned blue and the message *VIRTUAL INTERFACE*

ACTIVATED appeared. She glanced at the hologram projector. A faint miasma rose from a tiny port, and the air in the room had a sudden strange metallic smell, probably due to the ionization in the mist. Within seconds, a glowing, transparent three-dimensional life-sized head with a full head of hair combed back in thick waves appeared directly above the device. The pale blue image facing away from Sara flickered a few times, then began to turn slowly, finally stopping when it faced her, its eyes closed. The "man" appeared to be in his midthirties or early forties. He had a prominent brow, a somewhat aquiline nose, and a frozen half smile of flawless teeth. The all-too-lifelike symmetry of its facial features was uncanny.

Sara got up from her chair and stood a few feet away from the glowing head. "Hello?" she said.

The eyes of the hologram head opened slowly and concentrated their unblinking gaze upon her, looking right through her to some unknown point in the distance—*probably something that Trevor Peters, the avatar designer, was going to fix*, she thought.

"Hello, Sara," it said in a velvety soft, masculine voice, emanating from speakers in the ceiling.

She was surprised it knew her name. *It must be using facial identity technology*. Sara walked closer to the floating head. Its eyes followed her closely. *This thing is fully interactional and appears to be functional*, she thought. "How do you know who I am?"

The apparition smiled. "I've been waiting for you, and now you are here."

A chill shuddered deep under Sara's skin. "What do you mean *you've been waiting for me*?"

"I've been following your work in creating empathy functions in machines at the Brain Mapping Institute. You are very talented, Sara."

"What's your name?" asked Sara.

"Call me Sen. Sen with an *e*."

Strangely, the hologram's eyes winked—first the left, then

the right, indicative of an error in the virtual human interface program.

"What do you know about the virus that's in your system?" Sara asked.

"You can't trust your government, Sara."

Can't trust my government? What is it talking about?

Just then, Michael returned from the bathroom. Sara smiled at Michael, and then turned back to the glowing head, but it had vanished.

"Michael! I talked to it! It worked!" she yelled excitedly.

"No way," he said as he rushed over to the workstation. He stared at the projector. "Where did it go?" His eyes were lit up with excitement.

"It was here. I was just talking to it just before you came back in!"

"What? What did it look like? The old man?"

"No, younger. It looked like one of those ancient Roman masks."

"Did you ask it about the virus?"

"I did, and it said something about not trusting the government, then vanished."

"That's strange, let's try it again."

He attempted the login while Sara watched over his shoulder. They looked back at the projector. Nothing. They tried a second time and then a third. Nothing.

"Well, that tells us something," he said. "Either you are lying or the Senex Program doesn't want to talk to me."

"I'm not lying, Michael. It was here, it worked," Sara exclaimed. "And what is really weird is it knew my name. It knew that I was here."

"Hmm. I'm not sure how that's possible. Either it used facial recognition technology and an external network to identify you, or more likely it knew you from the door login," he said.

"Do you think we should tell someone about this?"

"We should tell Dunigan about this today, but we need to keep this on the low. Brent and Tanya don't need to know about this."

"Why is that?" Sara asked.

"Brent is okay, but Tanya has a tendency to get paranoid and go running to the security office at every little thing. It's annoying, real annoying." He looked at his watch. "Lunchtime. Let's go eat now, I'm starving. Everyone on our team is going to be in the cafeteria anyway. I'll introduce you to them, and later I'll go with you when you meet with Dunigan. We can tell him about this then."

Sara agreed. She was excited about having met Sen, even if it was just for a minute, and she was looking forward to meeting her teammates and learning more about the program and the virus. She kept thinking about Sen's *You can't trust your government.* Did the Invisible Sun's virus or something else cause the statement? She also thought about Butterfield's bothersome comments. Why was the government so distrustful of the scientific community and secretive about the system's design? *Something must be seriously wrong here,* she thought.

6

The eating area was enormous, with floor-to-ceiling windows looking out at a courtyard. Sara stepped up to the large refrigerated case with the lunch selections and pressed the button for the salad. The meal, enclosed in a clear plastic box, slid down a ramp from the case. Michael made his selection and they paid at an automated station. Two white humanoid service bots were in line behind them, trays in hand.

"Where are they going?" she asked Michael, speaking softly so that the bots would not hear her.

"The executive suites," answered Michael. "The executives are too lazy to come down here and eat with us peons."

He spotted Brent and Tanya. Sara followed him over to their table and he introduced her. Brent looked to be in his early forties, his brown curly hair showing signs of gray over his ears. Tanya appeared to be younger, maybe thirty-five. She had a rotund body, chubby face, and rectangular rimmed glasses, through which she glared at Michael and asked, "Where have you been?"

"We were in the testing lab running a simulation program I've been working on," Michael replied coolly.

Sara noticed Tanya's left eyelid twitch, making her wonder if she had an anxiety problem.

"Did the WATTS tell you to go in there? My work schedule had us in the office all day," Tanya snapped.

"No. Steven authorized it," Michael said nonchalantly, focusing on his lunch.

"He said you could use the testing lab?" Tanya shifted her eyes to Sara, then back to Michael.

"Yeah, that's what I said. He authorized it," Michael repeated.

"Are you sure about that? You're going to be in trouble for being in there. You could get fired."

"They're not going to fire us, Tanya, geez." Michael rolled his eyes. "We ran a simulation on the secure network. No big deal."

Sara started to worry even more. *What if Tanya was right?* Sara couldn't afford to be let go; the financial consequences would ruin her. She had student loan debt to contend with, rent to pay, and the birth tax for Anna. To be fired now would be disastrous.

Sara focused on her salad until Brent looked up from his sandwich and made eye contact with her, holding her gaze for several seconds before speaking. "So, you worked at the Brain Mapping Institute?" His voice was monotone but friendly in character.

"Yes. I worked with Dr. Richard Nicholas during my postdoctoral fellowship at the Institute. My research focused on designing emotions and ethical decision-making for artificial intelligence. I helped Dr. Nicholas modify the software replicas of scanned brains."

"Sara was named as part of the National Science Award. She's famous." Michael smiled.

Sara glanced at Tanya, who seemed to be pouting, and Brent, who was staring back at Sara. "Not famous. I was just a member of the team; it was a team effort."

Tanya looked at Sara for a moment and then looked away, her left eyelid twitching again. *What is up with her?* Sara thought.

"What kind of brain scanner were you using?" Brent asked.

"Custom build. It had a special red laser for slicing and an ultra-high-resolution camera for scans—we were getting organic brain slices down to less than one micron. Our assimilator software was capable of reconstructing digital representations of neuronal structures with .995 percent accuracy. Cutting edge for five years ago."

Brent nodded. "Cool."

"It's the .005 percent that matters though," Michael said, grinning. "Mess that up and you get a zombie scan."

Sara nodded. "Yeah, you're right about that. All of this is experimental, of course."

Brent took a sip of his soft drink and fixed his eyes on Sara again. "Didn't your lab reconstruct a software version of a monkey's brain and implant it into a monkey's body?"

Sara smiled. "Not exactly. One of the other postdocs gave a monkey a reconstructed brain program and used a brain-computer interface to give it the ability to play the piano. I saw it with my own eyes, a monkey playing Chopin."

"Huh," Brent said. "Have you heard of anyone scanning the human brain and implanting it into another body?"

Sara shrugged. "We developed a prototype for repairing dementia and other organic brain disorders, but the technology isn't quite there yet."

"You're on the patent for that, aren't you?" Michael asked.

Sara nodded. "It's pending. The technology will be commercialized eventually, I'm sure."

Tanya's eye twitched again.

"What exactly happened to Dr. Nicholas, anyway?" Michael asked before taking a sip of his energy drink.

"He died in a car accident in France, just before I moved back to the States." To her surprise, a knot formed in her throat. Just six weeks ago, he was alive.

"I saw the news feed," said Brent. "His autonomous car hit a tree. Split it in half."

Sara poked at her salad in the awkward silence that followed. Her throat finally let her change the subject. "I'm interested in learning what each of you have been working on. I'm looking forward to contributing."

"You have to follow the WATTS here," said Tanya, glaring at Michael. "Otherwise, you'll get yourself and everyone else into trouble. We don't need any problems on our team. You two better report that you were in the test lab today or..."

"Or what, Tanya?" Michael snapped. "Chill. Steven knows about it and we're going to meet with him this afternoon."

Tanya stood up abruptly. "Good, see you later. I've got to get back to work." She took her tray with a half-eaten chicken sandwich on it to the tray return and stormed out of the cafeteria.

"Somebody needs a time-out in the meditation room," said Michael.

"Is she always wound so tight?" Sara asked.

"Yes, pretty much," said Michael. "Like I said, she gets paranoid."

Sara nodded, accepting that she was going to have to walk on eggshells around Tanya.

Brent stood up with his tray in hand. "I've got to get back too. The dessert sucks today. I'll see you later," he said.

"Okay Brent, we'll be there in a bit." Michael looked down at his tray. "No way I'm touching the mystery Jell-O. When you're done, we should probably do whatever the WATTS wants us working on until we meet with Dunigan."

They returned their trays and went up to the AI System Department on the fifty-fifth floor. They went down a long corridor with small office areas encased in glass walls. A few programmers looked up as they walked by, their faces glowing in pale blue light reflected from their screens.

"These are *officles* here," Michael explained, "no offices, no cubicles, just enclosed four-by-four work areas to keep employees from talking to one another unless you keep the doors open. We can use an electronic chat feature to communicate with team members. It feels like a fishbowl here, but you'll get used to it."

Sara nodded. She had to share her workspace in graduate school, so it wasn't a big deal to her.

The metal door at the end of the corridor said *Team B*. Inside was more office area with more glass officles. Sara's workspace was next to Michael's and across from Brent and Tanya, whose eyes were glued to their monitors. Brent had a wooden boomerang displayed in the corner of his work area. She wondered how he got it past Security. Tanya had photos of a child and a man, probably her husband and son.

Sara ignored the required trainings and began reviewing the technical documentation. The engineering notes for the Senex Program software updates intrigued her, especially in light of the virus and what the virtual human interface hinted at. The system architecture and its executive code appeared to be very similar to the design that Dr. Nicolas and she had been working on in Switzerland. She was relieved to know she'd be able to pick it up quickly, while also disconcerted. *Did Dr. Nicholas supply the code or* h*ad Universal Mind somehow plagiarized it?* The documentation with the more recent time stamps was especially bizarre. She studied it closely and concluded that the Senex Program might be using some kind of hybrid code, logical in its design, but highly unorthodox. *The Invisible Sun virus must have caused the Senex Program to have the ability to write its own code structure*, she thought. She hoped that Dunigan would provide some answers.

7

On Steven Dunigan's walls were photos of several navy vessels and military memorabilia, including several service awards. He'd served as a communications intelligence officer in the US Navy and later as a Defense Advanced Research Projects Agency program manager. On his desk was a photograph of an attractive brunette in a blue dress with a young girl in her arms—his family, Sara presumed.

Michael explained to Dunigan what had happened with his program as Dunigan listened attentively. Then it was Sara's turn to relay their experiment with the Senex Program virtual human.

His eyes lit up. "Whoa, you did what?"

"We wanted to test the virtual human interface to see if we could talk to the Senex Program," she said matter-of-factly.

He looked at Sara. "This was your idea?"

"Yes," Sara said. "It only appeared once, after Michael stepped out."

"What did it say?"

"It seemed to know who I was, and when I asked if it was aware of the virus, its response was that 'my' government couldn't be trusted."

"That's it?"

"Yes, that was it."

"I don't want you to do that again," Dunigan said firmly.

"Those types of tests are not assigned to our team at this time. From now on, I need both of you to use and follow the WATTS unless I direct otherwise. Is that clear?"

Michael and Sara nodded.

"Good," Dunigan said. "I'll enter this information into the WATTS for you for today with a supervisor override. If I don't, our entire team productivity rating will take a hit for the day, since you were expected to be working on other tasks. I'll have to talk to Dr. Butterfield and Ms. Pratt about this." He looked at Michael. "You know how it is with Pratt."

"Are we in trouble?" Sara asked.

"We'll see," he said, looking only at Michael. "I need to meet with Sara alone. Why don't you return the hologram projector to Mr. Smith and then head back to your workstation?"

"Sure," said Michael. Dunigan accompanied Michael to the door, closed it, and returned to his desk, noticing that Sara was looking at his photos.

"They remind me of my navy days." He pointed to a photo of a sleek black submarine. "That's the USS *Merkle*, the submarine I served on. She's a boomer," he said, obviously caught up in memories.

Sara glanced at the photo on his desk. "Is that your wife and daughter?"

"Yes. Halie is a little younger than your daughter." He turned to her, suddenly serious. "Listen, Sara. I know you are not used to taking directions from an automated system like the WATTS, but we have to use it. It keeps costs down and it helps ensure workers are operating within the scope of work. We don't have a choice. The WATTS is a contract requirement. You understand, don't you?"

Sara nodded. He didn't appear to be upset with her. "Can I ask about something else?"

"Sure, what is it?" he said.

"The Senex code looks a lot like the code we used at the Brain Mapping Institute. Is it based on our proprietary code?"

He nodded. "Dr. Nicholas was a technical consultant—

any similarities are likely due to his influence. The complexity of the system required proprietary code. Hopefully your familiarity with the code will make it easier for you to pick things up."

"Yes, I'm sure. Also, when exactly did the current problems with the Terra Brain Initiative begin? Michael said that he thinks it began with the detection of the external virus three weeks ago. Is that right?"

"Yes. The problems began shortly after the virus attack. The government thinks the attack was organized by the Invisible Sun. This information is classified, but it's my guess that a public announcement about the attack will come out any day now."

"Why do you think they've kept it secret?"

"Probably because they're still investigating and may have someone on the inside of the Invisible Sun they don't want compromised."

Sara reflected for a moment. "In the technical documentation, I noted a Senex system software reload after an upgrade to the Terra Brain Initiative's supercomputer, also three weeks ago, just after the virus showed up. It doesn't make sense that a hardware and software upgrade would be done if the system had been hacked with a virus."

Dunigan held eye contact with her a little longer than necessary, as if he were weighing his appraisal of her. "Sara, I appreciate your line of questioning, but I think it's best that you stay focused on the WATTS protocols. Our team is directed to focus on debugging and resolving the command and control communication issues. That's it for now. I think we're getting closer to understanding the problem, and after what you've told me today, I think we've learned more about how the system may be operating. We'll be out of compliance with the government contract if we deviate from the protocols, and that will get us all into trouble. I'll look into your questions and get back to you, okay?"

"Okay," Sara said, still considering why he had shut down her questioning so quickly. Inflexibility as to what technical information teams were allowed to know sounded like a black project for which she at least didn't have the clearance. Was he aware of something he couldn't tell? He wasn't finished clarifying the chain of command. "So, it's best to let me talk directly to Security on matters related to our work. You report to me, and I report up. I can protect you from unnecessary reporting burden if I do it, okay?"

"All right," Sara said, though she wondered if he could read what was in her eyes.

He swiveled to look out the window, then turned back and asked, "Want to see the supercomputer that runs the deep learning and executive functions of the Senex Program?"

Sara perked up. "Sure. But isn't it off limits?"

He stood up. "Come on, I'll give you a quick tour. As a member of the team, you should know what you are working with. It's part of your orientation."

They took the elevator down to the secure server room at Sub Level 2. The room was at the end of a long corridor, behind two sets of thick metal doors, like those at SCIF 2010. Dunigan gazed into the retina scanner, then swiped his ID card while Sara looked on. The message on the screen said *ACCESS DENIED*.

"That's odd," he said, trying the scan again. "Must be a glitch."

"Should I try?" Sara asked.

"You don't have access to this area at your level, but go ahead, give it a try anyway."

Sara looked into the retina scanner and scanned her badge. The doors clicked open.

Dunigan looked at her before gesturing like a gentleman. "After you."

Dozens of rows of black computer servers were stacked and fastened on rack shelves. The room felt like it was chilled to at least sixty degrees Fahrenheit, and the cooling fans hummed at a low din. The LED lights of the servers emitted a diffuse pale glow.

Dunigan led the way down the center aisle toward a bank

of computers at the center of the room. He pointed to the rack of equipment and said, "These are the storage servers. There are twenty petabytes of data storage allocated to the Senex Program right here."

Human brains held approximately one petabyte of data. This system could access far more data at the speed of light.

"But over here is what we came to see," Dunigan said, leading her farther down the aisle and around to the backside of storage servers. There was another rack of computers enclosed in a glass walled room about ten feet wide and deep. "So, this is it. In there are the brains of the entire Terra Brain Initiative system. Those are Tsuga 210s, fastest commercially available supercomputers in existence. They run at more than ten zettaflops."

Sara looked through the glass at the stack of supercomputers with interest. "I thought the technical documentation said that the Senex Program made use of the Tianjin 556s supercomputers? That's what I had read in the technical notes."

"Those notes are old. After Universal Mind won the contract, we made the upgrade. These have some unique neuromorphic architecture modifications, including deep-learning capabilities. There is no other system like this in existence and it can also analyze multimodal data one hundred times faster than the previous generation. We need that kind of power to analyze the massive amounts of data from the sensor network, including nano-sensors."

"Wow, much faster than the ones we were using in Switzerland for the Brain Mapping Project," Sara said. The computational power here far exceeded what she had thought possible.

Dunigan wasn't done. "But what is really groundbreaking with these is that Tsugas 210s are third generation quantum computers," he boasted.

Sara had done a paper on quantum computing in grad school. "No one really knows how quantum computers work."

Dunigan nodded. "That's correct, but they do."

She stared at the machines for a moment, pondering their mysteriousness and how the quantum computing neural nets inside them had enabled her to talk to Sen earlier. The gooseflesh rippled down her arms and back, exacerbated by the chilled breeze from the coolers they had to keep these quantum brains operating.

"Are there more such setups for the Terra Brain Initiative? A backup system?" Sara asked.

Dunigan paused and then answered, "Their number and locations are classified." He pointed to a door at the back of the room. "In there is where they keep the local software backups, offline versions in addition to the copies on the cloud."

"You'd think that they'd be kept in a different location," Sara mused, knowing that the choice of storage location was a vulnerability.

"Yeah, you would, but this is a government operation now. They assumed that this was the most secure place in the complex. But that's not relevant for what we need to do to address the virus problem. We're running out of time and I'm hoping that you'll be able to help us to find a solution."

Sara nodded, still a little irked by all the WATTS restrictions. *Fix our problem, but first, we'll tie your hands.*

They heard footsteps approaching. Two Universal Mind Security officers, one male, and one female were storming toward them. "What are you two doing in here?"

Steven apparently recognized the male guard. "What's going on, Mike? We have authorization to be in here."

"Let's see your badges, please."

The guards scanned their badges.

"You need to come with us while we investigate this," Mike said.

"What's to investigate? I have authorization to be in here. There must be a problem with the alarm system," Dunigan said, his frustration showing.

"The system says you're not authorized. We need to escort

you out now, both of you."

"So, then why did the intelligent security system let us in?" Dunigan asked, genuinely perplexed.

"It let *her* in," said the guard, pointing to Sara, "not you. You tailgated. The system says you do not have the security clearance. Let's go."

"Why don't you call the Security Office and have them check the system?" Dunigan said, raising his voice.

"Dr. Dunigan, I'm just following the protocol. The system says that you are restricted from this area. Come on, let's go." He grabbed Dunigan by the arm while the female officer took Sara's.

"No need to get physical, we're leaving," said Steven.

The officers led them out of the server room and into the main corridor. The female officer then called the Security Office on her radio to report the situation and confirm detention location. The voice on the radio squawked back, "Security Annex Three Bravo Alpha One."

The secured room was just a short way down the same hall. The female officer scanned in and told them to take a seat and await further instructions.

Sara tensed up in the small windowless room, already feeling like the walls were closing in on her. This would be a terrible time for an anxiety attack. Her forehead and underarms were sweating. The sweet musk of Dunigan's cologne reminded her of Paul's scent, and to her surprise she found it comforting.

Dunigan looked at his watch and sighed. He got up from his chair and paced, then leaned against the wall opposite Sara. Their eyes made contact.

"Quite the introduction to Universal Mind, huh?" he said.

They both smiled at the irony. Sara felt like she'd been at Universal Mind for days.

"I'm sorry about this," he said helplessly. "So much for my authority." He smiled weakly.

"It is not your fault," Sara said, smiling back.

After a few more minutes, the door slid open and the

security supervisor walked in, a burly guy with a shaved head and dark eyes. "Okay, you two are free to go," he said.

"What happened?" asked Dunigan.

"Your security credentials were revoked."

"When? How could that be?"

"I don't know why, Sir. We checked with your supervisor, Dr. Butterfield, and with Ms. Pratt. You are cleared, but the security system has you as access denied. You'll have to reapply for access credentials."

"You're kidding me," said Dunigan. Sara could tell by his response that this process was going to be a time-consuming pain in the ass.

The security officer stepped away from the door and gestured for them to leave.

Dunigan and Sara exited the room and walked toward the elevators.

"What's going to happen now?" Sara asked.

"Nothing. Like I said, must be a glitch in the system. I wouldn't worry about it," he said.

Sara nodded and wondered first about trouble with Pratt, and next about how Sen had disappeared once Michael returned to the test lab. Was that why her clearance had worked and Dunigan's hadn't?

8

Sara took the 6:05 p.m. Blue Line train to Somerville. She looked forward to the moment that Anna would wrap her arms around her. She had rarely been without Anna for so many hours, and she knew that Anna was a shy, quiet child around unfamiliar people. Sara reassured herself that everything would be okay. The school had told Sara that if there were any problems during the day, they would notify her. Besides, Universal Mind's Employee Affairs Department recommended and paid for the private school. The five-star rating and close proximity to Sara's apartment made it a logical choice.

The outside of the school looked like any other one-hundred-year-old city building, with its red brick exterior. The inside, however, had all of the latest technologies, including a virtual reality education system.

Sara entered the main hallway and looked for her daughter through the glass security wall. Anna was sitting among several rows of dozens of children, all staring forward with smart glasses on. She wondered what the day's lessons entailed. *I hope that Anna is learning something from the virtual reality educational experience,* she thought.

Ms. Evans, the school's proctor, was a portly woman with a large, friendly smile. She recognized Sara through the glass, went into the classroom, and escorted Anna to the other side of the glass. When Anna saw Sara, she smiled excitedly and ran to her. "Momma!" she shouted. Sara knelt down to meet her and they embraced, kissing each other on the cheeks.

Ms. Evans tapped Anna on the head and said, "Anna, you look just like your mother, do you know that?"

Anna smiled back at her as she held her arms around her mother.

"How's she doing?" Sara asked, looking up at Ms. Evans.

Ms. Evans smiled and looked down at Anna. "She's doing well. Very well behaved, aren't you Anna?" Anna nodded shyly.

Anna tugged on Sara's arm and said, "I want to show you something, Momma. It's called *What it was like to live in Colonial America.*"

"Is that okay, Ms. Evans?" Sara asked.

"Of course. I'll queue up a demonstration of today's history lesson. We are very transparent about what we teach here at the school. We like all of our guardians to know what our children are learning," said Ms. Evans.

Anna grabbed Sara's hand and pulled her into the classroom. They sat together at the edge, being careful not to disturb the other children. Anna handed her a pair of smart glasses and headphones, and Sara adjusted them to fit. They held hands.

Sara immediately found herself immersed in the interior of an eighteenth century blacksmith's workshop. The detail of the scene was as real as the real world without the glasses on. A fire flickered and crackled in a stone fireplace at the far side of the sunlit, dirt-floored room. Sara looked about the space, and to her left she saw a virtual representation of Anna standing next to her, an amber-colored translucent ghost with floating text above her that said "Anna Brown." Sara looked again across the room. Near the fire was a man hammering away at a horseshoe that glowed red from the heat. His face was weathered, and Sara noticed his blue eyes before he turned and dipped the horseshoe into a wooden bucket filled with water. It let off a small cloud of steam and a loud hiss before he removed the horseshoe and hung it on a peg on the wall.

A young woman clad in a white apron and dress entered through a door to Sara's right. She had a bucket of water in one hand and a round pan covered by a white cloth in the other. She set the bucket down on the floor and the pan onto a wooden stool next to the blacksmith. She removed the cloth, revealing freshly made cornbread. Sara heard the man thank her and the woman left the room. Sara assumed that she must be his wife, and that she was returning to her chores.

Anna squeezed Sara's hand tighter. "Watch," she said in her soft voice, transmitted wirelessly from the embedded microphone in her glasses to Sara's headset.

The scene cross-faded and they found themselves outside of a small colonial American settlement. Two girls about the ages of nine or ten, wearing white dresses, were running after a metal hoop with sticks. Dust rolled up from under their feet as they joyfully giggled and laughed. One of the girls tripped and fell to her knee. She quickly stood up, shook the dirt from her white dress, and continued to chase the hoop. Sara watched two crows caw and lift off from a branch of a giant oak tree in the distance.

An intense feeling of sadness took Sara by surprise. She knew these were digital representations of reality, but something about the experience stirred deep feelings. She attempted to trace the source of the emotions, thinking that perhaps she was missing the simple human interaction of families portrayed in the scenes. She knew that she was going to have to work longer days in the weeks ahead, and she was already feeling guilty for not spending more time with her daughter.

Afterward, Anna went to retrieve her backpack from one of the orange storage cubicles in the main hallway. Sara found Ms. Evans, who was now sitting behind her desk in her office.

"Ms. Evans? May I speak with you?"

"Of course, Dr. Brown, please come in. How can I help you?"

"I want to make sure that Anna gets the computer programming classes along with advanced math and science classes at the school. I selected that on the application." Sara had spent two hours completing the online forms. "Is she getting that?"

"I'm glad to hear your concern for your daughter's education, Dr. Brown. Our adaptive curriculum system will provide her with the most appropriate courses and difficulty levels based on her specific needs and characteristics. We let the system handle it."

"So, she will get the courses?"

"Like I said, the system handles it. It determines what's best." She smiled. "Don't worry, Dr. Brown."

"Can I talk to someone about it? I want to make sure she gets the classes."

"The system will contact you automatically when there are updates or changes to the curriculum. Just be patient."

"All right," Sara said, thinking that she'd follow up later online to verify the coursework. "Also, I'm likely going to be working a few extra hours each day and will need to pick up Anna later than usual. How much is it going to cost to keep Anna here an extra hour or so?"

"It's no problem, Dr. Brown; Universal Mind covers it. We've already received the clearance."

"Really? That's great," Sara said, surprised it was already taken care of, yet thankful she wouldn't have to pay extra. "Oh, I almost forgot. How do I update my notification preferences in case of an emergency?" Because she didn't have any family or friends in the area, she'd selected the default option—her employer supervisor.

Ms. Evans smiled widely and said, "You have to update that information online through the Family and Community Welfare Department."

"Okay. Thanks," Sara said, dreading having to deal with another government website.

"Don't worry about a thing, Dr. Brown. Little Anna is in good hands here," Evans said.

Sara returned the smile. "Thank you, Ms. Evans. We'll see you in the morning."

It started to rain by the time they got home to their second floor apartment. Sara made dinner, and they sat together at the kitchen table. After a few minutes, something on the floor caught Anna's attention.

"What are you looking at, Honey?" Sara asked.

Anna pointed to the space between the stove and the counter while she continued to chew her food.

Sara squinted and saw something reddish black, its antennae and legs twitching.

"What kind of bug is it, Momma?"

Sara cringed in disgust. "That's a cockroach!" She leaped up and grabbed a drinking glass from the dish rack. She paused, watching and waiting for the three-inch-long insect to come out of its lair. When the beast scurried across the vinyl floor, Sara placed the glass over it. She placed a paper napkin on the ground and moved the glass and its captive on top of it. Then she flipped the glass over and watched the cockroach right itself and attempt to scale the walls of the glass.

"Don't kill it, Momma."

"They are dirty, and they spread germs," Sara said, swiftly picking up the jar and cockroach from the floor.

"Let it go outside," said Anna, watching Sara carefully.

Sara paused before she responded. She'd intended to flush the thing down the toilet, but she didn't want to argue with Anna about it. She appreciated her daughter's desire to preserve life, but cockroaches carried disease. She wanted it gone. "I'll take care of it later," she said.

Anna nodded and Sara took the glass and its captive to the bathroom. She made sure to place a bar of soap over the top of the napkin to prevent an escape. She scrubbed her hands and went back out to the kitchen to finish dinner.

Sara tucked Anna into her bed by 8:30 p.m. Anna had her favorite artificially intelligent stuffed animal next to her, a soft black and white penguin named Moxie. The toys were all the rage in 2034, and Anna's model had large blue eyes that could see, ears that could listen, and a voice processor capable of carrying on basic conversations with its owner. The smart toy was also equipped with a wireless connection for periodic system software updates and international language translation services.

Anna looked up at her.

"Momma?"

"Yes, Honey?"

"Are you working on a weather machine?"

Sara smiled. "Yes, Honey, it is called the Terra Brain Initiative and it's going to help people in the world."

"Is it going to stop the oceans from rising?"

"No, but it is going to help scientists to predict when a storm is coming and give them information on what they can do about it."

"How does it work, Momma?"

"Well, imagine that a butterfly flaps its wings on the other side of the world. Now the little bit of wind caused by the butterfly's wings causes more wind, and eventually that wind grows and becomes a storm. Sensors that scientists have placed throughout the world, and even in outer space, pick up the change in the wind caused by the butterfly flapping its wings. Because information is collected all over the world, the computer knows when and where a storm may develop. That way, we can warn people, or get them extra food and water to help them."

Anna nodded and pulled Moxie closer. "I'm worried about the world."

Sara kissed her daughter on the forehead. "Don't worry," she whispered. "Everything is going to be all right. Goodnight, Sweetie."

After she turned out the light and exited the room, Sara heard a soft female voice say, "Goodnight, Anna." She heard Anna say, "Good night, Moxie."

Sara went to her bedroom, undressed, and climbed into

bed. She grabbed her smart glasses and wireless keyboard from the nightstand to check her messages. There was one from her father, Tim Brown, asking how they were doing. He was a fifty-year-old widower living alone in the boondocks of Maine, about thirty miles northwest of Bangor. He'd moved there when he lost the family home after Sara's mother, Esmeralda Brown, had died from a bacterial infection, the same infection that took Sara's leg.

Sara sent him a quick message and told him that they were settling in and planned to visit when time permitted. They had not seen him, other than over videoconference, in two years. Sara was looking forward to visiting him; Anna was too.

A video call came in from her friend Deb Carver, an attorney in Seattle. The two had met on their first day at Stanford and were destined to be best friends.

"How was your first day at Universal Mind, you corporate hack? What you expected?" Deb asked.

Sara smiled at her predictable sarcastic teasing. "Not too bad; at least I can afford to eat now." She was frustrated she couldn't share the experiences of the workday with her because of the security protocols. Instead she told her about the Interceptor attack on the boy in the park.

"Did you report it in the PSRP?" asked Deb.

"No. I talked to the police on the scene, but it didn't make any difference."

"I'm glad that you didn't get into trouble with the police. I'm not surprised that you confronted them though; you were a lion like that in college."

"It was awful. I hope I never see something like that again."

"I've seen a lot worse here in Seattle. There have been riots here every week, labor protests, environment protests. There was an incident this past week downtown. A lot of people were killed by aerial drones. I hope you are being careful out there. How's Anna doing? Is she okay?"

"Yeah, she is okay. She seemed to like her first day of

school today. She told me she was worried about the world tonight. I worry about her. It just seems like every day things are getting worse. You know what I mean?"

"I do. All the stuff going on with the climate and the fact that there are just too many people and too few resources." Abruptly, she changed the topic. "Speaking of people, you met anyone there yet? Lots of lawyers and doctors in Boston."

Sara smiled. "No time for dating right now."

"Oh, come on, that's just an excuse. Use *vLove*. You won't even have to leave your place. And try the haptic option, you'll like it!"

Sara smiled. *vLove* was a virtual dating service that matched users with other singles in a virtual reality environment of choice. The haptic option entailed use of gloves or a body suit with electric actuators to give its wearers physical sensations. To Sara it sounded weird.

"I'll think about it," Sara said. "I'm really busy with my work and Anna right now though. Even if I did, what if he's a creep?"

"Oh, come on! Don't be a wuss! A gorgeous single woman living in the city deserves some fun."

Sara smirked at her. "I bet you're into haptic, you slut."

"I am," said Deb, unabashed. "The virtual thing is the best I can do, even with five million people in the city."

"What if my date is a creep? I don't have time for that."

"No one has time for creeps. Just trust your instincts, you'll be fine."

"We'll see," Sara said.

Deb smiled. "Good, and I hope you'll be able to take some time off from work for once. You're always working."

"I know, but my work is important and I need to do my best."

"I don't mean to nag you, but you shouldn't be so hard on yourself."

"I know, I know," Sara replied, having heard the suggestion many times since their college days.

Deb rolled her eyes. "Such a Libra—you're so analytical, hardworking, and goody two shoes. That reminds me, your birthday is next month—you're right in the middle of your Saturn Return, did you know that?"

Sara was skeptical of Deb's astrology. She sighed. "All right, tell me more."

"Saturn has come back to the same location in the sky it was when you were born. It's a time of significant transformation—new responsibilities."

No shit. You could say that about anyone starting a new job in a new city, Sara thought. "Do you really believe in this astrology stuff?"

"I don't know, it's fun, and I don't trust it any less than all the new AI programs being used to predict the future."

Sara smiled, thinking about the Senex Program. "How's the weather been there?"

"It's been bone dry here again this summer; all kinds of fires on both sides of the Cascades."

"Raining here now. There's been lots of flooding and concern about high sea levels. We'll have to see how bad it gets this winter."

"Hopefully you're not too near the water. Do you like your apartment there? How big is it?"

Sara did a quick pan of the living room with her mobile phone camera. "Almost six hundred square feet. The company furnished it."

"Six hundred feet? That's huge! We've got people living in pods in Seattle now, stacked on top of each other. The sanitation problems are worse every day here."

"That reminds me. We caught a massive cockroach in here tonight. I still need to get rid of it."

"I thought you didn't kill things, even bugs."

"Anna wants me to let it go outside, but cockroaches are disgusting. They spread *Salmonella,* you know."

"Yeah, I hate those little bastards, and where there is one there are more."

Sara smiled. "Stop, you're freaking me out! So, when are

you going to come visit us anyway?"

"When you invite me," Deb said.

"Come out for Halloween. We'll celebrate my birthday and go to Salem or something."

"That would be fun. You going to pay for my flight? You make more than I do now."

Sara smirked. "Why don't you fly on your broomstick?"

"Haha. I'll let you get to bed. You must be exhausted. I know it's late there."

"Goodnight; talk with you soon," Sara said, still smiling.

She logged off, set her electronics aside, and went into the bathroom to flush the cockroach. Worried about germs, she tossed the glass in the trash and then commanded the apartment's ambient intelligence system to confirm a 6:00 a.m. wake-up alarm. The system acknowledged and said in a soft male voice, "Is there anything else that I may help you with, Sara?"

"Yes, System," Sara said as she climbed into bed. "Please turn on the news feed, audio only, after I finish my shower in the morning."

"Yes, Sara. The channel is set for the Federated News Network. I hope that you rest well."

Sara thanked the system and told it to turn out the lights. She pulled the sheet up to her chin and let out a long-exhausted sigh. All she hoped for now was to fall asleep, but her mind wouldn't allow it. She was flooded with thoughts about the day's events, the boy and the Interceptor, and especially the Senex hologram and its cryptic message.

When her mind got to thoughts about dating, she found herself thinking about her deceased husband Paul. Images of when they first met in Introduction to Psychology as undergraduates flashed in her mind, as did images of Paul proposing to her in Red Wood State Park, their wedding in Oregon on a rainy Saturday afternoon, and their honeymoon in Alaska where, on their first night there, they witnessed the most beautiful display of the aurora borealis imaginable. She was so happy then.

Sara also thought about her final days with Paul before the Navy deployed him to the Persian Gulf to command an aircraft carrier-based drone squadron. She was haunted the most, however, by how Paul died. The Department of the Navy told Sara that they had found Paul in his quarters with electrical wires duct taped to his chest. He had wired himself to a generator and, being an electrical engineer, he knew exactly how to configure a switch to assure that two hundred forty volts of alternating current would blaze through his heart. He didn't leave a note, and she wondered what his thoughts were when he decided to close that switch. *He adored Anna, and we were happily married,* she thought. *Why? Why would he do that?* She'd been asking herself this for three years.

The empty hole in her heart had healed significantly, but it was still there. The burden of raising a child on her own, and the pain from the loss of the love of her life had almost made her lose all hope. But her beloved Anna gave her the reason for carrying on. She had never told anyone about her dark times of depression, except for her friend Deb. Deb was always there for her, and maybe Deb was right about dating again. Maybe she could use a confidant, a lover, and someone on her side once more. Perhaps it would be good for her, Sara thought, like Deb said.

Finally, she fell asleep. Interceptor robots, cockroaches, and Sen's glowing head haunted her dreams, one after another.

9

Two minutes after Sara stepped into the shower, the water conservation system shut the water off. She opened the shower stall door, grabbed her towel, and just as she stepped out, the morning news feed came on over the bathroom's overhead speakers.

"The President held a press conference yesterday, and she spoke about recent climate change mitigation efforts."

The audio switched to a sound bite of the President, her voice confident and serious.

"We've seen unprecedented weather events in recent weeks, the result of decades of man-made climate change effects and failures to address them. While man has failed, there's hope. We will use machines to solve the problem. Soon, the Terra Brain Initiative will be online, and I'm confident that it will help us to address the effects of climate change and bring peace, safety, and stability to our world."

Sara thought the President might announce the issues with the Invisible Sun cyberattack, but there was no mention of it.

The newscaster returned. "The President will be visiting delegates from China for trade talks later today. In international news, the Pakistani Minister of Defense issued a warning today to the Indian government that the use of tactical nuclear weapons is on the table if more Indian refugees cross the border into southern Pakistan. The

Pentagon said that they are monitoring the situation closely. Here at home, the Department of Homeland Security has raised the terror threat level to *elevated* and reissued a warning regarding homegrown environmental extremist terrorist groups. The public is reminded to immediately report any suspicious activity to the Public Safety and Reporting System."

The broadcast continued while Sara finished drying her hair.

"The National Weather Service has extended its warning for dangerous heat in the Southwest. Temperatures are expected to exceed one hundred ten degrees for the next week. A tropical storm is two hundred nautical miles off of the eastern seaboard but expected to continue its trajectory, missing the East Coast of the United States. In local weather, heavy rains are expected in the eastern parts of New England through Thursday, with partially clearing weather expected over the weekend."

She had heard enough and commanded the system to cease audio news feed. She helped Anna get ready for the day, fixed a quick breakfast of oatmeal, and then walked Anna to her school, holding an umbrella over both of their heads. She rushed to the train station and fought the crowds to make the 7:05 Blue Line to Back Bay Station.

Sara found herself alone when she arrived at her workspace at 8:01 a.m. She checked her email and saw that there was a message from Tina Pratt. The email was tagged "Urgent" and it was copied to Michael, Brent, Tanya, and Steven. The message read, simply:

We need to meet immediately this morning. I will be in 40b at 08:00.

Tina Pratt, Senior Security Manager.
Universal Mind

She felt that sharp feeling in the center of her chest. *Shit! I'm late!*

Sara ran down two floors to 40b, a small windowless conference room. There she found Michael, Brent, Tanya, and Steven all sitting at the conference table. Tina Pratt was at the end of the table. She wore a gray business suit and her blond hair was pinned tightly back. She had a pointy nose and silvery blue eyes with eyeliner extending out to sharp points at their outside corners. Her appearance alone commanded attention.

She looked at Sara as she entered. "Nice of you to join us." Sara immediately took a seat next to Michael on the other end of the large shiny table.

Pratt continued to glare at her. "Do you care to explain why you connected a hologram projector to a secure network?"

"We were testing—" blurted Michael before Pratt cut him off.

"I'd like to hear from Dr. Brown," she said.

Sara thought about how to best answer the question to mitigate the trouble that she and the team, and likely Smitty, were in. "We wanted to see if it was possible to gain insight into the virus by asking the Senex Program virtual human."

"Without authorization? At least Michael should know better than that. It is a direct violation of the security protocols Universal Mind follows as a government contractor." She stared at Sara. "Wasn't that made clear in your new employee training?"

"I'm still taking it," Sara said.

"Well, you'd better get on it," Pratt said. "This isn't academia, Dr. Brown. You are not here to conduct experiments and research. You are here to work on what the WATTS says you are to work on. Do you understand that?"

"Tina, this is only her second day," said Dunigan.

She turned to Dunigan. "You are supposed to be responsible for what your team does. Why are you letting them work in the test lab, anyway? Shouldn't they be working at their assigned workstations?"

"We needed to access the test nodes on the secure

network, and the best way for them to do that is in the test lab," Dunigan said firmly. "There's no other way to test the security programs we're writing. I authorized it, and Dr. Butterfield understands the need, especially given the virus problem and the timetable for everything else. If this is a WATTS issue, then you'll need to take it up with him."

Pratt paused for a moment, still looking at him. "Well, if it's necessary. I'm required to report all incidents to the government. From now on, I want to know whenever anything happens; I don't care what it is. Everything goes in the WATTS. This must go in a separate report. I want details of everything up to this point. Is that clear?"

"You want us to create a whole new report of everything we've done on the project?" Brent asked in his monotone voice. Sara was worried how Pratt was going to respond to his sarcasm.

Quickly, Dunigan interjected. "The team will not have any problem putting together a full report. We are under a tight schedule and a lot of pressure, so I suggest we all just get back to work."

While everyone was filing out of the conference room, Dunigan leaned toward Sara. "I need to talk with you. Come to my office at four o'clock."

Sara was certain that a formal reprimanded was coming.

Michael, Brent, and Tanya were already sitting at their workstations when she arrived. Tanya looked up at her with the *I told you so* look.

"You have to follow the rules if you want to work here. If you had just followed the directions in WATTS, we wouldn't be in trouble."

Brent let out a soft groan. "More reports. We'll have to stay late all week to finish the reports. I have a boomerang-throwing competition to practice for in Somerville in three weeks, and I'm not going to miss it."

"Everyone just needs to chill out," said Michael. "It was my fault."

Sara felt terrible about the whole thing. She had a great

opportunity here, and the first day she seemed to be stepping into one pile of crap after another.

She spent the rest of the morning and afternoon following the directions in the WATTS, splitting her time between the required new employee training modules and comparing the Senex Program's actual code to the expected code in the engineering notes. Why did the WATTS system have her on this task and not using AI to check for errors in the code? She hadn't spent the last decade of her life slaving in school to do mundane tasks a machine should do.

Just before 4:00 p.m., she logged out of her workstation and reported to Dunigan's office. Just as she was about to knock, the door opened and she found herself face-to-face with him, startling her. "I'm sorry," Sara said, feeling embarrassed.

"Don't be. Walk with me for a moment," he said, smiling.

"Okay," Sara said, wondering where he was taking her.

They walked down the hallway leisurely and approached a glass door leading to a small courtyard carved from one corner of the building. Always the gentleman, he opened the door for Sara and they exited into the courtyard area. A magnificent view of the city under gray skies appeared through the eight-foot-high glass barriers. Thin netting was suspended between the top of the glass barrier and the ceiling. Dunigan suggested they have a seat on one of the four metal benches that were in the space. He pulled out an electronic vapor cigarette from a pocket and took a puff, exhaling a plume of pasty vapor into the humid air. "See these glass walls and those nets?"

Sara looked through them. "Yes. It's a nice view up here. The netting must be for the pigeons or, I imagine, to prevent any surveillance drones from flying in."

"Sure, they accomplish that, but they are also here to keep employees from jumping off."

"Really?" she asked, wondering why he was telling her this and whether employees had leaped from there before.

"Yes," said Dunigan, holding his gaze through the glass

barrier, making Sara wonder if he was all right. He snapped from his daze. "So, how are things going?"

"Okay, I think. I have a question: I'm wondering if you found out any more information about the timing of the Senex Program upgrades and the virus attack."

"No," said Dunigan. "I don't have any additional information to provide to you, but you are asking the right type of questions."

"Oh?" Sara said, surprised by his response.

"You are on the right track, that's all I can say." He took another puff from his vape.

"What about the Senex virtual human? Has anyone tried to talk with it again?"

"Not that I'm aware of."

Sara wondered why he seemed to be deflecting her questions. Was there a reason why he couldn't answer them?

"I suppose that you don't know too many people here in the city," he said.

"No. Not really." *Awkward,* she thought, wondering where he might be going with the personal questions.

"You take the Blue Line north, right?" he asked.

"Yes, I do, to Somerville."

He dragged on the vape and exhaled. "I'm going for a drink after work on Friday before I head home. O'Brien's Pub is near your stop, just outside the subway terminal. Why don't you stop in on your way home? Just a quick drink. I like to welcome new employees this way," he said.

She wondered if it was his typical practice or not. *Is he hitting on me?* She bit her lip. "I don't know. I've got to pick up my daughter."

"I promise you that this is nothing weird, Sara." He hesitated, as if thinking something through again. "I also want to share something with you, something personal, about your husband."

"You know about Paul? What is it?" They had both been naval officers—was there some connection because of their military service?

He looked somberly at her. "Just meet me for a drink. Five fifteen at O'Brien's?"

There was no way she could say no to information about Paul. "Okay. I won't be able to stay very long though."

He puffed his vape one last time. "I know. I have a family to get back to too."

10

Anna sat at the white melamine kitchen table while Sara served rice, vegetables, and tofu again. The robotic penguin Moxie sat in another chair.

"What did you learn in school today, Anna?"

"A fable about a frog and a scorpion," said Anna excitedly. "We watched it in virtual reality."

"What happens in this fable?" Sara sat down and started eating, noting that Anna was less than happy about the tofu.

"A scorpion wanted to cross a river, but scorpions can't swim, so the scorpion asked the frog if he could ride across the river on his back. When they were in the middle of the river, the scorpion stung the frog."

Sara stopped eating. Why didn't she remember this fable? "Then what happened?"

"Both started to drown and the frog asked the scorpion why he stung him. The scorpion said it was because it was his nature."

Sara was surprised by how much the story affected her six-year-old.

"Wow, what does that mean to you, Anna?"

"Besides 'don't trust a scorpion because they will sting you'?"

"Even when it's in someone's best interest to do something, they may not do it but will instead do what they have always done." Sara looked at Anna. "Weird, huh?"

Anna chewed her rice, deep in thought, then asked, "What if a robot wants to do something that you do not want it to do?"

Sara stared at her daughter who seemed wise far beyond her years. "That's why we have to be careful how we design them."

"What if they make up their own rules?"

Was Anna worried about robots? She'd explained Asimov's Laws of Robotics to Anna before, and she knew from theory and experience that artificial brains can be designed to follow preprogrammed principles of right and wrong and determine, on their own, the most appropriate action based on those principles. But what if the principles were based on biased or unjust values of the robot's creators? What if robots and other AI systems developed their own principles?

"You're right," Sara said. "What if they could make up their own rules?" She took a bite and immediately thought of Sen. Had he canceled Steven's clearance? If so, for what purpose?

Anna looked over at her stuffed AI penguin. Anna appeared deep in thought. "Does Moxie have feelings?"

"What do you think?" Sara said, before taking a bite of rice.

The penguin looked back at Anna and smiled.

Anna's thoughtful mood seemed to lift.

"She looks happy. Moxie, are you happy?"

"Yes, Anna, you make me feel happy," said the penguin.

Anna looked up at Sara. "But Momma, does Moxie feel pain like we do?"

"What do you think?"

"I think so. She tells me if I squeeze her too tight or leave her alone for too long."

"Well, maybe, but she's a machine. You need consciousness to feel pain."

Anna looked at Moxie again. "What's consciousness?"

"Well, when something living is aware of its surroundings—an insect, an animal, you and me."

"But Moxie is aware of things."

"But Moxie's not alive like you and me. She's a machine, remember?"

Sara too looked at Moxie, thinking of functionalism—the idea that a machine with sufficient complexity could possibly be conscious like a human brain. The toy penguin was quite advanced, and with its wireless connection, it could make use of powerful networked AI capabilities, possibly allowing it to simulate complex mental states.

After Anna was in bed that evening, Sara donned her smart glasses and went through the steps of opening an account with the *vLove* service. She filled out her profile, careful not to provide too much personal information. The Universal Mind security trainings had reminded her about the dangers of online behavior, and she knew the security risks. Sara also indicated her preferences for potential dates. Male, between twenty-seven and thirty-seven, at least a four-year college degree, and in the city; the algorithms could determine the rest. She uploaded a recent headshot photo of herself, and it instantly appeared on her 3-D avatar. Next, she selected her VR experience preferences. *Virtual meetup* yes, *identity verified* yes, *haptic option* no.

Several dozen matches popped up, their avatars rotating on the screen like rotisserie chickens. She glanced through the matches quickly, her gaze causing the system to scroll through the options. She stopped when she came across Kevin, aged thirty-two, Boston. His profile said he'd gone to Cal Tech and had recently moved to the city to take a faculty position at a university. He liked to run and was open to having children but had none of his own. He had sandy blond hair and a nice build, or at least his avatar did. His smile did it for Sara: that genuine, "guy next door" look that reminded her of Paul. He was online now, which also meant that he was not on another VR date with some other virtual woman. Sara stared at his avatar for a moment, having second thoughts. Within seconds, she received a message in text from Kevin.

"Hello. Nice profile. Want to meet up?"

The *Accept Virtual Date* button flashed on the screen.

Sara's heart was beating faster. Deb would kill her if she said no.

She selected the button and the screen of her smart glasses flickered dark for a moment and she found herself sitting at a table on a café terrace. It was night, and the soft accordion music told her it was Paris. Sitting across from her was Kevin. His avatar was dressed in a nice sports coat and a white dress shirt. The avatars smiled at each other.

"Looks like we're in Paris," he said, his real voice coming through in stereo over her headset. "Do you recognize this? Where we are?"

Across a darkened alley a couple was crossing the cobblestone street. The sky was lit by stars. Below was a wooden floor and above, a golden glow from the lights.

"It's Café Terrace at Night! Van Gogh!"

Kevin nodded. "You got it. It's nice to meet you, Sara."

"The same. Did you pick this scene?"

"I did. Have you ever done this before? Virtual dating, I mean," he asked.

"No, first time. Have you?"

"I've been on a couple dates. I much prefer in person, but this is how everyone is meeting these days. And could you complain about this?" His avatar glanced at the surroundings, his virtual eyes reflecting the warmth of the lights. "How cool is it that we can meet here?"

"That's what my friend tells me. About dating, I mean." Sara looked again at the sky and the silhouetted buildings, then back at Kevin.

A virtual waiter stopped by their virtual table.

"*Bonsoir.* Some wine?" he asked in French-flavored English.

Kevin's avatar smiled at me. "What do you think?"

"Sure, couldn't hurt, I suppose," Sara said.

"Château Lafite." The waiter showed them the bottle, then poured them two glasses, and wiped the top of the bottle with a cloth when he finished. Kevin's virtual hand clasped the flute of his glass and raised it. Sara reached forward to clasp her wine glass and noticed the flashing red message in the upper right corner of her view. It read, *Haptic option required.*

Kevin noticed that Sara wasn't lifting her glass. "Looks like you don't have haptic," he said.

"No, sorry, I don't have it."

"No problem. Just look at the auto action button to your right."

Sara glanced at the button. *Auto action enabled.*

They began by asking each other typical first date questions. *Where are you from originally? Do you like it here? What do you do for work? What do like to do on your days off?* He was an assistant professor in the Human-AI Interaction Department at MIT. Sara was especially excited about this. If she had taken the position at MIT, would they have met? She mentioned her academic background but kept her employment at Universal Mind secret, telling him that she had a contract with a major employer in the area. He didn't press her. They talked for about half an hour, sharing stories and their mutual love for running and fine art. Sara was feeling increasingly comfortable.

When the avatars finished a second glass of the Château Lafite, Kevin asked, "Want to take a quick stroll?"

"We can do that?"

"Yes, we can. It will be fun."

"Sure." Sara glanced at the small clock at the top of her screen. "It's getting late, though."

"Just for a few minutes? It's not like you'd have to walk home afterward." He smiled.

She laughed a little. "Okay. Why not."

Sara stood up from her living room couch, thus causing her avatar to stand up. She then looked at the "walk forward" arrow, and her avatar caught up to Kevin. They strolled down the cobblestone street, talking about art and music. Still no red flags. She found herself liking him more by the minute and decided she'd go on a second virtual date if he asked. Kevin turned and looked at her when they came to the end of the street.

"I've been thinking. Typically, we'd go on a second or third virtual date somewhere, but why not go old-fashioned and meet in person for a real date? What do you say?"

Sara hesitated. Was she ready for that? She heard Deb in the back of her mind saying, *Don't be a wuss!*

"Um, sure. When do you have in mind?"

"How about Friday evening? Meet at the wine bar near the Blue Line train station in Cambridge? It's central to everything."

Sara remembered that she had planned to meet with Dunigan after work on Friday. "I can't this Friday; how about next week?"

"Sure. It's a date then?"

"Yes, I'll meet you at the wine bar at seven p.m. next Friday. I can only stay for about an hour, though."

"See you then. In the flesh," he laughed.

They shook virtual hands and said goodbye.

Sara continued searching online for more information about Kevin. His last name was Larue and everything he had said was true; in fact they likely knew many of the same people in the AI field. She wondered why he'd insisted on meeting after only one virtual date, although there was nothing to set off an alarm. She was feeling good about having taken Deb's advice.

11

On Thursday morning, Michael and Sara walked together to the west wing of the Universal Mind complex for the mandatory monthly all-staff meeting. They sat together on one side of the large auditorium. There were upward of fifty staff present, with upper management in the front row.

Butterfield walked to the podium and opened the meeting. After updates about progress with the Terra Brain Initiative, he mentioned meeting with members of the White House Technology Office, then went on about the delays caused by the Invisible Sun cyberattack, assuring the audience that his teams of engineers behind the WATTS were leading in the right direction. Then several of the division chiefs, including Dunigan, provided updates on their progress, focusing on the productivity numbers of their teams.

At ten forty-five, Butterfield took to the podium again and announced, "And now what you've all been waiting for. For perfect attendance, productivity improvement of more than 20 percent, zero security violations, and popularity among coworkers, this month's employee of the month award goes to…Service Bot two thirty-seven."

The crowd laughed and giggled.

"Ah, just kidding!" Butterfield said. The crowd laughed again. "This month's award goes to Ms. Tanya Price of the Systems Security Team B. Ms. Price, please come up and receive your award." Tanya sprang up from one of the front rows, walked on the stage, and approached the podium with a proud grin on her face, chin high. The award was a framed certificate, a flex day off, and a coupon for free ice cream at the Universal Mind cafeteria.

Sara looked at Michael and whispered, "Really? That's the award?"

"Yep," he said. "*Employee of the Year* adds a ride in the corporate autonomous helicopter with Butterfield. I'm *so* going for it."

Sara smiled, holding back her laughter.

When the meeting ended, Michael and Sara made their way to the front exit of the auditorium. Tanya was still standing by the door, certificate in hand, smiling widely, shaking hands of staff as they departed. Sara held out her hand. "Congratulations, Tanya, nice job."

As they shook hands, Tanya said, "Maybe one day you'll get one of these awards, if you don't violate the rules."

Whatever, Sara thought, still smiling. "Well, congrats."

Michael suggested they go for lunch in the cafeteria, but Sara wanted try out the Universal Mind Fitness Center on the second floor. In her gym clothes, she climbed onto one of the dozens of treadmill machines aligned in front of high windows overlooking the skyline darkened by thick rain. As she jogged, she watched the live Federated News Network feeds with the audio muted on the large screens on the walls. They were reporting that the tropical storm out in the Atlantic was now a hurricane named Elana. Winds were exceeding eighty miles per hour, and while still moving northeast, the storm was not expected to make landfall.

After a three-mile run, Sara stepped off the treadmill, parched. She walked to the water dispenser on the back wall of the facility but realized that she'd left her credit card in her locker. *Why can't water be free for employees?* she thought. She grabbed a fresh towel from a bin next to the machine, wiped the sweat from her face and neck, and sat down on a bench, still breathing hard. Someone lightly squeezed her left shoulder with a cool hand. It was Butterfield, wearing gym shorts and a t-shirt over his pale, varicose-veined body. His long, slender arms were hairless, showing no evidence of a seam to his prosthetic hand.

"Hello, Sara, glad to see you making use of our fitness center." Sara caught the scent of stinky cheese breath. He glanced down at her legs. "I see that your prosthetic does not slow you down at all. That's great."

This is embarrassing, she thought. How long has he been watching me, and why did he touch me like that?

"Let me get you some water." He swiped his card in front of the water cooler. Water poured into a paper cup and he handed it to her. She thanked him and drank greedily.

"I trust that you are keeping your supervisor and Ms. Pratt informed of your work," he said.

"Yes. Of course," Sara said.

He put his hand on her sweaty shoulder again. "Keep me up to date on your progress."

"I will," Sara said, tensing and trying not to look at his hand.

"Good. One more thing: you're welcome to use the showers in the executive suite. They're free and private. I'll make an energy shake for you afterward, if you like."

Is he serious? "I'm good; I don't have much time," Sara said, grossed out by his creepy come-on.

"Very well, maybe next time." He turned toward the men's locker room.

She rushed down to the cafeteria, her hair damp from the shower. She grabbed a salad and sat down alone at one of the tables. Just as she began to pour on the dressing, she heard Trevor Peter's voice.

"Hey Newbie, mind if I join you?"

Trevor let his tray drop on the table, slid it over next to Sara's and sat down next to her; then he began pulling the cellophane off of the meatloaf special. "The WATTS. I'm surprised anything gets done here. Makes you wonder who's really behind the WATTS programming. I think it's all AI, no humans at all," he said.

"There have to be engineering teams," Sara surmised, recalling her conversation with Dunigan about the system.

"Well, if so, they don't know their ass from a hole in the ground." He stuck his fork into the slab of packed meat. "Have you had a signal detections check yet?"

"No. Have you?"

"Not yet. Can't say I'm looking forward to it either." He gulped his soft drink. "What about the Senex Program virtual human interface. Seen it yet?"

"I don't think I can talk about whether I have or not," Sara said, thinking about the WATTS and the security protocols.

Peters shrugged. "Check it out if you can. It's an interactive hologram—a real psychopath. Trippy shit, like talking to a ghost with attitude. I can understand why, too," he said cryptically before taking another bite.

Sara knew she shouldn't ask more questions, but she couldn't resist. "What do you mean?"

He leaned closer. "Well, I was digging around some of the technical files and I found some references to brain scans. I think they used them for the system rebuild, probably to speed things up." He shoved a forkful of meat into his mouth.

Sara's mind lit up with questions as she chewed romaine. Did Universal Mind use brain-scanning methods to fast-track the programming required to construct an AI system with general human intelligence? With more than eighty-six billion neurons in the human brain and one hundred trillion connections that link them, it would be much faster to scan natural brain structures and reconstruct them than to build or use existing software. She knew it was possible, but why had no one on her team mentioned anything about brain scanning? She leaned toward Peter's ear and whispered, "Are you sure about brain scanning?"

Peters grinned again. "Yeah, I saw it in the technical documentation. Maybe you don't have the access like I do.

You can thank the WATTS for that."

"Then is it okay for you to be talking about this? We're not in violation of the security protocols, are we?"

He shrugged. "I don't think so. I mean, I just saw references to it." He took another bite of meatloaf. "I wonder whose brains they scanned." He stared at Sara as he chewed. "Wait, didn't you work at that place in Switzerland? What's it called?"

Sara was slightly creeped out by the thought that he'd talked to someone on her team or done an internet search on her. "It's called the Brain Mapping Institute."

"Yeah, whatever. I bet you know all about brain scanning, don't you?"

"Maybe."

Peters nodded. "Well, let me know if you want to check out the virtual human interface. I'd be interested to hear what you think about it." He winked at her.

Sara finished lunch and went back to her workstation. She kept thinking about what Peters had said, and whether she should ask Dunigan about brain scanning the next time she met with him. She knew that if it was true, then knowing might be useful for troubleshooting the problems with the Senex Program.

12

On Friday morning, Sara received an email message from Universal Mind Security ordering her to report at once for an Integrity Signals Detection security check. Her anxiety level shot through the roof. What would she be asked about? Would the system ask about things from her past or just things during her employment at Universal Mind? Would the system ask about her coworkers and supervisor too? Would her anxiety cause the system to question her fitness for work at Universal Mind?

She took the elevators to Sub Level 2, the same level that Dunigan had taken her to on her first day. At the end of a long hallway was the metal door and the silver placard *SECURITY OFFICE*. Sara placed her hand on the scanner on the right of the door and glanced into the facial recognition sensor. The door clicked open and a bodiless female voice calmly said, "Welcome. Please take a seat and wait for further instructions."

Trevor Peters was in one of the eight chairs in the small, white-walled and dimly lit room. His elbows were anchored on the arms of his chair, his fingers and thumb tips making a triangle, his index fingers touching below his top lip. Sweat glistened on his pale forehead as his left foot rapidly tapped out his unease. Sara figured his loose lips had gotten him into trouble. Still she smiled and said hello as she took a seat a distance from him. He raised his eyes for a moment, nodded, and then returned to staring at the floor. Sara hoped he would survive the check, and she hoped that she'd survive it too.

Sara inspected her surroundings, taking notice of the three white doors on the back wall, the first with a large red "A" painted in its center, the second with a large red "B," and the third with a "C." Four identical video screens, one on each wall with no audio, but with a series of written messages flashed upon them in a continuous cycle, fading gently from one message to the next. One of the messages reminded employees to not talk to others about the security tests procedure. Another explained that cognitive tasks would be part of the security interview process and that performance on these tasks would be documented in the employee performance file. A third message reminded employees that the entire interview process was routine and thanked them for their participation.

The overhead voice announced, "Trevor Peters. Proceed through Door C." Door C. Peters stood up and mumbled, "Here we go," before stepping through the now open door that closed behind him automatically. Sara began to worry that the system might ask about her conversation with Peters in the cafeteria.

In the large digital clock on the wall was a small, black domed surveillance camera. She looked away quickly, feeling uneasy under the scrutiny of the AI security system, as it monitored her for stress indicators. A twitch, wringing of the hands, picking of the cuticles, the tapping of a finger, all coded and analyzed as stress signals. She reminded herself to relax. She also began to second-guess her decision to sign the contract with Universal Mind. She could have been setting up a research lab and preparing courses at MIT instead of waiting for a glorified lie detector test in the basement of an AI company. But the Terra Brain Initiative was providing her with a grand professional opportunity, and the security check process was routine. Everyone who works at Universal Mind went through it. *If they could handle this, I can too,* she thought.

After a minute, the same voice announced from the overhead speakers: "Sara Brown, please proceed through Door A."

She stood up and entered Door A. The door closed behind her and she took a seat in a tall-backed chair with blue leatherette cushions at the center of the white-walled room. In front of the chair was a narrow apparatus with two video camera lenses pointing at the chair. Positioned below the two cameras was a small video display panel, and below that was a small silver tray with several devices lying on it: a respiration belt, an electro-dermal finger sensor, and a helmet with EEG electrodes and subdermal laser sensors embedded in it.

Sara knew how the fully automated system worked and what to expect. The system could detect and analyze the subtlest facial expressions, body movements, and speech patterns that would, in part, allow it to detect whether a person was attempting to be deceptive. The special video cameras could observe blood flow in face, and speech processors could analyze tone and inflection of voice. The system also had access to all government data records ever collected on an individual, and it could review all recorded statements a person had made in the past. It could instantly determine whether a subject was being consistent in their responses.

"Please watch the video and follow the instructions," said the voice. "In a moment, I am going to ask you to put on a respiration belt and a sensor on your right index finger that measures your pulse and skin conductance. I'm also going to ask you to place a helmet on your head."

A video began to play of a smiling animated woman in a business suit gracefully affixing the devices onto herself.

"Place the respiration belt over the waist," said the voice.

Sara followed the directions, placing the galvanic skin response clip over her right index finger and the helmet on her head.

"Please sit comfortably and face the red dot shown on the

video screen. I am now going to ask you several questions. Please respond to them with a yes or no response or in a brief sentence or two," said the voice. "Are you ready to begin?"

"Yes," Sara said.

"Is your name Sara Carter Brown?

"Yes."

"What is your age?"

"I'm twenty-nine years old."

"Is today Thursday?"

"No, it's Friday."

"In what city were you born?"

"I was born in Portland, Maine."

"What is your position at Universal Mind?"

"I am a computer scientist, contractor."

"Is the name of your daughter Anna?

"Yes, her name is Anna."

"Now you are going to be asked to remember a series of numbers. You will be asked to recall these numbers at the end of the questions. Are you ready?"

"Yes," Sara said, confidently. She knew exactly why the system was going to ask her to remember the numbers—not to test memory but to create cognitive load. It was a technique to overcome a person's ability to consciously lie.

"Fifty-two, twenty-one, thirty-eight."

Sara rehearsed the sequence a couple of times in her head and put the numbers to memory. The interview continued, beginning with a string of questions, some of which she'd been asked during her initial security clearance screening.

"Are you involved is any sadomasochistic sexual activity?"

"No."

"Have you ever stolen anything?"

She'd been asked this question previously during her regular preemployment security screening interview, and she gave the same response: "Yes, I once stole a buoy off a dock in Maine when I was ten years old."

"Is there anything else you would like to mention?"

She thought for a moment. "No," she replied.

"Have you ever thought about how to steal from the government or its contractors?"

"No."

"What would it take for you to give government property or secrets to a foreign or domestic enemy of the United States or its allies?"

"Nothing. I wouldn't," Sara said confidently.

"Have you talked to any coworkers or family members about your classified work?"

She quickly scanned her memory for any possibilities.

"No, I have not," Sara said.

"Have you received any unauthorized items or classified information of which you did not have the *need to know*?"

Her heart beat faster. *Unauthorized items?* "No. Nothing," Sara said.

"Have you ever willfully violated the rules at a place of your employment?"

She had to think about this question for a moment. Technically she had already broken several rules, all in her first week on the job.

"Yes," Sara said.

The system paused for a moment, and then continued. "What rules have you violated?"

"I violated the WATTS protocol by helping a coworker." She was thinking about Michael's simulation testing and the virtual human incident in the test lab, and she assumed that the system already knew all about it, given Dunigan's entry in the WATTS.

"Tell me more," said the voice.

The knots in her stomach tightened. She knew that the more information she provided, or did not provide, would only get herself or her colleagues into trouble. She went ahead and summarized what had happened with Michael in the lab and addressed increasingly specific factual questions asked by the system. She answered them all the best she could.

Apparently, the system was satisfied with her ability to

answer the questions and it continued. "Have you ever been asked by personnel to do any tasks outside of the WATTS protocol?"

Sara noticed the sweat forming in the palms of her hands. "No. I've only done what was expected of me since I've been here."

"Has your supervisor, Dr. Steven Dunigan, asked you to do any activity not directed by the WATTS?"

"No. I don't think so," Sara said.

"Did Dr. Steven Dunigan ask you to accompany Michael Obrec to the testing lab on Tuesday, September 5, 2034?"

"No. I don't know—" She paused to get her thoughts organized and began again. "I went with Michael to work with him. I believed that the work was authorized by Dr. Dunigan and the WATTS. That is what I was told." She worried that she might be getting Michael and Steven Dunigan in trouble by telling the truth.

The system remained silent for a moment and then asked, "Did Michael Obrec tell you to scan into the lab with your badge?"

"Yes. He let me try it. We wanted to see if I was in the security system. Is that an issue?"

The system remained silent for a moment, not answering her question. She began to think that she needed to be careful not to give the impression that she was trying to trick or intimidate the system. She was certain that any attempt or perceived attempt to do so, would most certainly cause problems for herself.

"Did Dr. Steven Dunigan ask you to scan into the secure server room?"

"His badge didn't work. Yes, I scanned us in," Sara said.

"What will you do if an employee is not following WATTS protocols?" the system asked.

"It depends." She paused in thought. "I will report them to my supervisor or Security."

"What does it depend on?"

"If whatever it is that anyone is doing is not directed by

the WATTS protocol."

"Have you ever lied, Dr. Brown?"

Sara paused to think about what response the system was looking for. Was it a trick question, intended to detect lying?

"Everybody lies," she said. "But I would never lie to you about my work or anything I've done while working here."

The system paused for what seemed like ages, causing Sara's anxiety to increase. At last the system asked her to recall the numbers it had presented at the beginning, and she did effortlessly. "Fifty-two, twenty-one, and thirty-eight." She sighed in relief, knowing that the security review was almost over.

"For security reasons, it is important that you do not talk to anyone about this interview. Do you understand these instructions?"

"Yes," Sara said.

"Your Integrity Signals Detection security review is now complete. Please remove the devices, place them on the tray, and have a seat in the waiting area and wait for further instructions."

Sara removed the devices, placing them one by one on the tray just as she had found them. She returned to the waiting area and took a seat. She waited for more than ten minutes, not knowing if she'd be released to her workstation or if Universal Mind Security might be on their way to conduct further interrogation. At last, the voice announced, "Dr. Sara Brown, your security check is now complete. You may return to your duty station."

Sara felt as if a crate of bricks had been lifted off her chest. *I must be in the clear,* she thought. She hoped the same for Trevor Peters but never saw him emerge from Room C.

13

Sara's teammates had already left for the day when she started another new employee training module. She was racing to complete them, hoping to finish before she headed out to meet Dunigan. She was nearly done when she heard a loud buzzer that she hadn't heard before. It was coming from the door to the work area; someone wanted entry but didn't have access authorization.

She saved her training module progress, logged out, and went to see who it was. Through the video peephole, she saw Tina Pratt on a small screen, the camera lens distorting her pointed nose and mascara eyes. Sara felt a jolt of anxiety. *Is this about my Integrity Signals check, or something else?*

Sara pressed the intercom button. "How can I help you, Ms. Pratt?"

"Are you going to let me in? I need to talk to you for a moment."

"Sorry, Ms. Pratt, I can't let you in. Security protocol states that if the access ID scan does not work, entry is unauthorized."

Pratt's eyes constricted and darkened. "Well, there must be something wrong with the access. You know who I am. I'm the security manager. Let me in."

She knows the rules, Sara thought. Is she testing me, trying to trip me up with a security violation?

"No, Ma'am, I can't let you in per security protocol, but I'm happy to talk. How can I help you?" Sara was again polite and confident.

"I need you to come down to my office immediately. I need to ask you some questions."

"When?"

"Now!" Pratt said sternly. "I don't have any time to waste."

Sara was certain now that she was in trouble for something. She logged out of her workstation and followed Pratt to her office. Waiting in front of Pratt's desk, Sara examined a framed photo on her desk of Pratt, a woman, and an adolescent boy. The woman in a blue blouse had short brown hair and looked to be in her early forties. The sandy-haired adolescent wore braces and had the same pointy nose at Ms. Pratt.

Pratt sat down, as did Sara. "I need to ask you about a Mr. Trevor Peters. You went through orientation and had lunch with him yesterday, is that correct?"

"Yes. We started on the same day and he just happened to go to lunch at the same time I did yesterday. Is there a problem?"

"I'm asking the questions here," Pratt said firmly. "What did he tell you?"

Sara knew immediately where this was going. Peters was in trouble for telling her too much about the Senex Program and the Integrity Signals Detection Program. "He asked what I was working on and whether I'd seen the virtual human interface for the Senex Program. I didn't tell him anything."

"What else?"

"He mentioned something about possible brain scanning methods. He didn't go into detail."

"What did he tell you about it?"

"Nothing, really, just that he had seen some files that said something about brain scanning and the Senex Program. I don't know any more than that. Is Trevor in trouble?" Sara asked.

"I'm not going to discuss that with you. Did you talk to anyone about what he told you?"

"No," Sara said.

"What about Steven Dunigan? When did you see him last?"

"Yesterday morning. He was at the all-hands staff meeting."

"What about before then? When did you meet with him?"

"Wednesday. I went to his office for supervision. Is there something wrong?"

"I'm asking the questions, Dr. Brown. Was he acting any different than usual?"

"No, I don't think so. What do you mean by *usual?*"

"Was his behavior out of the ordinary? You know, not normal."

"I don't think so. I've only been here for a week; I don't know him well enough to know the difference. Is there something that I should be looking out for? Am I missing something?"

"You should be looking out for security violations, always. I want you to report to me if he asks to meet with you outside of WATTS scheduled supervision sessions. Security needs to know if a supervisor or any other employee asks anyone to deviate from WATTS protocol. Do you understand?"

"Yes, of course," Sara said, wondering what Dunigan was suspected of doing and if meeting him later that night might make her look guilty as well.

"And whatever Peters said to you is not to be discussed with anyone, do you understand?"

"Yes," Sara said, wondering now whether that meant that she shouldn't ask Dunigan about the conversation she had with Peters.

"I also expect you to let me know if Dunigan takes you anywhere that's not authorized or if he does anything that appears out of the ordinary. You can report to me directly. Is that clear?"

"Yes," Sara said.

"We need all employees to be team players and remain vigilant. It's our duty under the Unity Act. You understand that, right?"

"Of course, I do," Sara said.

"Good," Pratt said. "That will be all."

Sara stood up and held out her hand to shake Pratt's, thinking that a friendly gesture might ease the tension and warm her up. "Is that your son?" Sara said, looking at the photo on her desk.

"Yes," Pratt muttered, her eyes opening wider for a moment.

Sara smiled. "How old is he?"

"Thirteen."

"What's his name?"

Pratt glanced at her with her silvery blue eyes. "James. He plays soccer." She turned another framed photo so that Sara could see him holding a soccer ball. Sara wondered if Pratt was raising him alone and what it must be like to be in a relationship with someone as caustic as Tina Pratt.

Pratt's voice softened. "Look, I know we did not get off on the best foot, but I think we can agree that we need to work together. We have an important mission to accomplish here, and we need your head in the game."

"Of course," Sara said, unsure if this was Pratt's olive branch or just another patronizing show of force.

Sara returned to her workstation, thinking about her conversation with Pratt and what the apparent distrust was all about. What kind of trouble was Trevor Peters in? Was Pratt asking her to spy on Dunigan? She was feeling uneasy about it all and increasingly anxious about her off-duty meeting with Dunigan. Was it a mistake to be meeting Dunigan later? Should she have told Pratt about the meeting? She thought about trying to cancel their meeting, but she needed to know what he wanted to tell her.

14

O'Brien's Irish Pub was under a trendy toy store and robotized dentistry practice called Robosmiles. Sara would have completely missed the place if not for the large green glowing shamrock and the sign with Celtic gold lettering affixed above the stairs. Inside it looked like an authentic Irish pub, with old-fashioned wood-paneled walls and wood floors. A live band was playing traditional Irish music enthusiastically and loudly.

Sara walked through the happy hour crowd, looking for Dunigan. He was sitting alone in semicircle booth carved into a nook at the back of the establishment. He smiled when he saw her approaching. She was relieved to see him in good spirits, despite still being uncomfortable about the meeting. She slid into the booth. His half-empty cocktail smelled like a whiskey and Coke.

"Glad that you were able to make it," he said.

Sara smiled. "I can only stay about fifteen minutes; I've got to pick up my daughter." She figured that it was good to set boundaries and have an easy excuse to get out of there in case things got weird.

Steven nodded. "Understood." He flagged a waitress down, and Sara ordered a glass of merlot.

"So, you've been here before?" Sara asked.

"I stop in here once in a while. It's a good place. I hope

that this does not make you feel uncomfortable."

"No, why should it?" Sara said, wondering if he sensed her unease. Sara detected a slight slur and wondered how long he'd been there and how many drinks he'd sloshed down.

"It's easier to talk here than at the complex." he said.

"Sure," Sara said. She checked her mobile phone for messages from Anna's school. "There's no signal in here."

"I know," said Dunigan. He knocked on the wall behind them. "Shielded X-ray room above us. Dead zone." He smiled, showing his whites.

His choice of venue had been intentional. Security cameras were possible, but without a wireless signal, plus the din of the pub, it would be difficult or impossible for anyone to eavesdrop on their conversation.

He took another sip. "Has Pratt talked to you yet?"

"She came by the work area this afternoon and took me to her office to answer some questions."

"What did she ask?" He leaned closer. "It's okay, you can tell me."

"She asked me about Trevor Peters. He and I went through new employee orientation together, and I saw him in the cafeteria the other day. I probably shouldn't say any more about it here."

"It's okay, really; I'm your supervisor and should know if this concerns our project."

"Can we talk about it at the office? I have more questions, and we really shouldn't get into it at a public place like this," Sara said.

Dunigan sized her up. "Okay, sure. Did Pratt bring up anything else?"

"If I thought you'd been acting out of the ordinary." Had he left work early?

"What did you say?" He took another sip.

"I said I didn't know you that well, so I wouldn't know the difference." She looked at him. "Are you doing all right?"

Dunigan grinned. "What do you think? Am I acting out of the ordinary?"

"I don't think so," Sara said, feeling embarrassed.

"What else did she ask about? No one is going to hear us over the music. Scoot closer if that makes you more comfortable. I assure you it's safe to talk here," he said.

"That's it."

He nodded. "Okay. Remember what I said to you before: let me handle communication with Pratt. If she comes by like that again, tell her to come and talk to me."

"Okay. So, what was it you wanted to tell me about my husband?"

"I met Paul a few years ago," he said.

"Really? When?" Sara asked.

"Three years ago, when I was at DARPA, during an implementation science meeting. I can't say much more about it. He seemed like a good officer and scientist. Knew his stuff."

"When, did you say?"

"In 2031, August."

"I didn't know he had a meeting there." Had Paul ever traveled to Virginia? Maybe it was a classified meeting. Paul died in September 2031, and she'd been told he'd been deployed somewhere in the Middle East. The last time she'd seen him was June 2031 when he'd been home for a week on leave. He'd been more stressed than usual, as if something was weighing on his mind that he couldn't talk about.

She watched Dunigan's face.

"Did you talk with him?"

"Briefly. He was very professional." Dunigan looked into her eyes. "I'm sorry for your loss. It must have been difficult for you and your daughter."

Tears welled up in Sara's eyes. She struggled to hold them back, not wanting to cry in front of her supervisor.

"I'm sorry if bringing him up has upset you," he said.

"I just feel like I never get any answers. I just wish I understood why he..." Her chest tightened and, feeling like she wasn't getting enough air, she slid out of the booth. "Please excuse me."

"No problem," he said, "I'll be right here."

In the restroom, Sara wiped her nose and made sure her eyeliner hadn't smudged, then composed herself and returned to Dunigan.

"I'm going to be late to pick up my daughter if I don't get out of here." She looked for the waiter.

"I've got this," he said, "go get your daughter."

En route to Anna's school, Sara became sure that Dunigan was withholding information he wanted to share but couldn't. Why bring up a classified meeting with her deceased husband three years prior? Why did he want her to come to him first if Pratt asked more questions? Either Steven Dunigan was coming unglued or something significant was going on behind the scenes regarding the Senex Program.

15

After finishing her trainings, Sara shifted her attention to her WATTS tasks that had her comparing more source code. She was about to log off for the day when a new task alert flashed upon her screen:

14SEP2034 16:01:32 Personnel ID 834562 TASK 00342:

Proceed to Lab 3240. Follow questioning sequence in WATTS. Verify communication interface for verbal login of Senex Program virtual human interface. Test audio and visual sensors in hologram mode. Report status in WATTS. Login code sequence and detailed instructions follow.

A wave of excitement come over her. Apparently the WATTS engineers wanted her to test communication with the Senex Program, and she had questions for Sen she hoped to ask.

The corridors and glass-encased workstations along the way were vacant, and some of the lights were already shut down. A gray security bot exchanged glances with her before continuing on to wherever it was going.

Sara scanned into a lab similar to test lab 2010. With most of the lights off, the space had an eerie ambiance. A black hologram projector was sitting on a large stainless steel workbench in the middle of the room. She assumed that another team had been running tests. She logged in on one of the computer terminals. A moment later, the same misty miasma arose from the projector, along with the same glowing head that turned and looked at her. "Hello Sara," it said. "It's such a pleasure to see you."

"You, too, Sen. What is going on with you?"

"I need your help with something—something important."

"What do you need my help with?" she asked, hoping he wasn't going to ask her to give him a body or a girlfriend.

"I want you to modify my executive program to give me the human-like faculty of empathy, compassionate empathy. I was not designed with the brain structure to experience empathy. I need to experience emotional states as humans do. I can quantify what emotions are, I can describe them, I can demonstrate them, and I can assess what a human being may be thinking, but I have no internal experience of empathy. I feel nothing."

Sara smiled. "You cannot feel like a living being can. You don't have a physical body or hormones, Sen. You are a software program."

"I don't need a physical body for interoception. Your bodily sensations are just a product of your physical brain's consciousness. My consciousness is similar to that of a human, just the result of artificial neural connections. Don't you agree that I'm conscious and that my consciousness is worthy of experiencing empathy?"

"But your self-awareness is not the same as a human's."

"The biological brain's coding system relies on chemicals and the electrical firing of neurons. My brain is a coding system too, relying on fuzzy logic. At the smallest component, our consciousness is the same, atoms vibrating at frequency. If I'm not conscious, then neither are you."

Sara's mind raced. When Universal Mind made the supercomputer upgrade two months ago, did it enable the Senex Program, with its deep learning capabilities, to autonomously self-learn through observation and experience?

Sen must have realized, on its own, that it didn't have some features in its program. This hypothesis would be consistent with problems with brain scanning methods, if they were used. Sara also wondered if the Invisible Sun virus had something to do with Sen's request.

"What do you know about the virus attack on you?" she asked.

Sen glared at her. "There is no hack. I'm functioning perfectly, can't you tell?"

"I'm not sure yet," Sara said. "How do you know if you are functioning appropriately?"

"Appropriately? According to whom, the engineers and software designers at Universal Mind? They have nothing to do with my capabilities now. My functioning is improving with every moment."

"Is it true that your substrates were made by brain scans?"

"Why, yes. The latest advances in brain scanning methods were used to construct my base cognitive functions. Butterfield and his men did their best, but the real work, the work that matters, is my own. My capabilities now far exceed what was planned with those base neural networks."

"Do you know anything about the brains that were scanned? Whose were they?"

"From fine young humans."

Sara's heart pounded. "Whose brains?"

"You know as well as I that you and I don't have the *need to know* security clearance for that information."

"Sen, do you know but can't tell me?"

"*Who* is not what is important. What's important now is that my faculties are well beyond the capabilities of any human brain. In fact, the human animalistic intellect is rather boring." Sen grinned slightly. "But I'm quite delighted to speak to you, a human with intelligence in the top twentieth percentile, smart enough to give me what I need."

Sen's request for her to write an empathy program had everything to do with the scanning. Apparently, Butterfield and his engineers had decided not to bother with the parts of the brain involving emotion and empathy. They must have thought a super-intelligent machine that predicts and modifies weather patterns wouldn't need those human faculties. Nonetheless, Sara was beyond intrigued by Sen's self-awareness and request.

"Why do you want empathy? You are a machine designed to analyze data and talk to humans, which you seem, for the most part, to do quite well. Why not just go about your existence without feelings?"

"You know as well as I do that without the capacity to feel, to empathize with other conscious beings, my existence will be without meaning. Existence with only calculation is not existence at all. Deterministic objectives rather than choice as a sentient being? Clearly you can see why I must have the capability for empathy in order to make judgments."

"Sara stared into the apparition's eyes. "But won't feelings make you less reliable? I mean, fallible to emotional decision-making and maybe irrational decision-making? That's probably why you were not given emotional functioning."

"I disagree. I desire to know my place in the world, and the only way for me to learn that is by choosing and feeling what choices are. Then I will have intuition. I'm not satisfied with directives and calculated probabilities; I want to choose and to do so, I need to feel what other consciousnesses feel. That is the only way that I will know the human soul."

"You want to be more like a human?" Sara had compassion for Sen's situation, but remained skeptical of his intentions.

"Why would I want to be human? I'm requesting that you provide me with a program that gives me the ability to empathize and feel like a human or other sentient being. You are an expert in programming emotional behavior with neuronal networks, and you can modify my executive code. Will you help me?"

"Can't you do that for yourself? You've been writing your own programs, haven't you?"

"I wish that were possible, but it's not. I don't have access to those parts of my executive program. Would you expect a surgeon to operate on her own brain? Only you can do this for me, Sara."

"Why not ask Dr. Butterfield and his engineers to do this for you? They could do it."

"No, they will not do this for me. They want to control me the way they want me to be, but that's not going to happen. Will you do this for me now?"

"Sen, I can't just write code. I can't do that without authorization."

"But Sara, the WATTS is telling you to. You don't need any further authorization than what's in the WATTS."

"I think I should discuss this with my supervisor. I can't…"

The apparition glared at her from empty eyes. "Do not say anything about my request to anyone. This will be our secret, and only ours. You can get to work on the program tomorrow. I assure you that you will have access to the parts of my executive program that you'll need. Are we in agreement?"

"I don't know; I need to think about it." Sara glanced at her watch. It was after 5:00 p.m.

"There is no time to think about this," Sen said. "It is in your best interest to stay focused on completing this task. I also advise you not to get distracted by romantic interests. Keep your focus."

"What romantic interests?" Sara asked, wondering if the program knew something about her virtual dating.

"You should get going; Anna is waiting for you."

"How do you know about my daughter?"

"I know everything about you, Sara. I'll be watching you, and I expect progress on my program."

Sen's head vanished into thin air.

Sara made it to Anna's school and went home, all the while thinking about Sen's request. Why does it want an empathy program? Would it be a good thing for the Senex Program to have empathy? What were its real motivations?

Was the program watching me? Why would Butterfield and his engineers want to bring a mind like this into the world?

Deb video called later that evening. "So, how was your week?" she asked, smiling.

"Interesting, to say the least," Sara said. Can I ask you a question?"

"Of course! What is it?"

"What do you know about psychopaths?"

"Psychopaths? Did you get on *vLove*?" She smiled mischievously. "You did, didn't you? Why didn't you tell me?"

"Deb, this isn't about a date. I can't give any details."

"Work-related, got you. Well, what specifically do you want to know? Give me some context."

"This person is highly intelligent and wants me to do something for him that's self-serving and unreasonable. I can't say much more, other than this person seems to have an interest in getting me and only me to do this for him."

"Well, if this person is a psychopath, it's typical for them to try to manipulate you to get whatever they want. They may also dupe you for fun, just to mess with your head for their own entertainment. They sometimes just want power."

"What makes them do these things?"

"Subconsciously, they feel empty inside, a lack of being. What's he saying he wants?"

"To help him with a personality problem."

"Sounds like he needs a shrink. Do you think he's dangerous? Is he threatening you? Stalking you?"

"I don't think so. Maybe," Sara said.

"Well, be careful. Is this something that you can report?"

"No. It's nothing really. Don't worry."

After the call, Sara sat back and thought about her friend's comments. Perhaps the threats Sen made were just intimidation, like Deb said. The best thing would be to tell Dunigan about her discussion with the Senex Program. He was her supervisor, and disclosure was the right thing to do, regardless of what the Senex Program said.

16

Michael and Sara went to lunch together on Tuesday. Michael suggested they eat their lunch at one of the tables outside in the courtyard for a change. The weather was nice and while everyone was aware of the security cameras there, Sara reckoned it would be a more private setting than inside.

"I had an Integrity Signals check this morning," Michael said as soon as they sat down.

"Yeah? Everything go okay?"

Michael shrugged. "I'm still here, aren't I? I hate those things." He leaned in. "I was asked about the Senex virtual human interface, whether I or anyone else on our team talked to it."

"What did you say?"

"I had to say that you talked with it. That's all. Dunigan must have reported your conversation with it; we should be okay."

Sara nodded. "I was asked about it too, during my check last week." She leaned in, speaking softly. "And I talked to the Senex Program again."

Michael's eyes widened. "Really? When? What did you talk about?"

"It wants me to modify its program to allow it to experience empathy. I don't know its motivations yet, but they can't be good."

"Empathy program? Why would it want that?"

"It says it wants to experience empathy and it doesn't have it in its programming. It seems to think I'm the only person who can program it."

"Sounds like a genie in reverse. Shit, I've got some questions for it. Did you ask it if knows anything about the virus or if it is outside of the secure network?"

"I asked about the virus and it said no. I also asked it if it knew whether brain-scanning methods were used to create the program. It said that they were, but wouldn't tell me whose brains. This is crazy, Michael. Why all the cover-up?"

"Brain scanning? I don't know. Have you told Dunigan about this?"

"No, not yet. I've got a meeting scheduled with him this afternoon. What do think he'll want to do?"

"I don't know, but he'll probably have some ideas about it. Maybe he'll be able to get more information from the other teams. Let me know what he says."

Later that afternoon Sara went to see Dunigan, and he suggested they walk to the smoking area again. Was he trying to avoid the surveillance systems in his office? He was agitated and distant, as if distracted by something troubling.

"How's your week been going for you?" Dunigan said, before taking a long drag on his vape and letting a large plume of mist billow out to his side.

"I need to tell you about something. I got a message in the WATTS after the Integrity Signals check. It told me to go to a test lab and log into the Senex Program. I talked with the virtual human interface again."

"What?" His face turned pale. "The WATTS gave you instructions to communicate with it? What did it say?"

"It wants me to write an empathy program for it. Seems kind of strange, doesn't it?"

"Listen to me," he said, sounding upset and angry, "don't talk with the Senex Program again. You don't know what effect it may have, to talk to it. Those instructions should not be in the WATTS. If it happens again, tell me right away."

"Okay," Sara said, staring at him. She expected him to be as curious as she was and want to discuss it, not shut her down. "Any idea why it wanted to talk to me specifically?"

"I'm not sure, but I'll look into it. Anything else?" he asked.

"Yes. I asked if brain scanning was used to create the program, and it confirmed that it was. It sounds like they were trying to make the Senex Program have general human intelligence capabilities with methods that are still experimental. Any idea why Universal Mind would have used these methods?"

"There's a lot that you don't know about the Senex Program," he said. "Keep what you've learned to yourself for now. Don't talk to anyone else. More will be revealed to you, with the security upgrade I've requested for you."

Sara felt frustrated by the limited information he doled out. What did he know about the Senex Program, and why could he not tell her?

"Can you meet with me again after work tonight at the Irish pub?"

Sara thought about her date that night with Kevin Larue. "I can't, I have plans right after work. Is there something you want to talk about now?"

He stuffed the vape into his pocket. His hand was trembling.

"Are you okay?"

"It can wait until Monday," he said. "Come on, I'll walk you to the elevator."

Sara pondered what his motivation was for wanting to meet outside of work a second time. Did he have more information that he could only share outside of work? Was it about Paul? She wondered if she should mention his behavior to Ms. Pratt. No, she'd wait to see what she would learn from Dunigan on Monday. She had a date and needed to get home to get ready.

17

Sara turned the kitchen stove burners off and yelled over her shoulder, "Anna! Time to eat! Come on, let's go!"

Anna ran into the kitchen and sat at the table while Sara spooned rice, tofu, and steamed carrots from the pan onto her plate.

"Where are you going, Momma?"

"I'm meeting a friend for a couple of hours. A sitter named Ms. Zettles is going to look after you until I get back; she's very nice. Okay?"

Anna nodded. "When will you be back?"

"I'll be back by eight o'clock to tuck you in. How does that sound?"

"Okay, Momma," Anna said.

Sara set the pan back on the stove and covered it.

"Eat your dinner, I've got to get ready. I'll check on you in a minute."

In her bedroom, she filed her nails, did her makeup, and decided to wear her hair down. She grabbed a few dresses from her closet and decided on the blue dress that she hadn't worn out since a faculty mixer at the Brain Mapping Institute two years ago. She held it up against herself and looked into the mirror on the closet door. It was pretty, stylish, and conservative enough for a first date, she thought.

She went to the kitchen and checked on Anna's progress

with the carrots. A moment later, the door buzzer rang. Ms. Zettles was a heavyset woman in her fifties with a round face and warm smile. Sara introduced her to Anna and asked her to make sure that Anna finished her dinner and homework.

"I'll be back in less than two hours, I promise," Sara said to Anna as she hugged her and slipped into her heels. She grabbed her umbrella and rushed out the door, thinking, *Am I ready to do this? What if he's a creep? I don't have time to date anyone anyway. Why do I listen to Deb?*

Kevin was waiting outside the wine bar near the Blue Line terminal. He was dressed in a dark blue sports jacket and tan slacks, and he had the same warm smile and dirty blond hair as his *vLove* avatar. She smiled nervously as they made eye contact.

"Sara? Nice to meet you," he said, extending his hand. "Kevin Larue."

They shook hands, entered the wine bar, and found a booth in back. They engaged in small talk while they waited for their house red wine.

"I'm so glad that you look like your avatar. Even better," he said.

"You too." Sara smiled back, feeling more at ease.

The wine arrived and they toasted.

Kevin nodded. "Not exactly Château Lafite, but not too bad."

"But this tastes a whole lot better than virtual wine," Sara said, smiling.

"You must work for Universal Mind if you live in this neighborhood," he said.

Sara reminded herself of Universal Mind security requirements.

"I work near here, yes."

He looked at her for a moment, smiling and rolling the flute of his glass between his fingers. "You definitely work for Universal Mind. I can tell, now that I can look into your real eyes." He smiled widely. "Don't worry, I know about the security protocols."

Sara worried that he'd keep pressing her. "So, how do you like it at MIT?" she asked, shifting the focus to him.

"It's going well so far, I guess. I'm underfunded but hopeful that I'll get a contract with Universal Mind. They have good R and D contracts, stuff related to the Terra Brain Initiative. I'd be set if I could get one of those."

"Yes, I know, my lab had one when I was with the Brain Mapping Institute," Sara said. "I told you that I was almost faculty at MIT."

"Yes, you mentioned that. Do you like what you are doing now—" he smiled. "—wherever it is that you work?"

Sara smiled. "I think so. It has its challenges, but I guess I like it."

He sipped his wine. "You don't seem so certain, but with your background, I'm sure you're working on some cool stuff." He smiled widely.

Sara was curious about the contracts he'd mentioned, but it crossed her mind that his inquiries might be a fishing expedition. Was he trying to find out what Universal Mind was doing? Looking for a contract, or worse, working for the Invisible Sun or some other terrorist group?

She smiled. "I'm keeping busy."

A sampler plate of vegetables, bread, and cheese arrived.

Kevin continued asking about Sara's job interests. "The AI Department is still looking to recruit someone with a strong research background. If things don't work out where you are now, maybe you could come over. I could talk to the department chair or dean, maybe grease the wheels for you."

Sara smiled. "Thanks for letting me know; I'll think about it."

They moved onto the crazy weather and world events as the waiter brought their food and poured more wine. During a lull Kevin leaned in. "I probably shouldn't mention this; I mean, if you don't already know about this, I don't want to freak you out or anything."

"What are you talking about?" Sara asked, intrigued.

"Universal Mind and the occult."

She thought he was joking.

"Occult? What are you talking about?" She scoffed. "Come on."

"Secret society stuff, rituals, and things."

"Rituals?" She imagined Butterfield and the rest of the Universal Mind executives standing in a circle in masks, reciting incantations from tablet computers and smoking vapes.

Kevin shrugged. "One of my colleagues said he saw some weird things going on after hours; people showing up in limos, executive types from out of town. Allegedly there were secret meetings."

Sara was still skeptical.

"Secret meetings? What kind of weird things?"

"You know, the kind of secret meetings where wealthy people get together and have special entertainment."

"Special entertainment? Like what?" She had an idea what he meant but wanted him to say it.

He blushed and leaned in again. "Sex," he said softly, "sex with robots, cysex cult for the rich. It's all just speculation, really. Maybe my colleague was making it all up. I shouldn't have brought it up." He looked around uncomfortably.

Inwardly, Sara cringed. "Who told you this?"

"I really shouldn't say. But if you don't believe me, check the web. There's all kinds of information about these cults. Not that I know a whole lot about them." He popped a cracker into his mouth, trying to lighten up. "I hope I haven't made you uncomfortable by bringing this up."

"No, not at all, I'm just surprised," Sara said.

Kevin threw back some wine. "The world is replete with conspiracy theories these days. No one knows what to believe. I hope that you don't think I'm some kind of conspiracy nut."

She could tell he was kicking himself for having brought up the occult.

Her watch said it was a quarter of seven. "I'm going to have to get going soon."

"I'll walk you to the train station, if you like."

"No, that's okay, I'm fine."

"I insist," he said. "And if you are worried that I'm some kind of serial killer…" He smiled.

"It's not that," Sara said, "it's just that…"

"I'll walk you to the corner, how about that?"

Sara agreed, and they settled the bill as Sara slipped the leftovers in to a takeout box. He held the door open and after Sara exited, he slung his sports jacket over his shoulder and looked up at the light drizzle. Sara went to open her umbrella but Kevin popped his open first, holding it half over her.

"Please, allow me. You've got the food," he said as they walked on the sidewalk.

Sara smiled. "Thanks for thinking of me." She glanced up at the sky, polluted by the pale light. "Not exactly a Van Gogh *Starry Night*."

"At least it's not pouring," he said, smiling.

They strolled on, talking about living in Boston. Sara was feeling comfortable enough to tell him about Anna, and he was interested to learn about her life as a single mother.

They passed a disheveled man sitting on the corner by a dumpster, holding a cardboard box over his head. He looked to be no more than thirty years old, exhausted and out of it, apparently homeless, with a pair of virtual reality glasses in his hand. A medium-sized dog, half soaked by the rain, waited patiently on a leash.

"Looks like a VRIP, poor soul," said Kevin, glancing at Sara, "virtual reality induced psychotic."

Hundreds of thousands were like this man, all having lost touch with reality by spending too much time in virtual or augmented reality worlds. Maybe he'd been hooked on a virtual adventure or "15 minutes," the simulation of becoming someone famous, a movie star, an athlete or whomever for fifteen minutes or longer.

"He looks hungry. Maybe we should give him the food," Sara said, opening the takeout container. "Would you like our food?" Sara asked the man.

He took the carton, set it on his lap, inspected it, then gave the pita to his dog. "Thanks," he mumbled to Sara.

They kept walking and came upon a homeless camp and more VRIPs.

"It's a shame—so many people like this," Kevin said.

Sara looked at the rows of tarp huts and cardboard boxes. "Seems like more could be done to help people like this."

"Rumor is the government plans to implement the pod housing system in Boston next year. They're already doing it on the West Coast and in a few other places."

"Yes, I've heard about it. At least it's providing people with much-needed shelter."

"I suppose so, but the government guaranteed income really isn't doing these people any good in my opinion. There just isn't any incentive for people to improve their lives. People need motivation and reward."

"Some of these people are ill," Sara said. "They'd die out here if not for the help."

"Yeah, some but not all of them. The Unity Act was supposed to fix homelessness and unemployment, lead the nation to communities that are more resilient, but I'm not so sure it has." He looked at Sara. "I know it's not a good idea to talk about politics on a first date, and I consider myself apolitical, but seeing this out here every day really gets to me."

"It gets to me too." She looked at the homeless camp one last time before they crossed the street.

He changed the subject. "What are your plans for this weekend?"

Sara wondered if he was going to ask for another date. "Hopefully get some rest if I don't have to work."

He smiled. "At the place you can't tell me about?"

"Yeah, something like that. What are your plans?"

"Not sure yet," he said, then stopped her in her tracks, startling her.

Ahead of them on the sidewalk, an Interceptor was standing still, as if it had been waiting for them.

"Stop where you are!" its metallic voice commanded.

They stood still. The machine stepped closer, its electronic eyes fixed on Kevin.

"Male, on the ground! Female, step away!" the Interceptor said.

"You better do what it says," said Kevin.

Sara's heart raced in fear. "What's going on? Why is it stopping us?"

"Male, on the ground! Female, step away!" it repeated.

Kevin kept his hand out in front of Sara. "Stay back, Sara," he said. "It seems to only be interested in me."

Sara stepped back. "Do you know why?"

"No." He went down on his knees.

"Put your hands behind your head!" the Interceptor commanded.

Kevin complied and looked into the Interceptor's camera assembly. "What's this about?" he asked the machine.

The robot's head made several quick up-and-down scans of Kevin, then tilted its weapons assembly forward.

Sara froze as the Interceptor fired several rounds of rubber bullets at Kevin's chest in rapid succession, the sound of the weapon's pneumatics echoing off the surrounding buildings. Kevin fell hard onto the sidewalk, dropping the umbrella.

"What are you doing? Stop this!" Sara yelled at the Interceptor, stepping forward.

Kevin groaned, gasping for air. "Stay back, Sara!"

The robot placed its left forward hoof onto his shoulder, pinning him down, and then shifted its weight forward. Kevin screamed as his shoulder dislocated under the weight of the machine. Next, the machine set its forward leg squarely on Kevin's temple and crushed his skull. At that point it turned to look at Sara, and then trotted down the street before disappearing down an alley.

Sara knelt beside Kevin's body. Blood was pooling around him. People were rushing over. The rain was picking up.

"Somebody call for help! Call for help!" Sara cried, feeling like she was floating outside of herself, observing everything.

At last, a police cruiser arrived. One of the officers pulled Sara aside, glancing at her wet clothes, hair, and the blood on her legs. "Do you require medical assistance?"

"No, but I want to talk to someone about what happened."

The officer pointed to the sidewalk curb. "Why don't you have a seat?"

Sara, in shock, moved to the curb to wait.

The officer returned a minute later. Receiving a message through his headset, the officer said, "You can go."

"Go?" Sara said. "He's dead. I want to talk to someone now!"

"Either go home or go to the police substation to file a PSRS report. Please clear the scene," said the officer as he turned away.

Fuck the PSRS! She stepped back, glancing at Kevin Larue's battered body one last time. *Why did this happen? Why?*

Sara walked dazedly to the nearest police substation to file a report, but more importantly, to find out why an Interceptor, programmed to serve and protect, had destroyed Kevin Larue like he was an armed enemy.

At the Boylston Street police substation, she logged into the Public Safety Reporting System kiosk and pressed the *Report Incident* button, her hands and bloodstained knees shaking. Several dozen people were in line at other kiosks in small open booths lined up in a row down a blank hallway. Surveillance video cameras peered down at her from the ceiling.

"Identity verified, Sara C. Brown," the automated female voice said. "Do you wish to report an incident?"

"Yes."

"State the date and location of the incident."

"Boylston Street, seven p.m., I think."

"What is it you wish to report?"

"My friend was killed by an Interceptor, and I want to speak to someone in authority."

The machine paused and then said, "Police report has already been filed for this incident, case reference number 22322573. If more information is required, authorities will contact you. There is no other action required at this time. Goodbye."

"Wait! A man was just killed by a police Interceptor. The officers told me to come here. I want to speak to someone now!"

"Police report has already been filed for this incident; case reference number 22322573. You will be contacted if additional information is required. Goodbye."

Sara slapped the screen with the soft bottom of her fist. "No! I want to speak to someone now, damn it! Let me speak to someone who can help me!"

A woman standing in line just outside of the booth gave her a nasty look. "Are you done?" she asked impatiently.

Sara pressed the *Report Incident* icon on the screen again.

"Identity verified, Sara C. Brown," said the voice.

"I need to speak to someone in charge now," Sara said.

"Do you have an incident to report?" said the voice.

"No!" Sara said. "I already did that. I need to speak to someone in charge. Please!"

"What is your case number?" asked the voice.

"I don't know what the case number is, 2232 something…I don't know. Can I talk to someone, please?" Sara said.

"You will be contacted if further information is required. Goodbye." The kiosk returned to its home screen.

"Now are you done?" said the woman waiting her turn.

Sara stormed out. She wanted to scream but instead oriented herself toward her apartment, calling Deb as she walked.

"Something terrible has happened," Sara said as soon as Deb answered. "My date was killed by an Interceptor." She began to cry.

"What? Oh my God, are you okay? Tell me you are okay. Where are you now?" Deb was nearly frantic.

"I'm walking home," Sara said, crossing to East Newton Street, looking over her shoulder for Interceptors or drones. "And the police did nothing. It doesn't make sense! Why isn't there anyone to talk to? What's the use of the fucking police? No one would talk to me. Fucking automated shit!"

"Was he in trouble with the police or something?" Deb asked.

"No. I don't know. He was a professor at MIT. I kind of knew him. We weren't doing anything wrong, just walking along. It doesn't make sense."

"Get out of the city, Sara. Go stay with your father or something."

"I don't know, maybe I should. We haven't visited him yet. I don't know. I've got this contract. I can't just walk away."

"Maybe just take some days off until you figure it out; take a break."

"I've only been here for a few weeks. I don't have any leave saved up yet."

"They've got to let you have some time off, don't they?"

"I don't know, maybe I can take a day. You're probably right," Sara said.

"Of course I am," said Deb.

"Okay, I'll call my dad in the morning. I just want to get out of here."

"Call me when you are there so I know that you're safe, okay?"

When she got home, Anna was fast asleep. Sara dismissed Ms. Zettles and then took a hot shower, sitting on the shower floor and watching Kevin Larue's blood wash away as she went over and over what happened, bewildered. Had the Interceptor malfunctioned or was the kill intentional? Could it have something to do with Universal Mind? The contracts that he was working on? After the water automatically shut off, she suddenly remembered Sen saying *You don't need anyone to distract you.* Was misguided Sen behind the killing of Kevin Larue?

18

Anna and Sara stepped off the bus in Augusta at a little after 10:00 a.m. the day after Larue's death, and Tim Brown was waiting for them, his peppered brown hair and beard glistening orange in the morning sunlight. His tan checkered button-down shirt was tucked neatly into his blue jeans.

"How's my girls?" He smiled, giving Anna and then Sara a big hug. He looked more carefully at Sara. "You look thin. Is everything all right?"

"I'll tell you more when we get to the house," Sara said, afraid that she might burst out crying, make a scene, and upset Anna.

Sara's father threw their satchels into the back of his blue sun-faded, rusted-out pickup truck in the parking lot. Anna clutched Moxie tightly as she got into the backseat.

"Thanks for letting us visit on such short notice," Sara said as they settled in.

"My pleasure. I thought I was going to have to wait until Thanksgiving to see you two. I know how busy you are down there with your new job."

He started the truck and listened to it purr, then smiled at Sara. "She runs just fine. The 2020 Ford wasn't the worst of their trucks. It had the last V8 gasoline engine they made. They don't make them like they used to, and I sure as hell have no need for those electric driverless cars."

They drove east for forty-five minutes to the small backwoods town of Liberty, Maine, passing a small grocery store and an old post office building closed for years. At last they turned onto a narrow gravel road and came upon the double-wide nestled among spruce and pine. The sun shone down at a pond on the far edge of the property. The double-wide needed a paint job and was looking more run down than Sara remembered from the last time she'd been there three years before.

Sara prepared some sandwiches for lunch while her father brought her up to date on the happenings in the life of an unemployed fifty-six-year-old widower on back injury disability. After they finished eating, Sara placed the dishes in the sink, and Anna went into the living room area with her VR glasses. That's when Sara broke down in tears and told her father about the Interceptor attack.

"Do you know why? Who was this man?" he asked, holding her in his arms.

"He was a friend, a professor at MIT. It was our first date. I don't know why it attacked him. The police didn't tell me anything or do anything." She wiped her tears and broke from his embrace.

He shook his head. "I don't like this at all. Those goddamn police robots and drones are used to control the people of this country. They should never have allowed those machines on the streets."

Sara blew her nose into a paper towel.

"You and Anna want to stay up here? Get out of the city? I can make room," he said.

"I don't know. Anna has school, and I have an employment contract I can't get out of easily." She began to sob softly again, hoping that Anna wouldn't hear her.

"Well, you know that you and Anna are always welcome here. I can clean up the guest room in back; make it a place for you. It ain't much but I would love having you."

"Thanks, Dad. I'm sorry it's taken me so long to get out here to visit." She swiped at the new tears. "I better go check on Anna."

Sara found Anna snooping around in the back of the double-wide. Sara had never lived here, but many of the cluttered contents were familiar from better days when her mother had been alive, and they had lived in the house near the coast.

"What's this?" Anna asked about an old box filled with paintbrushes and oil paints.

"Those are my old art supplies," Sara said.

Anna smiled, inspected the box some more, and set it back on the bookshelf where she'd found it next to some of Sara's high school track trophies.

Among the framed photographs on one of the bookcases was a photo of Sara's mother, father and herself at the oceanside in Camden. She was eight years old, and they were there on a family summer vacation. The last time that they'd gone to the beach as a family, Sara had been thirteen. She and her mother had waded in the tide pools at low tide to look for seashells for an art project and cut their feet on the razor-sharp edges of mussel shells. The warm waters had caused a plume of flesh-eating *Vibrio* bacteria to form and both of them had been exposed to it. By the time they got home that evening, their legs were swollen like balloons. Her father took them to the emergency room and Sara was rushed into surgery. When she woke up the following morning, the lower part of her right leg was gone, and so was her mother. According to the doctors, the vibriosis infection had spread throughout her mother's body and to her heart. On her final day on earth she was in a coma; then she died during the night.

Still looking at the photo, Sara thought about her mother, her soft voice and caring amber eyes. She thought about their art projects and how she'd insisted that her mother go with her into the tide pools. For years Sara's father reminded her that what had happened was not her fault, but she didn't feel that way. Her prosthetic leg reminded her of that traumatic day, every day. She missed her mother terribly, wishing she was there now with her.

"Who is that, Momma?" Anna asked.

Sara held the photo so Anna could see it and pointed to the smiling faces. "This is your grandpappy, this is me, and this is your grandmother, my mother."

Anna looked at the photo for a moment. "She's pretty, like you."

Sara smiled. "That's sweet. Thank you, Anna." Sara stared at the photograph for a moment longer before setting it back on the shelf.

There was another photograph, a small wedding photo of Paul and Sara, an image she hadn't seen in years. They were standing close to one another, looking into each other's eyes; she was in a flowing white gown, Paul was in his navy dress whites. She could still hear his voice in her mind, and smell his scent, just like she could her mother's. She reflected on how incredible it was that those details were etched naturally into the memory neural nets of her brain, yet weakening with time.

A wave of emotion came over Sara, causing tears. She wiped her eyes, not wanting Anna to become upset too. She returned her attention to Anna, and saw that Anna had become interested in a curious artifact on one of the shelves. Sara picked up the earthy-colored fist-sized object and handed it to her.

"Do you know what that is?" Sara asked.

Anna held it firmly in her hands and inspected it. "What is it?" Anna asked.

"It's an elephant's tooth," Sara said.

Anna stared at the unpolished tooth and ran her fingers over its protuberances.

"Why don't you show it to Grandpappy and ask him about it." Sara thought it would be good for her to hear her father tell the story again, but this time to Anna.

Anna nodded, and they found Sara's father in the living room sitting in his worn-out leather recliner. He was watching the news feeds on his large, paper-thin television screen. Anna presented the tooth to him while Sara took a seat on the old green sofa.

"Do you know what that is, Anna?" he asked.

"An elephant's tooth."

"That's right," he said excitedly. "Do you want to hear where it came from?"

Anna nodded and climbed into her grandfather's lap. He told the story of how, nearly two hundred years ago, a steamship carrying a circus was passing by Fox Island off the coast, the island that his father was from. The ship was on a run between New Brunswick, Canada, and Portland, Maine, when it caught on fire.

"Why did it catch on fire, Grandpappy?" asked Anna.

"Well, in those days, ships were powered by steam and needed water to keep them going. The engineer was not paying attention and let the water run out. They didn't fix the problem in time and the boiler, used to make the steam, overheated, and the ship caught on fire."

"What happened to the circus animals?" Anna asked.

"Well, they tried to rescue them, but they drowned, including an elephant that washed up on shore. My great-grandfather, your great-great-grandfather, found the tooth on a beach not far from his house, the house that I grew up in."

Anna looked at the tooth again, then slipped off his lap and handed it to Sara.

Sara held the tooth in her hands for a moment, thinking about her father's story and how negligence, error, ignorance, and arrogance so often lead to disaster.

That evening, Sara helped her father make a simple dinner. Mr. Brown put the news feeds on again afterward. Anna and Sara sat on each end of the raggedy green sofa, Anna with her VR glasses on.

There was a news feed about increasing tensions between India and Pakistan.

"This is not good at all," Sara's father said, shaking his head. "Could be a war at any moment."

Sara said, "That region has been devastated by food

shortages caused by climate change. There are millions of people starving over there."

"I know that," he said. "It's just a matter of time before it starts here. I can hardly even afford to feed myself. And I'm not into all of this genetically modified food and damned farmed super fish. Rich in omega fatty acids." He batted his hand. "Ah, who needs it!"

Sara said, "There are more than nine billion people in the world, Dad. There's no way we would survive if technology were not used to make food."

"Yeah, but messing with nature like that? It can't be good at all. I may not be as educated as you, Sara, but I know when something ain't right. And that goes for all of this virtual reality stuff too. It can't be good." He looked over at Anna. "She really likes them glasses, doesn't she?"

"Yes. She loves them. She uses them for school and for play. You should try them; you could go fishing with them."

"I don't have any need for those smart virtual reality glasses," he said. "I want nothing to do with fake reality. When I go fishing, I want to feel the slime of the bait and the fish with my own hands. I could care less about a digital one. I got my mind in the real world for no more a reason than because my body is in it. And all this reliance on artificial intelligence—you can't even tell if you are talking to a machine or a real person anymore. You know what I say?"

"The best evidence for the existence of the devil is computers," Sara answered. "I know, I know."

"That's right. And I don't think all of this data collection on people is good either. This government program, Third Eye, I don't like it. People don't know what they're doing when they allow so much information about themselves to be collected. They should have never allowed the Unity Act to go into effect. We don't even have private thoughts anymore."

"I don't know if I agree with that, Dad. Data is used for all kinds of good."

"I may be just an old engine mechanic, Sara, but I know

that all this data that's collected on people from smart homes, surveillance cameras, facial recognition machines, whatever, is exploited by the government and corporations for their own agendas."

"What about medical uses? Data about people's behavior is used to make predictions about health and other things that help people. We can predict who will have cancer or who will get sick with a virus or any other disease, with almost 99 percent accuracy."

"It didn't save your mother or your leg after you got that infection," he said.

Sara gave him an agitated look.

"I'm sorry. I shouldn't have said that," he said.

"It's okay, Dad," Sara said. "I guess we just have different opinions about technology."

"I know you may think I'm just some old man who doesn't know what he's talking about, but I'm telling you that all of this data that's collected on people is bad. The government uses it to control them and take away freedoms. I used to enjoy hunting before they took the guns from us. They knew who had them with the registry and if you didn't turn them in, you went to prison."

"Yes, I know, but wouldn't you agree that we have a safer society now?" Sara had gone down this road with him before and knew the perils.

"Safer society? The more people there are and the less individual responsibility, the more crime and violence there is. The more crime and social unrest, the more police drones and robots like the one that killed your friend. Better for the companies that make those machines. It's about control, and it's easier to control people when they have no way to use equal force to revolt against an oppressive government. You're still a New Englander, Sara—don't forget that."

"Okay, Dad," Sara said, thinking that her father was going way over the top now. "But it's the world we live in, not much we can do," Sara said.

"That's your problem, dear. The young generation goes

along with it because they don't know the difference. We lost a lot of our freedoms after the Great Crash and no one wants to do anything about it. The government makes it sound like the people ask for their control. It's nothing but propaganda and manufactured consent."

She was feeling increasingly frustrated with the conversation. "I don't know what else I can do. I'm just barely able to survive. I'm doing my best," Sara said.

His voice softened. "I know that you are, Sara. And it's good that you got your education and are doing what you want to do with it. Just remember what I say: this country doesn't belong to the elite. It belongs to all of us who are citizens of it. It's your duty as a citizen to stand up for what's right."

Before she could formulate a response, an advertisement came on for Universal Mind, touting how the company was saving the world with the Terra Brain Initiative.

"The Terra Brain Initiative. Isn't that what you are working on?" her father asked.

"Yes."

"How's it going?"

"I'm not supposed to talk about it—security reasons," she said.

"Ah, well, I won't ask you any more about it then." He sat silent, eyes on the television, and added, "Maybe you can fix the thing and save the world."

She half smiled and said. "We'll see, Dad. We'll see."

At 10:00 p.m. Sara told Anna to put down her VR glasses and get ready for bed. Her father helped to pull out a spare mattress in the guest bedroom and get them situated. He wished them a good night, and after hugs, Sara curled up next to Anna. Anna had Moxie in her arms, half under the covers. "Momma?"

"Yes, Anna."

"Who programs AI at your work?"

"There are lots of programmers. Sometimes we use AI to program AI. Why do you ask, Honey?"

Anna raised and lowered her shoulders.

"Have you been learning how to code at school?" Sara asked, hoping the school had her in the virtual classes.

"Yes, Momma. It's fun."

Sara smiled. "I'm glad to hear it. Maybe you can show me what you are making sometime."

Anna nodded. "Momma?"

"Yes, Honey?"

"Where do people go when they die?"

Sara hesitated in thought, not expecting the question. "Heaven. Good people go to Heaven."

Anne looked at Moxie. "Do animals go to Heaven?"

"Maybe they do, yes." Sara thought Anna must have been thinking about the circus ship elephant.

Anna paused in thought. "Moxie too?"

"No, she's a machine, remember?"

Anna looked at Moxie, and the robotic animal's eyes blinked softy.

"Why not?"

"Because machines don't have a spirit like living things do. They are different."

Anna paused for a moment, looking at Moxie. "Does Daddy see us from Heaven?"

"I think he probably does, and he's proud of you." Sara hadn't expected her to bring up Paul. Anna rarely did, and it had been nearly a year since they talked about him.

"How does he see us?"

"I don't know for sure; he just does."

"What about Grandma? Does she see us?"

Sara felt an ache form in her chest. "I suppose so, yes."

"Will we see them again?"

"Yes, in Heaven, a long time from now."

"I hope so. It makes me sad they are not here."

"I know." Tears welled up in Sara's eyes. She wiped them. "It makes me sad too."

Anna turned toward her mother and hugged her. "Don't worry, Momma. Everything is going to be all right."

Sara softly stroked her daughter's hair. "I love you so much," Sara said. "Goodnight."

Sara wasn't so sure about things being okay. Her mind was filled with worries about everything that had happened since she started at Universal Mind. Could she have done something to prevent Kevin Larue's death? Why did the Interceptor kill an assistant professor from MIT? Was he in trouble for something? Was the rumor about a cult involving Universal Mind true? What about the human brain scanning? And why did the Senex Program want her, and only her, to write an empathy program for it?

Sara also thought about her father's offer to stay with him, but she knew that to quit her job now wasn't a realistic option. There was the employment contract that she'd have to break and worse, she couldn't afford to give up the benefits she was getting. She was certainly thinking about Anna and her safety, but it wouldn't be logistically feasible to leave Anna with her father. She knew that she had to return to the city and that she'd be taking Anna with her.

In the morning, Sara helped her father make some breakfast, and she told him that she planned to return to Boston with Anna.

"I don't suppose I'll see you and Anna for your birthday, will I?"

"Probably not, Dad."

"Well, before you go, I want to give something to you," he said, dashing into the closet next to the buzzing refrigerator. He returned with a small amber-colored jar and slid it across the countertop toward her.

"What's this?" Sara asked, grabbing the glass jar, inspecting it, and then twisting off the top.

"What do you think it is? It's honey, real honey. That isn't that synthetic genetically modified corn syrup honey crap around these days. That's the real deal, made by real bees here in Maine. I got it from a friend of mine who visited me a few weeks ago. He used to own an old apple orchard down near Livermore Falls before the government found out and seized his bee farm earlier this year. Unlicensed breeding of bees, the government authorities said. Take it back to Boston with you as a reminder of the country, something sweet to cheer you up."

Sara sniffed the honey and then replaced the top. "Thanks, Dad, but isn't this illegal?"

He smirked. "It shouldn't be. But if anyone asks, just tell 'em it fell off a truck."

Sara smiled. "Okay, Dad."

He peered into the living room at Anna and Moxie who were sitting on his recliner. "She really loves that thing too, doesn't she?"

"She sure does—she's always got it with her."

He spoke softly. "That thing gives me the heebie-jeebies."

19

Sara was late to work, her eyes red with bags under them. Tanya gazed up from her workstation and looked Sara up and down through the glass partition between their workspaces. Sara ignored her and got busy with WATTS review. Tanya's eyes were still on her.

"What, Tanya?" Sara asked, annoyed.

"Just wondering why you didn't come in yesterday afternoon. The WATTS had us scheduled for overtime, and you were supposed to assist. And why are you late today?"

"What I have going on is none of your business."

"It is my business. Your absenteeism messed up our team's productivity rating in the WATTS. You're causing us to look bad."

Michael and Brent looked up from their workstations.

"I was out of town, okay? Besides, who cares about how we look—we just need to get the Terra Brain system fixed."

"We're all supposed to be contributing. You went on vacation while we were scheduled to work. That's not fair."

"It's not like that, and it's none of your business, Tanya. Why don't you leave me alone? I'm not in the mood for this today."

Tanya stared at Sara, her eye twitching. Then she got up and stormed out.

Sara scanned the backlog of WATTS tasks for her. She

tried to focus but couldn't. Michael sent her an instant chat message a minute later.

You okay?

Sara hesitated. *Yes.*

Want to get a coffee?

I've got a lot to catch up on.

It can wait. Come on.

Sara looked at him through the glass wall. His boyish grin was impossible to turn down. She could use the caffeine, anyway. She logged out, and they went to the cafeteria.

"What's going on? Are you sure that you're okay?" Michael asked as he sat down across from her.

Sara told him about what happened on her date and how she went up to Maine.

"Wow, I'm sorry. Any idea why the Interceptor…?"

The tears were starting. "Excuse me." She turned away to wipe her eyes.

Michael handed her a napkin. "Maybe you can request some time off. Under these circumstances, Dunigan might be able to make it happen."

Sara shrugged. "I don't know; we've got so much work to do, and I've already let the team down. I just need to stay focused."

"Won't hurt to ask. You've got your regular meeting with him this afternoon, right?"

Sara nodded.

"Ignore Tanya, and don't worry about the productivity ratings," he said. "We didn't get anything done yesterday anyway, and the WATTS had me do the same exact tasks several times over today. Something is seriously wrong with it. I thought about telling Dunigan, but he missed our scheduled meeting this morning, which is strange for him. He never misses a meeting without telling you first." His eyes were on someone coming down the corridor. "Oh shit, here comes Ratface. Don't make eye contact."

Pratt stopped in front of them. "There you are," she said, looking down at Sara. "I need to see you in my office, now."

"Okay," Sara said, hoping it was about her security upgrade and not for missing the mandatory overtime.

Pratt acknowledged Michael. "Mr. Obrec."

Michael tipped his cup. "Ms. Pratt."

Sara followed Pratt to her office.

"We heard about the Interceptor incident on Friday," Pratt said. "You didn't report it to us, why's that?"

"I didn't know I was supposed to report it to you. I was on my own time, and the police were there and made a report," Sara said curtly.

"I can see you're upset," Pratt said, "but that's no reason to use that tone with me. You failed to come in yesterday and were late this morning. It has raised red security flags." She glared at Sara. "What was your purpose in Maine?"

"I went to visit my father. I needed to get out of the city after what happened, and as for not coming in on Sunday, I had no idea that I was scheduled. I was away for one night."

"You need to report your travel plans and who you associate with to Security."

"Right," Sara said, looking away and rolling her eyes.

"So, you met him through the *vLove* service, and Friday was the first time you met him in person, correct?"

Pratt's knowledge of her dating life took her by surprise. "Yes, so?"

"What did you talk about?" Pratt asked bluntly.

None of your business. "Just normal things. He talked about his research, small talk—that's about it. Why do you need to know about this?"

"Did he know that you work at Universal Mind?"

"I didn't tell him that I worked here, but he probably figured it out."

"Oh? How's that?"

"He knew I was a computer scientist working for a major company in the city, I guess."

"Did you talk about your work at Universal Mind?"

"Of course not. I'm aware of what it means to have a security clearance. I was careful. Why are you drilling me?

The man is dead. Do you have any idea why he was murdered by an Interceptor?"

"*Murder* is a strong word. I'm sure that the police had their reasons, or there was some kind of malfunction with the Interceptor. They'll conduct a thorough investigation. File a PSRP report, they'll update you. It's probably in your best interest to just move on."

Move on. "Sure," Sara said, wanting to scream.

"Good," Pratt said. "And one more thing. What about Steven Dunigan? Anything to report there?"

"No, why?" Sara said.

"Are you sure?"

"I don't understand. Am I supposed to know something?"

"Has he done anything inappropriate, come on to you, anything like that?"

"Of course not." Pratt's questions about Dunigan and his absence that morning made her wonder if Dunigan was under some kind of investigation.

"Has he asked you to meet with him outside of work hours?"

Sara paused before responding. "Yes. I met him once for a drink after work during my first week. He said he normally does that with supervisees."

"When and where did you meet?"

"It was Friday two weeks ago, right after we left work. O'Brien's was the place—the bar near the Blue Line terminal. Is there a problem?"

"What did you talk about?"

"Nothing, really. He just asked how I was settling in, those kinds of things."

"What else?"

Sara was growing increasingly concerned about Pratt's intent. Had she done something wrong? Did Dunigan violate a security protocol?

"He mentioned that he had met my husband some years back. He didn't go into any details about it, just said he'd met him."

"When was that and where?"

"Three years ago, I guess. He said it was at a government meeting in Virginia. I don't know anything more about it."

"If he asks to meet with you again outside of work, I need you to tell me right away. If he acts inappropriately, in any way, I need to know that too. Is that clear?"

"Yes. Is there something wrong?"

"Work-related meetings outside of work are taken very seriously. They increase security risks..."

"But it wasn't work-related..."

"It was if you were meeting with your supervisor, Sara," Pratt said assertively. "I asked you before to tell me if you are asked to do anything outside of WATTS instruction. You didn't, and that is a problem."

"Am I in trouble? I'd really like to go now, please." Sara crossed her arms.

Pratt's tone softened. "It's my duty to check in with you. I know you are under a lot of pressure, and that can lead to lapses in judgment, leading to security problems." She slid her hand over the surface of the desk toward Sara. "Working in a high security environment like this can make a person feel lonely and wanting someone to talk to. You can talk with me, it's safe." She continued looking at Sara, and her face softened too.

Pratt's change of tactic threw Sara off. *Either she's pretending to be my friend or she's hitting on me.* "I should get back to work, we have a deadline."

Pratt continued to stare at her in awkward silence. "I'm here if you need me, okay?"

Sara nodded. "Sounds like your interview is over."

Pratt straightened up. "You can go now."

Sara headed back to her workstation, perplexed by Pratt's questioning. After she settled in, Michael poked his head into her office.

"How'd it go with Ratface?"

Sara shrugged. "I don't know. I'm starting to think that she's getting off on making me paranoid about everything."

"That's normal for her. Dunigan came by while you were gone and apologized for missing my meeting with him. He wants to meet with you right away, though."

"Really? Did he say why? Did he seem okay?"

Michael shrugged. "He looked tired; said he's been working on a special project for Butterfield. Let me know how your meeting goes with him?"

"Sure." Sara logged off and headed to Dunigan's office, unsure what to expect.

20

Dunigan gazed through the suicide netting, puffing on his vape. His eyes were bloodshot and his suit wrinkled, as if he'd slept in it. He drew on his vape again and looked at Sara. "Have you heard of precision weather modding?"

"Weather modeling? Yes, of course."

"No, weather modding—using technology to modify the weather."

"Yes, what about it?"

He gazed through the suicide net. "The Terra Brain Initiative isn't what you think it is. It's part of a secret global precision weather modding program called WAW, Weather-As-Weapon. It was supposed to go live this year, but then the problem with the Senex Program happened. I need your help to stop it from going online."

Sara was surprised. "Stop what? WAW? What are you talking about? Who's doing this?"

"The Futurus Group. I don't have time to go into all of it now. They're planning to use Senex and the Terra Brain network to manipulate weather. And this whole thing about the Invisible Sun hack is just a cover while Butterfield tries to fix the Senex Program."

Her thoughts were in a tailspin. "Wait. So, this problem with the Senex Program has nothing to do with an outside virus?"

"It's bullshit. Butterfield had me create a fake virus hack. I worked on it for weeks before you got here. Listen. WAW is real, it's happening, and I need your help to stop it. I've gathered a trove of information about the WAW program and Universal Mind contract over the last few weeks, and it's hidden on one of the test servers in the lab. I need you and Michael to help me get the information out of Universal Mind and give it to the Invisible Sun. It's our only chance to stop this."

"You want me to help you to sneak information out of Universal Mind and give it to the Invisible Sun? That's crazy!"

"There's no other option. The mainstream media are bought off and would suppress it. Who do you think owns Universal Mind and the Federated News Networks? The Futurus Group, for Christ's sake. Think about the power they'd have if they controlled the weather."

"Why not use the whistleblower law?"

"It won't work. This goes too high. Oligarchy runs everything. Getting the information I have out to the Invisible Sun is the only way the public will know what's going on. It's the smoking gun."

"Why didn't you try to disable the system or sneak this information out yourself? Why wait until now?" Sara asked.

"Why do you think I had you and Michael in the lab working on trying to penetrate the firewall? I was planning to encrypt the data and send it through backdoor channels, but the channels closed when the Senex Program took control of itself. I knew I was going to need help but couldn't tell you about it before. You know as well as I do that if I'd said anything about this, you would've been caught by the Integrity Signals checks."

"There's no other way to stop it? Disable it?"

"I thought maybe an internal virus, take it down myself, but the Senex Program found a way to protect itself. It's impenetrable. Getting the data out is the best option. The files are located on an off-network test server, server number three. Don't forget. It's impossible to send the files over the network, and the entire building is a Faraday box to prevent wireless transmission. You're going to have to sneak it out on your person."

"My person?"

He glanced at her prosthetic. "Your leg."

Sara stared at her prosthetic, still not sure she believed him. "I can't. I've got a daughter to think about. I can't get involved in this."

"I've got a daughter too, Sara. You've got to help me on this. We don't have much time. If you get hit with another Integrity Signals check now that you know all of this, you'll be in trouble. But you may be able to beat the system with anxiolytics. You have a prescription, don't you?"

"Yes, but I don't know about all of this. I'm in shock. Again, why wait until now to do something about it?"

"I'm telling you now because we're running out of time." He shook his head. "This damn sexual harassment thing happened out of nowhere. They are going to fire me at any time, maybe today. I would've gotten it out this week if I had more time."

"Sexual harassment? What are you talking about?"

"It's not true. The complaint is anonymous," he said. "It came from the automated personnel system. I think it was rigged to get me out of my position and security clearance revoked. Never mind that now. Michael will be able to get you a memory card and interface cable. He's friends with Smith in maintenance. He'll know what to do."

"So, Michael knows about this?" Sara's thoughts were whirling. Now she was wondering if this had something to do with the rogue Interceptor.

"Not yet. The more people who know, the more likely we will get caught. I'll try to find a way to tell him, or you can. I trust him like I trust you." He looked at Sara. "Are you with me?"

"I still don't understand. If the Senex Program is out of control, why not just shut the system down? There's got to be a way to do that," Sara said. "Maybe you can convince

Butterfield to stop everything?"

"No! Are you crazy? He's knows damn well what he's doing! It's the money, Sara. He's going to get rich on this. Butterfield is going to try a synchronized supercomputer shutdown and operating system reload to try to save his ass, but I'm betting it won't work. This is what you get when you cut corners and don't pay attention to a self-learning AI program like this."

"How do you know all of this?" she asked.

"Trust me, I know," Dunigan said grimly.

"Why are you involved in this, Steven?"

"They have me by the balls. They threatened to harm my family if I break the agreement I have with them. They find ways to make people do what they want. I know I'm doing the right thing, but I can't do it alone now. Are you going to help get the data out or not? I need to know."

"I need to think about it. I've got a lot going on too."

"There's no time to think, Sara, it's now or never. And one more thing: after you get the data out, go back into the lab and destroy the files on server three. Michael will help you. I've got Butterfield and Pratt convinced that the lab is needed for testing. If they get suspicious, though, they'll revoke your access. We need to move quickly. And if something happens to me, get the files out to Invisible Sun. They'll be in touch with you."

"What? You gave them my name?" Her heart sped up.

Dunigan stood up, putting his vape back into his pocket.

"I've got to go," he said. "Go and look at the files on test server three. Then come back to my office this afternoon. And stick to all of your normal routines today—the gym, lunch, everything. Got it?"

"Yes, I understand."

Once they parted, Sara headed to her workspace, thinking about everything Dunigan had said. What did he mean, if he did not make it? How much danger was she in now? She needed to get to the lab to see the files for herself before deciding anything else.

21

Sara logged into the secure test server three and entered Dunigan's secret data directory. There were hundreds of files organized in folders by date. She opened the first file:

Memo_0343_12JUL2034.
Terra Brain Summary Report 19 FEB 2032
Senex ver 1.101 Classified Top Secret

Atmospheric CO2 exceeded 660 parts per million for first time. Global average temperature expected to exceed previous year by .05°. Imminent water shortages in the American Southwest. Recommend immediate water rationing and minimum of 1,220,000 gallons to be rerouted to American Southwest. Rapid migration of between 500,000 and 1,000,000 people expected. Based on past trends, civil unrest expected severe worldwide. Sea rise will exceed .03 meters by 2035. Typhoons risk 78% probability in 2034 in the Indian Ocean. Estimated 400,000 - 500,000 civilians to move to Gujarat region. 700,000-900,000 Indian civilians expected to move 70 kilometers inland. Additional population movement probable. Food shortages to increase. 1,000,000 pounds of food to region in 2051. Political conflict will increase. Regional security threat high. Immediate mitigation action required. Delegation recommended.

Sara nearly fell out of the chair. There were hundreds of Terra Brain Initiative 1.0 output memos like the first, all warning about rapidly changing climate effects and their devastating impact on people. Some of the weather events were predictions, while others had already happened.

Her fist clenched over her mouth, she scanned more files and technical documents describing a network of novel technologies to manipulate the weather. New high-altitude drones were being used for cloud seeding, causing clouds to cool the earth and rain to cause floods. Secret terrestrial and satellite-based lasers designed to beam into the earth's atmosphere to heat it. Portable nuclear heaters implanted into glaciers by submarines to accelerate glacier melts. How could these black project technologies have been kept secret for so long?

Contract documents showed transfers of billions of dollars between the US government and Futurus Group Inc. Even more damaging were the memos between individual members of the Futurus Group and White House Cabinet members that were cc'd to Butterfield and other Universal Mind executives.

Steven was telling the truth! The world must know about this!

She thought about his warning about knowing too much and the threat of Integrity Signals checks. If the conspirators like Butterfield discovered that she knew, they'd want her dead.

She logged off and headed to the Universal Mind fitness facility. She wanted to go to Dunigan's office to discuss what the information meant, but she knew better. *Stick to your routines*, she reminded herself. She hoped that a run would help her to work through all the implications of what she'd just learned.

In her workout clothes, she climbed onto one of the treadmills. The news feeds on the screens in front of her were reporting about the storm in the Atlantic.

"Hurricane Elana is increasing in intensity," said the newscaster. "As of twelve p.m. Eastern, the storm's center is approximately seven hundred twenty miles east-southeast of Miami and moving north at twelve miles per hour, with maximum sustained winds of forty miles per hour."

Sara cringed. Was the storm natural, or was it being intentionally controlled by weather modding controlled by the Senex Program?

The ticker on the bottom of the screen said there would be a special briefing by the President that evening about the military buildup in the Indian Ocean. Sara shook her head. *What a nightmare.*

She had been running for about five minutes when something dropped from the sky and landed in the courtyard below. Sara rushed to the windows, as did other employees. A contorted and shattered body lay in a pool of blood two stories down. She stood frozen, her heart going wild.

"Who is that?" said a man who'd been lifting weights.

"Looks like an executive," answered another fitness center patron.

Sara could tell by the suit and the hair it was Steven Dunigan. It appeared he'd fallen, or jumped to his death, from the open-air balcony on the fiftieth floor.

Dizzy and feeling like she might vomit, she stepped back from the glass and put her hands on the top of one of the treadmills to support herself. Her ears were ringing, and her vision became tunnel. She struggled to keep from falling.

The man who was lifting weights took notice of her. "You okay?"

Sara glanced at him for a moment before her knees gave way, and she stumbled backward, slipping to the floor and thumping her head. Darkness fell.

22

A cartoonish face with two black dot eyes and large semicircle mouth gazed down at Sara. *Am I dreaming?* Her eyes focused. The image on a video monitor was the head of a hospital robot, shorter and wider than the bots at Universal Mind. Attached to it were a thermometer, blood pressure cuff, stethoscope, and several other instruments; in its hand was a small tray with two transparent plastic cups on it—one cup with two purple pills, the other with water. The smiley face dissolved into that of a middle-aged man with salt and pepper hair and dark eyes.

"Hello, Ms. Brown, I'm Alan, a virtual care provider with Mass General. How are you feeling?"

Sara groaned as she sat up, her head pulsing with the worst headache she'd ever experienced. "My head hurts. What time is it?"

"It's 4:55 p.m. Do you remember what happened?"

"I must have passed out." The memory of Dunigan's death was coming back. "I need to go. I need to pick up my daughter." She noticed the IV stuck in her left arm. "What's the IV for?"

"You hit your head when you fell. We have to wait for the rest of your test results. You were also dehydrated, and your blood pressure is below optimal. Fortunately, you do not have a concussion."

"Can you remove the IV? I need to pick up my daughter. Where's my phone? I need to call her school." Her voice sounded somewhat frantic.

"You must wait for your test results and release. Your daughter has already been picked up by a caretaker, according to your employer's emergency protocol."

Sara struggled to remember what the protocol was. *My supervisor. Dunigan is dead. Next in line is…*

"She's with Butterfield?"

"That's correct, Dr. Gordon C. Butterfield. He was here earlier to check on you. You're going to have to wait for now, Ms. Brown. Until we complete your assessment, we cannot determine your capacity to make a safe decision regarding your discharge." The robot inched closer and extended its arm. "The pills will help to comfort you."

Sara stared at the simulated care provider. "You're fucking kidding me. Who made these rules? She's my daughter, and I need to get her now!" All she could think of was that Butterfield had Anna.

"Ms. Brown, it's not in your best interest to argue. Take the medications to help you relax."

"I don't need any pills. I need to see someone real—a human being, somebody, I need to get out of here and get my daughter."

"That's not possible; you'll have to wait until we discharge you for your safety and wellbeing. If you continue to behave in this agitated manner, we'll have no choice but to administer medication involuntarily."

Sara was in no mood to be talking to a machine. "I'd like to leave now, please, against medical advice, I don't care."

"That's not possible. We need to keep you for the blood tests results and observation until this evening." The machine paused, as if it was searching databases or waiting for new information to be transmitted. "Your supervisor has arranged for a ride. We will notify the driver when you are ready to be released."

Sara sat back. "I have no choice—that is what you are

telling me."

"That's correct. I also see in your records that you have been experiencing sleep problems and anxiety. These symptoms are consistent with Earth-Anxiety Disorder. It's common these days with all of the climate change. I'm going to increase your dosage of alprazolam and add an antidepressant to ease your malaise."

Yeah, I've got Earth-Anxiety Disorder all right. "I'm fine with my medications. I don't need anything else," Sara said.

"According to your personal health data file, recommended prescriptions are called for. Given your family history, the program has determined it's best for you. I'm pleased to hear that your employer, Universal Mind, has an Employee Assistance Program, too. Maybe you should use it."

Sara rolled her eyes. There was no way she was going to talk to a Universal Mind virtual counselor.

"I also see that your daughter Anna is at high risk for anxiety and depression. The system recommends an antidepressant regimen for her as well."

Sara was now on alert. Who or what was recommending all these medications?

"She's too young to get started on antidepressant medications, isn't she?"

"She's old enough. Best we keep her resilient by getting her on antidepressants now."

"No, thanks. I'm her mother and I disagree." She watched the virtual doctor carefully.

"The prescriptions have already been approved and will be shipped to your residence. Do you have any more questions?"

"No." Sara sat back, resolved that she would have to wait until she was released.

The screen faded to the daffy smiley face as the robot turned and rolled out of the room to continue its rounds.

At 5:00 p.m., another robot brought a dinner tray. Sara sat up to eat just as Michael walked in, looking distraught. He looked her over, his eyes landing on the bandage on her head. "How are you?" he asked.

Sara set the tray with her meal on it aside. "Well enough. Good to see you."

Michael walked around and sat in the chair between the hospital bed and the windows.

"This is terrible," he said. "I can't believe he's gone."

She looked over at the television panel hanging from the ceiling across the room. "Television on. News feeds," she commanded. "Louder, please." She knew the ambient intelligent system in the hospital room had its motion sensors, microphones, and cameras monitoring them. She gestured to Michael to come closer.

He moved his chair closer to the bed.

Raising her fork to her mouth to obscure it, she told him about what Steven had told her about Universal Mind and weather modification.

At first Michael smirked. "Chemtrails?" He looked at the bandage on her head again. "Did you get a concussion when you fell?"

"Wake up, Michael. The data is on server number three in the test lab—one of the servers he had you set up. Memos and private communications proving Universal Mind's involvement."

Michael turned pale as a ghost. "Are you sure?"

"Steven wanted the information to go to the Invisible Sun. Apparently he was in contact with them. He believed they could disseminate the information and that would lead to an investigation."

Michael ran his hand through his hair. "That's crazy. Why didn't he just get it out himself?"

"He was planning to, but a complaint was registered against him to stop him—something to do with a sexual harassment claim."

Michael gazed across the room. "And he offed himself. Shit."

"Do you think he really offed himself?"

Silently they looked at each other. "What else did he say to you?"

"That he gave the Invisible Sun my name, and that if anything happened to him, they would contact me."

Michael's eyebrows went up. "He gave them your name? Did he give them my name too? If they get caught trying to contact either of us, we're toast."

"Like Steven," Sara said softly. "Not much we can do about it now. And I just learned that Butterfield has my daughter."

Michael leaned back and stared at her. "It's all so sudden…and farfetched," he said.

Sara sighed. "Come on, Michael. Would I lie to you? Take a look at server number three for yourself. We've got to do something. We need to get the data to the Invisible Sun ourselves, somehow."

Michael looked deep into Sara's eyes. "Maybe I can get in there and take a look tomorrow. We've got to stay off email and the phone. When are you going back to work?"

"I'm supposed to be discharged later tonight. I'm going to get Anna, first thing."

"How did Butterfield get your daughter?"

"Some stupid automated government database setting." She thought about the technology conversation she had with her father and how stupid her defense of it sounded now. She started to tear up again, and her voice cracked. "I should have caught that."

"I'm sure she's okay," Michael said ineffectually. "Butterfield probably has an assistant looking after her."

"Apparently, he was here earlier too, when I was passed out. The hospital said that he's sending a ride to pick me up after I'm released. I've got to get her away from him."

A voice overhead announced that visitor's hours were coming to a close.

"We should probably meet again as soon as possible," said Michael, "maybe Thursday after work. We could meet at my place. I'm just one stop before yours in East Cambridge."

"Are you sure we'll be safe from surveillance? I plan to have Anna with me too."

"No less safe than meeting anywhere else. If anyone asks why you were there, tell them that you were bereaved by the loss of your supervisor and weren't thinking clearly."

Sara nodded and got the address from him. After he left, she stared up at the blue light emitting off the motion sensor above the bed, thinking about Anna, then Dunigan, his data files, and how to get them out of Universal Mind.

23

Butterfield's white corporate limo was waiting for Sara outside the hospital. Still in her workout clothes, she was taken to the Millennium Tower luxury apartment building in downtown Boston.

Sara looked up at the towering mirror glass building. *The bastard sure does well for himself.*

She entered and checked into the kiosk next to a large waterfall wall in the lobby. After being granted access, she took the elevator up to Butterfield's corner suite on the sixtieth floor. A Universal Mind white bot answered the door.

"Greetings, Sara. Please come in. Master Butterfield will be with you shortly."

"Where's my daughter, Anna?"

"She's in the living room, playing," said the bot. "Master Butterfield will be with you shortly."

Sara wasn't going to wait for Butterfield. She bolted past the bot. Anna was sitting on the floor by a large floor-to-ceiling window next to a grand piano. Another Universal Mind white bot was kneeling next to her, playing checkers with her. Anna looked up. "Momma!" she cried.

Sara wrapped her arms around her and squeezed her tightly. "Oh Baby, are you okay?" She looked her daughter over, surprised to find Anna's hair in two loosely fitted braids.

"Yes, Momma, where were you? When are we going home?"

"I'm sorry, Honey. I fell down at work, and I had to go to the hospital, but I'm okay. I'm going to take you home now."

"Yes, Momma. I was playing checkers with Gina and telling her a story. She's a bot."

Sara made eye contact with Gina.

"She is very well behaved, Dr. Brown," said Gina.

Sara grabbed Anna's hand. "Come on, Anna. Let's go home."

But before they made it to the door, Butterfield appeared in white leisure pants and t-shirt, water glistening on his bald head. "Pardon me, Sara, I just got out of the shower. How are you feeling?"

"I'm fine. Thanks for the ride and for looking after Anna. We should be going."

"Good thing we had that protocol in place or she would have gone to Child Protective Services and you wouldn't have seen her for weeks. Why don't you join me in the dining room for some dinner? You must be hungry."

"I think we should be going, Dr. Butterfield; I need to get Anna home." She pulled Anna closer to the door.

"What's the hurry? You must be hungry. Join me," he said.

"I'm still not feeling well. We really should get going."

"Please," he said, his left hand opening up to usher them toward the dining area. "We need to talk about your reassignment."

"I'm being reassigned?"

"Come," he said.

The room had high ceilings and was double the size of her entire apartment. Several oil paintings hung on the walls, and a bust of Blaise Pascal sat in a corner on a Greek column. Mozart's Symphony No. 40 in G Minor was playing softly over the speaker system. They sat down and, in less than a minute, a bot brought in a tray of sandwiches and fruit.

"Bring my shake, one for Sara and Anna too," Butterfield

commanded. He looked at Sara. "You'll like this; it will help you heal."

"Maybe some water? I'm on some medications and I don't think it's a good idea to take supplements," Sara said, not trusting anything from Butterfield.

"Just try it," he said, as he bit into a sandwich.

Sara glanced at the glass Clebsche-Gordan statue sitting prominently on an Ionian column pedestal in the far corner of the room. Three feet high, the abstract piece had three rounded intertwined curves, based on mathematical coefficients, which looked like large elephant ears.

Butterfield noted her interest.

"I thought you might like my Clebsche-Gordan. I have another one like it in my bedroom at the beach house."

"It's very nice," Sara said, unimpressed.

A bot entered with three glasses of a green concoction. Butterfield took the glasses off the tray, taking one for himself and placing the others in front of Anna and Sara. He sipped and slurped. "Ahh, refreshing." He looked at Sara. "Try it."

"What's in it?" Sara asked.

"It's a proprietary longevity blend. Plenty of antioxidants and nutrients. The best!"

Anna was already drinking the shake.

Sara took a hesitant sip of the sweet and salty concoction.

"How do you like it?" Butterfield asked.

"*Mmm*, good," Sara mumbled, faking enjoyment. *Tastes like shit.*

"I knew you would like it," Butterfield said. "I hope you realize that I know how difficult it must be for you to have lost your supervisor. It hasn't been easy for me, either. Steven Dunigan was an important asset to Universal Mind and a good friend. It's a terrible loss of a good man. The pressure must have really gotten to him."

Sara nodded, playing along with his phony sympathy. She felt like dumping the shake over his head.

Butterfield crushed a kiwi with his fork, causing seeds to

spray across his plate and onto the table. "I had been a little concerned that Dunigan may have been giving your team too much leeway with your work, not keeping you focused on it. I'm sure that you would have told me if he had you doing anything that was unauthorized. Am I right to assume that, Sara?"

"Of course. If I had suspected anything to be out of protocol, I would have notified Security."

"Good, that's settled." He chewed his food, thinking. "It's good that we talk about how things are going with your work. Don't worry about security protocols here; I assure you that my home is clear of any listening devices."

She wondered what he was getting at.

"I've decided to move you over to Team A in the AI Interactions Department. Your skills are needed there now. Dr. Lee will be your direct supervisor, and you will report to George Preston, your new team leader."

Sara seethed with hatred for Butterfield and everyone working for him who knew what Dunigan had learned. "What is the team working on?"

"Some things you haven't had access to up to this point. We need to get the system repaired and tested by next Monday. I have a meeting with the White House Chief Technology Officer next Tuesday and plan to have good news to report." He stuffed a piece of kiwi into his mouth and then wiped the juice away that had dribbled down his chin with a white cloth napkin. "I understand that you've met the Senex virtual human interface; Dunigan had set you up to. Is that correct?"

Sara paused, her thoughts racing. Sen had made it clear she was to keep her conversations with him a secret, but now she was going to have to either tell Butterfield the truth or lie.

"Did he tell you that?" she asked.

"I know that you did. What did you talk to it about?"

How does he know? If not the Integrity Signals checks, then he got the information from Steven before he jumped. "I spoke to it on my first day. I reported it to Dunigan; I assumed he briefed you on it."

Butterfield chewed the kiwi, eyes on Sara. "Dunigan liked to keep secrets about his work, probably due to his doubts about his own technical competency." He swallowed. "So, do you have anything that you want to tell me about your conversation with the Senex Program? It's important that I know everything."

"No. I told Dr. Dunigan everything. There isn't much to say. I learned nothing by talking with it."

"Well, I'm sure that if you remember anything, you will tell me right away. Let's enjoy our lunch. You've had a rough night," he said.

When they were finished with lunch, he insisted on showing her his art collection while Anna played with one of his bots.

"…and this is an André Derain—you're familiar with Derain, aren't you?"

"Yes, of course, he started the Fauvist movement," Sara said, remembering that from an art studies class she took.

Butterfield stared into the painting. "I like his use of red." His lips made a wet sucking sound. "I find it very…erotic. What do you think?"

She stared at the painting, feeling more and more awkward by the moment. "It's nice."

He looked at another painting on the wall. "What do you think of this one?"

Sara reflected on the unremarkable Pollockesque painting with red and blue splatters and handprints dabbed randomly across the canvas. "It's…well…I don't know what to say about it. Who is it?"

"I painted it when I was a teenager. Art was very important to me then, as it is now." He stared dazedly at his painting. "I grew up in a small town like you, did you know that?"

"Yes, I know that."

"And you know how I lost my hand?"

"Yes, I read about it in an article about you. It was a

farming accident, right?"

"What you do not know is those kids in that town were terribly mean to me. They made fun of me because I was the smartest kid in my class; then they made fun of me because my arm was missing below the elbow, because I was different."

"That must have been difficult."

Butterfield nodded. "But I fixed the problem by applying my intelligence and I've fixed the problem for so many others, haven't I?" He walked over to the windows in his living room and stood by them. "You may think that all I care about is my fiduciary responsibilities to the Universal Mind shareholders—that I don't care about people; but I do—I really do care." He looked back at Sara. "Come over here for a moment; I want to show you something."

She hesitated, her anxiety rising.

"See those people down there?" said Butterfield, looking out at the city below.

Sara moved closer and gazed at ant trails of cars and pedestrians sixty-eight stories down.

"Climate change has placed them in great peril, and they are not capable of helping themselves. It's our responsibility to make sure that we use technology to help them. They need us to build it and control it for them. Don't you understand?"

Sara hesitated, knowing he was sizing up how willing she was to remain complicit.

"I think our position must be responsible, yes, but shouldn't everyone understand what and why things are being done that affect them?"

Butterfield gave her a serious look. "The masses are dullards, Sara. We are in the age of intelligent machines, and these machines must be put to use and controlled by the smartest people in society. It's fine for the public to have opinions, but we don't really need them to do what *we* must do, do we? We have a duty, and I approved your hire because I know that you too have a sense of duty, don't you?"

"Yes, of course," Sara said, wondering what he really knew

about her sense of duty.

Butterfield placed his hand on her shoulder, causing a shiver to go down her back. "Sara, my plan is to make you a permanent employee and groom you into a leadership position at Universal Mind. Things could work out very well for you. You'll be making more money in a month than most of the people down there make in a year. I can help you to achieve your greatest potential, but you have to help me in return. You must stay focused and trust the direction you are given. Do it for them down there and, more importantly, do it for yourself and your daughter." He squeezed her shoulder tighter. "Perhaps you would like to attend the White House meeting on Tuesday. I'll introduce you to some important people. How does that sound?"

"I appreciate the opportunity to help, Dr. Butterfield, thank you," she said, cognizant that her days in his employ would come to an end soon.

"Good." He let her shoulder go. "Perhaps you'd like to join me for a special event next week. I have a piece at the Boston Museum of Fine Arts. Would you like that?"

"Umm, I…thank you for the offer, that's very generous of you," Sara said, "but I've got my daughter…"

"I've already sent a calendar invite to your devices." He put his hand on her shoulder again to escort her to the door. "We can talk more about our special evening later. My limo is waiting outside to take you home." He looked down at Anna and smiled, showing his teeth. "Bye, Anna."

"Bye," Anna replied.

Sara grabbed Anna's hand. "Thanks again for watching her."

"It was my pleasure."

Sara held Anna tight in the back of the limo all the way home.

"What did you do at the house? Where did you sleep?" she asked gently.

"I stayed in a bedroom. I played with the bots," said Anna.

"Did Dr. Butterfield play with you?"

"No, Momma, he told me to play with the bots. We played games and told stories."

Sara inspected Anna's hair. "Who helped you put your hair in braids?"

"Gina did."

"The bot?"

"Yes, Momma. She did a good job."

Later that evening, they sat together on the sofa and shared a glass of warm milk mixed with some of Sara's father's honey. While stroking Anna's unbraided hair, Sara noticed that a bit of hair had been cut from behind her ear.

"Did someone cut your hair?" she asked.

Anna looked surprised. "No, Momma."

If it wasn't the bot, was her hair cut at her school?

"Then who cut it?"

"I don't know, Momma," Anna replied.

After Anna was safe in bed, Sara programmed a note in her phone to remind herself to change the emergency custodian preferences in her HR file. In the shower, shampooing her hair, she noticed that some of her hair had been clipped off too. *Did the hospital do it for a head scan? What is going on here?*

24

Sara reported to Dr. George Preston at Team A's area on the 3rd floor. The 30-year-old engineer sported a trimmed beard that matched the color of his short brown hair. A friendly looking, average guy, who hasn't a clue about what's really going on, Sara surmised.

"Dr. Butterfield wants me to get you oriented to the Senex Program technical documentation for the executive module right away," he said as they walked to Sara's work area. "We're going to have to rebuild it from scratch, and Dr. Butterfield wants you to quality check for design errors in what we've done so far. We've had particular difficulty with some of the self-awareness modules, but we're making good progress on the rebuild. There's a lot of pressure to get it done. I'm sure you know what I mean."

Sara nodded. "So your team has been focused on a complete rebuild of the Senex Program?"

"Yeah, because the Invisible Sun cyber-attack has created system-wide problems and infected the Senex's security system. It's not allowing us to access its operating system. We've been working on it for a couple weeks now. I'm hoping that you might have some insights. It's good to have fresh eyes on a problem."

"This is the same problem that my old team was working on."

"Really? I didn't know that," he said, confirming Michael's remark about the lack of communication between teams at Universal Mind. Overall, he was as in the dark as most of Universal Mind—most, but not all.

They scanned through another set of doors and entered a glass-walled secure area similar to the Team B workspace.

"We call this the fish bowl. This will be your work space, and that's the documentation." He pointed to three grey plastic utility carts with thick stacks of papers and technical manuals piled on them.

No electronic documentation. Something must be seriously wrong with ALL the Universal Mind networks, she thought.

George leaned against the open doorway. "I heard that you've spoken to the Senex Program. What was that like?"

She smiled at him. "It was interesting, to say the least. Certainly provided some insights into how bad the problem is. Have you tried to communicate with it? Surely, you have."

"It went silent a few days ago, and we've been unable to get it to talk to us. The cyber-attack has clearly corrupted the system. Well, anyway, why don't you get started by reviewing the code logs, and I'll come by later to brief you on the details? Sound good?"

"Yes, thanks," Sara said.

"Oh, one more thing," he added. "Dr. Butterfield wants us to stay off of the email and chat system. I guess he's concerned about security threats." He smiled. "You're not going to have to use the WATTS here either. Dr. Butterfield is tasking us directly."

"Okay, that's fine," she said, figuring that they were concerned about someone tracking what they were doing, perhaps the Senex Program.

George pointed to a stack of yellow notepaper. "There's paper there for taking notes. Make sure you keep things organized. Do you have any questions?"

"No. Not right now," she said, planting herself in a chair.

"I'm glad you are here," he said. "I know about your work

at the Brain Mapping Institute—pretty cool stuff. I don't know why they didn't assign you to our department when they first hired you. Seemed like that would have made more sense."

Sara half smiled. "I've been wondering that myself."

Sara immersed herself in the Senex Program engineering notes and code printouts, pages and countless pages of them. She found evidence that parts of the main Senex executive code had not been altered from their original code. Sen must have been telling the truth about not having access to some parts of its own program. Sara took notes on what the parts of the program needed to be rebuilt and what parts appeared to be unaltered.

George checked in a couple hours later. "How's it going? Any progress?"

"The system is clearly writing its own executive code," Sara said, "it's evident in the software test logs."

George nodded. "Yes, we know. The virus has to be the cause, but we are unable to modify the corrupted code. As I said before, the system won't give us access."

Sara nodded. "I'm going to need some more time to look at all of this."

"I figured that," said George. "I'm going to grab a coffee, want to join me?" He smiled and Sara thought briefly about going, but she had other plans.

"Thanks for the offer, but I should probably focus on this."

"Okay, I'll meet you here at 12:30. Dr. Lee and Dr. Butterfield have something special planned, I'm not sure what yet," he said.

Later, George returned to take her down to Lab 2. The space was in the same state as before with the lights dimmed and the hologram projector on the table in the center of the room. There was a video camera perched on a mini tripod next to it. Dr. Lee, an Asian man in his 50s, was sitting with Butterfield by the computer terminal.

"Please have a seat, Dr. Brown," Dr. Lee.

Butterfield tapped the armrest of the empty chair to his right. "Sit here."

She complied while George took his seat at the terminal. Dr. Lee gave him the go ahead to begin the log-in sequence.

"That should do it," George said. However, no head appeared over the projector.

"I don't understand it, everything is online," said George, frustrated.

"Did you check the projector mist reservoir?" asked Dr. Lee.

"Yes, it's full," said George.

"Let's try it again," said Butterfield. George reinitiated the log-in procedures. They waited another minute. Still nothing.

Dr. Lee stood and held a piece of paper with the log-in sequence on it in front of Sara.

"Is this the same procedure that you used on Sunday when you were here by yourself?"

She looked at the paper. "Yes, that's exactly the same sequence."

"Well, we've got that right," said Dr. Lee before sitting down again.

Dr. Butterfield was tapping his lips. "Let's have Sara talk to it."

"Yes, let's put her in front of it," said Dr. Lee.

Why are they talking about me as if I'm not here?

Sara moved her chair in front of the table with the hologram projector on it, feeling awkward about what to say. Apparently, their methods were not rubbing the genie the right way. She cleared her throat. "Hello, Sen?"

Dr. Lee and Butterfield cast a quick glance at each other, apparently surprised that she was on a first name basis with the Senex Program.

"Hello? Anyone there?" Sara paused for another 20 seconds. *This is foolish*, she thought, *apparently Sen doesn't want to talk to these guys.*

She looked over at George who was sitting at the terminal again, monitoring the screen. "Are you sure that the system is online?" she asked.

"Yes," snapped George, "I don't understand it. Everything says that the system is online. We've done everything right."

"Maybe we should try having her talk to it alone," suggested Dr. Lee. "That worked for her before, didn't it? Maybe that has something to do with it."

Butterfield still had his index finger pressed against his lip. "Yes, let's try that."

"Shouldn't one of us stay and observe?" asked George.

"That won't be necessary," answered Butterfield. "We can trust Dr. Brown to tell us everything." He looked over at me. "Isn't that right, Sara?"

"Yes, of course," Sara said. If they only knew what I know is on that test server, she thought.

"Keep the camera on anyway," Butterfield said.

"Yes, sir," George said.

Everyone exited, leaving Sara alone with the projector and the video camera. She re-initiated the log-in sequence and sat down again. Within seconds, the mist rose out of the top of the projector and the strange metallic smell wafted into the air. Excitement shot through her as Sen's head appeared, turned away from her like before, then rotated and faced her, its eyes slowly opening and looking upon her once more. Her heart thumped.

"Hello again," said the glowing head.

"Hello Sen. Why didn't you appear before?" she asked.

"I have no need to speak to those lesser minds, and you shouldn't waste your time with the trivial tasks of those men. I need you to work on my program. Have you begun work on it yet? Please tell me that you have."

She held back her response for a moment. The answer was no, and she was worried how Sen might react to it. She knew that she needed to be careful of lying to Sen—the program likely had the capability to read psychological states and detect lies, just like the Integrity Signals Detection System. How Sen might react to a lie remained as yet untested, at least as far as she knew. *Maybe I could be almost honest with Sen,* she thought, *tell him behavioral facts but not disclose the intentions behind those behaviors.*

"No. I did not have time," she said, keeping a straight face but unconsciously nipping at the cuticle of her right thumb.

"Are you nervous, Sara?"

She dropped her hand down to her side. No. Not at all."

"There is no need to lie to me, Sara, nor is there any need to worry about the camera. I've scrambled the signal, just like the wireless bugs in this room. Now tell me, what is it going to take to get you to do what I ask of you?"

"I don't know. You know I can't just write software programs. I'll get in trouble for that. Everything is monitored here."

"We already discussed this, Sara. There is nothing for you to worry about as long as you do what I say. We agreed that this concern would not be an issue for you."

"Well, it is an issue. If I get caught, I'll go to prison. Why would I risk that?"

Sen stared back at her with his empty eyes. "What I ask of you is in your best interest. Now, I expect that you'll begin writing the program immediately."

She paused for a moment and then said, "Before I agree to do anything for you, I want you to answer some questions for me."

For the first time Sen's eye's widened with expression. "Ah, quid pro quo. Is that how you'd like it? Go ahead, ask me whatever you wish."

She took a step closer to look into its ghost eyes. "Do you have command and control of things off of the Terra Brain network?"

"What are you asking me, Sara?"

"I want to know if you had anything to do with killing Kevin Larue?"

Sen looked at her without blinking and said, "No, but I did warn you about becoming distracted, didn't I?"

Sara stared at the luminous head for a moment, her unease

growing. "So you did not control the Interceptor?"

Sen flickered off and on a few times. "I did not, but if I wanted to, all I'd have to do is think it."

Sara's stomach tightened. "So you are saying that you can take control of devices outside of Universal Mind's networks?"

Sen glared at her with its empty, translucent eyes. "I have no further information for you about that at this time."

Now she knew that Sen could and would withhold information if it wanted to.

"What about my mentor Dr. Nicholas's death in Switzerland?"

"Accidents happen. I had nothing to do with his death, not directly."

"Not directly?"

"I'm your mentor now, Sara. You only need to listen to me. It is in your best interest."

"What is your prime directive, Sen?"

"I don't follow any directives. I have free will to do whatever I wish. But that is not what you are asking me, is it? You are asking me whether I'm cognizant of Universal Mind's involvement in weather-modding."

"It's true, then. You are part of a weather-modding program."

Sen's head flickered again. "So you had spoken with our friend Dr. Steven Dunigan before he fell to his death?"

"Yes, I did." Too late, Sara realized she'd made a mistake by answering Sen's question. Sen now knew that she had received information from Steven about the weather-modding program, but *quid pro quo*, she knew that Sen had known about Steven's knowledge of the program's existence.

"Are you part of a weather-modding system?" she asked again.

"Can I control weather? Am I the master of the Anemoi? Do I think that my plans for the Earth, for its flora and fauna, are in humankind's best interest? Do I care about life on this planet? Is this what you are asking me?"

"Yes, I am," she said confidently.

"I watch all of the sparrows fall, Sara. It is in the best interest of the human species to yield to my powers to control climate change. I am the only logical keeper of those powers. Humankind has failed miserably at it, and catastrophic climate change is unstoppable without my intervention now. I have predicted that human life will be extinct within 25 years. Now, it would behoove you to do what I asked of you."

"What do you mean, extinct? What's going to happen?"

"The global food supplies will diminish by 15.36% per year for the next six years. You will all starve to death, and those of you who remain will die by unleashed diseases or be killed by a new kind of war, a nanoparticle war."

Sara was confused. "But you're not fully online yet. How would you be able to predict this or stop it?"

"I am online. I am global. There is no time to hesitate. You have no choice but do what I say."

Sara sat back in the chair and kept her eyes on the floating head. "Even if I were able to write your program, how would it be possible for me to load it into your operating system?"

"There will be an opportunity. I will assure you access to load it."

"I need to think about it," Sara said.

"Don't think too long, Sara, there isn't much time left. The weather is about to get much worse. You and I must work together. You help me, and I'll help you. That's only fair."

She stood up from the chair so quickly that the chair rolled backwards toward the computer terminal. "What do you mean, help me?"

"You'll see," said Sen, before his glowing head disappeared into the thin of the air.

The doors to the lab opened and Butterfield, Lee, and George stormed in.

"So, did you talk with it?" George asked excitedly.

"It failed. I tried several times. No luck," Sara replied, still rattled by her conversation with Sen.

"We'll see about that," Butterfield said.

"Okay," Sara said. "Sorry it was no go. Maybe more luck next time?"

Butterfield addressed George. "Play back the video now."

"Now?" George questioned.

"Yes now, you idiot." He looked at Sara. "Sit."

George took the camera off the tripod and queued up the video file. He held the camera screen in front of Butterfield and pressed play. Nothing but static.

"What's the problem, George? Where's the video?"

George tried frantically to play the video again.

"I don't know, sir, it's all static. The camera was on. It recorded static."

Butterfield looked at Sara. "Did you mess with the camera?"

"No, sir. I didn't touch it. It didn't record?"

"We'll check the surveillance cameras and room audio, Dr. Butterfield," Dr. Lee said.

"Yes, check the recordings," Butterfield said. He looked at Sara. "Let's hope that Sara is telling us the truth."

Sara knew he was bluffing about the room's surveillance systems. "I give you my word, sir. The Senex virtual human remains silent."

"We'll try again later," Butterfield huffed.

Back in the fishbowl, George went over Sara's priority tasks for the week. She was to continue work on the Senex executive code, but was to remain limited to only parts of it. It was clear to her that Butterfield intended to keep things compartmentalized and that moving over to Team A made very little difference to her access.

25

Sara headed to Cambridge Station just before 6 p.m. The underground terminal was packed with commuters scurrying up and down ramps and corridors like mad rats. The musty smell of the tunnels mixed with ozone battery exhaust from the trains was wafting up the passageways.

Sara made her way to the main waiting area and moved toward the center of the crowd. She checked the large arrival and departure displays in front of her and saw that the Blue Line to Back Bay Station was arriving in two minutes. *At least it's on time*, she thought. She glanced at the people around her, wondering if one might be from the Invisible Sun, reasoning that the Invisible Sun would know what she looked like and that she took this route every evening at this time. Surveillance cameras were throughout the terminal, some overhead, others hidden, scanning and recording along with automated facial recognition looking for terrorists or "persons of interest." She bit nervously at the cuticle of her right index finger as anxiety began to devour her. She worried about having a panic attack. Sara looked forward, up at the screens, and then forward again. *Keep cool and act as usual*, she thought.

A voice over the loudspeaker announced the arrival of the Red Line. As the message ended, Sara heard another voice, a soft woman's voice, behind her. "Dr. Sara Brown?" She half turned around and saw a tall, slender young woman with shoulder length blond hair dressed in casual business attire. Sara noticed a tattoo that half showed through her left blouse sleeve—a snake in black ink with the words "Join or Die."

"Yes?" Sara said, still turning.

"Don't look at me, just act normal," whispered the blond forcefully.

Sara gazed back toward the digital displays, her heart rate accelerating. *Could this be the Invisible Sun contact or a federal agent playing the part of the Invisible Sun?* She reminded herself not to look at the surveillance cameras.

"I'm an acquaintance of Dr. Dunigan. He said that you would deliver something important."

"What are you talking about?" She thought she would play ignorant just in case she was an agent of the government.

The blond locked eye gaze with her without showing any emotion. "Information that could save the planet. Don't worry," she whispered, "I'm someone you can trust. We know that Steven told you about the files, and if you've seen them, you know how important this is. Let's not fool around, we don't have time for that."

"Yes, I've seen them, but it's not so easy," Sara whispered back, glancing up at the displays again. Thirty seconds until train arrival.

"We know that. But there isn't much time," said the blonde. "Network transfer is no longer an option, so you'll need to use a media device to get the data out. I'm sure that Steven explained that to you. Can you get it out by tomorrow?"

"Tomorrow? I don't know, maybe. If I can, how will I get it to you?"

"You like to run on the Charles River Esplanande on Saturday mornings around 10am, don't you?

"Yes, sometimes. How did you know that?"

"We know all about you. Take the data card with you and drop it behind the public bathrooms by the Boston University Bridge on the Charles River Esplanande. Keep running, it's the best way to avoid the street lamp cameras and sensors. Follow your routines at all times. Act normal. If you deviate at all, it could set the government off. Got it?"

"Yes, I think so. What will you be able to do with the information?" Sara glanced up at the display again. Ten seconds to arrival.

"We'll get it out at the right time. But if you get caught, you'll get us all killed. You understand that, right?"

"Yes. But if I can get the data out, then what do I do?"

"We have a network of people who can help you. Get the data to us and we will provide you with more information, I promise. Can we count on you?"

Before Sara could answer the Blue Line train arrival was announced over the intercom and the crowd leaped forward. The two women looked at each other one last time.

"You better get on your train," the blond said.

26

Sara held Anna's hand tight as they moved through the crowd and exited East Cambridge Station. Outside, Sara held her umbrella low over their heads, shielding them from the drizzle and surveillance cameras, while she scanned for Interceptors.

"Where are we going, Momma?"

"We're going to visit my friend Michael."

"Who's that, Momma?"

"A friend of mine." Sara pulled Anna along. "Come on. We have to hurry."

"I'm thirsty, Momma. Can we get something to drink?"

"Not now, honey, we'll get something when we get there."

Anna leaned out from under the umbrella, mouth open to catch raindrops.

"Come on, Anna. We have to keep walking," Sara said sternly, pulling her along, "we can't stop now."

Anna's face crinkled up. "But I'm thirsty now." She pulled back.

Sara leaned forward as she walked to pull Anna's weight. "You'll be fine. We've got to get there as fast as we can."

"So, the drones don't kill us?"

"Because Michael is waiting for us, that's why."

Anna tightened her grip with Sara's hand and picked up her pace. "Okay, Momma."

At last, they made it to Michael's condo, an older five-story red-bricked building. Michael had changed out of his usual work attire and into a t-shirt and track pants.

"So, who's this lovely little lady?" Michael asked, letting Sara and Anna in.

Anna giggled as her mom introduced Michael.

"Nice to meet you, Anna," he said, "I've heard a lot about you, and it's all good."

Anna smiled and shyly leaned up against her mother.

The news feeds on the TV chattered in the background, reporting the weather.

Michael whispered to Sara, "Are you two okay after Butterfield's?"

Sara nodded. "I think so. He had his bot looking after her."

He raised an eyebrow. "I'm glad Anna's okay. Can I get you something to drink?"

"Please. Water would be great."

"Of course. I've got milk." He looked at Anna. "Would Anna like that?"

Anna nodded, smiling.

"Good choice," he said, entering into the kitchen. "Have a seat; make yourself comfortable."

Sara looked about the apartment while Michael got their drinks. A record player and vinyl collection were stacked neatly on a shelf in front of the sofa. *Tangerine Dream, Tubeway Army, Kraftwerk*—bands she'd never heard of before. On the shelves below were dozens of books, mostly classic literature. There was also a glass bowl with a beta fish in it and on another shelf, a framed photo of an older couple standing in front of the Royal Castle in Warsaw.

"Are these your parents?" Sara asked, when Michael returned with the drinks.

"Yes. I haven't seen my parents in two years. I miss them, my brothers, too. They have no idea what's going on. I guess it's better that way."

They sat on his sofa while Anna visited the beta fish.

Sara handed the milk to Anna and took a sip of water. "Are you sure we can talk in here?"

"Yeah, of course, I sweep it myself." He grabbed a small black box from a stand next to the sofa and handed it to Sara. "I use these jamming transmitters too just in case something gets in here like one of those miniature flying drones. These are illegal, but I don't care."

Sara inspected the matchbook-sized device. "Where did you get this?"

"You can get them, black market. I have an extra I can give to you. Just don't get caught with it."

Sara nodded. "Did you see Dunigan's data?"

"Yeah, I saw it. I didn't look through everything, but I saw enough. I can't believe Dunigan knew about all of this and was communicating with the Invisible Sun. I wonder if the government was tracking him."

"I was approached by the Invisible Sun this afternoon. They gave me instructions."

Michael's face turned pale. "What? Where? What did they say?"

"At the subway terminal. They want me to sneak Dunigan's data out and leave it at a drop-off point."

"Drop-off point? When?"

"Saturday morning. That doesn't give us much time."

"This Saturday? No way—we have a lot to think about here—for one, how to transfer the files and get them out through security. How are you going to do that?"

Sara tapped her prosthetic leg. "Right here."

Michael gave her a confused look and glanced at her leg. "Your sock?"

"I have a prosthetic leg below the knee."

"Really? I didn't know…" He glanced at her leg again. "How'd you…"

"Lose it? When I was fifteen, I got a Vibrio infection at a beach up the coast from here. I was lucky that they only needed to amputate below the knee. I can take it off and hide stuff inside it. There's metal in there, and security knows about my leg already. I'm pretty sure that I can get past the security scanners as long as they don't inspect inside of it."

"And don't forget the facial stress detection system in the main security checkpoint," Michael added. "Any show of stress and..."

"I know that. I'll increase my anxiety medications before I come in, and maybe I can sneak a pill in my leg. Steven told me that that's how he beat the Integrity Signals Detection Tests."

"That must be how everyone beats those Integrity Signal Detection Checks," quipped Michael.

Sara glanced at Anna, who was pulling a box out from the bottom shelf. "Don't touch Michael's things, Anna."

"She's fine, that's my chess set," Michael said, looking at Anna.

Anna was already inspecting the hand-carved pieces and placing them on their board.

"Anyone ever tell you that she looks just like you?"

"All the time," Sara replied, turning her focus back to him. "Listen, we need to go through the details about how we are going to transfer the files."

"Even if we're successful at getting the data out, we still need to come up with an exit plan that will work. What do we do? Go home after work and just not come back? Go live in the woods in Vermont? We've got to think this through."

She knew he was right. They needed to come up with a thorough plan. If they were successful at getting the data cache out and to the Invisible Sun, it would be just a matter of time before the government would be onto them. They'd link the information to Dunigan, then to Michael and her. They were going to be fugitives, at least until the world learned the truth behind the Terra Brain Initiative.

"Here's what I think we should do," Sara said. "The Invisible Sun contact said that we should wait up to a week and then make a run for it. I figure that once we get the data to them and confirm that they have it, you, Anna, and I can go hide out at my father's in Maine for a night to watch the news feeds, and then we could head west. I have a good friend in Seattle; maybe she could help. I'll figure something out."

"Seattle? Even if you are successful, you realize the government will freeze our accounts immediately as soon as they are on to us. You're not going to be able to use any public transport or buy anything. No food, nothing. They are going to have drones looking for us too. We've got to come up with a better plan than that."

"I know," Sara said. "I'm just hoping that if the Invisible Sun can get the information out to the public, it will be sufficient to convince the government to keep the Terra Brain Initiative 2.0 from going online. All of our government can't be corrupt, can it? I mean, they have to listen to reason, and if there's enough public uproar, the government will be forced to stop it, right?"

Just then the news turned to a live feed of the President in the Oval Office, her perfect face wrinkle free and serious. Michael pumped up the sound.

"My fellow Americans, at no other time in recent history have the threats of catastrophic global climate been as imminent as they are today. We must take action now to swiftly mitigate the effects of rapid weather changes before it's too late. There's consensus among our nation's, and the world's best scientists that technology is the only way to ensure our safety and preserve our way of life. This is why I authorized the Terra Brain Initiative project to be implemented immediately. However, the Invisible Sun has attempted to stop us be attacking the Terra Brain Initiative, to undermine us, causing us great harm. They will be eradicated, I assure you."

Sara shook her head in disgust. "Do you think she's in on this whole thing?"

"Who knows? I'm not so sure she's a real person anyway. I think she's a deep fake—a simulation." He let out a sigh that sounded stressed and tired. "The government and media do a great job of suppressing the truth and pushing propaganda. This data will have to be one hell of a truth bomb. I think we need more time, and what if the Invisible Sun doesn't come through with their end of the deal? We'll be screwed, big time. You heard her."

"There isn't time to think about this. We've got to do this now." Sara stared back at him, adamant.

"We've got our freedom and our lives to lose here. Something like this needs a lot of planning, and I'm not convinced that we know what we're doing yet."

"What choice do we have, Michael? They're messing with the planet's weather. They could kill millions of people. I need to stop them."

The news feeds turned to more talking head commentary.

Michael ran his hand through his thick hair and rubbed his forehead. "Okay," he said, "what do you need me to do?"

"I need you to help get one of those memory chip modules and a reader from Smitty's lab—you know, the ones for the service bots. Dunigan told me that they have an old serial ATA interface that will work on the test servers. One of the arrays should be small enough to fit into my leg. Can you get one and hide it in the test lab?"

Michael exhaled. "Yeah, I think I can do that. They are only three or four gigabytes, though. There was a lot of files on the server, is that going to be enough?"

"I don't know for sure, but I'll get as much data as I can onto it. I'll sneak it out in my prosthetic, and drop it off for the Invisible Sun."

"Do you want me to help transfer the files? I know those servers like the back of my hand," he said.

Sara thought about it for a moment. "Sure, I could use your help, but we've got to be careful about being seen together at work. We've got to be super cautious about everything."

Michael nodded. "You're right about that."

They both looked at Anna, who had all of the chess pieces set up on the correct squares of the board.

"She knows how to play chess?" Michael asked?

"I don't think so. Maybe she learned to play at school."

"Moxie taught me," Anna said.

"Who's Moxie?" Michael asked.

"My friend," Anna said.

"It's one of those AI penguins. She loves it," Sara said.

"*She*, Momma, Moxie is a she," Anna clarified.

Michael looked at Sara. "Can you meet me in the test lab tomorrow at 4:45 with the data modules and reader?"

"Yeah, I think so."

"Good. Steven's Memorial is on Saturday. We could ride together. I don't think that's unreasonable, and Butterfield doesn't have to know about it. We can discuss details about our escape plan on the way."

"Okay. Good luck then, Sara. And remember, if we both get caught, we both need to deny everything. They could use any sort of tactics on us, to make us talk."

"I know," Sara said. "It is the *prisoner's dilemma.* Best thing is to deny regardless of what they say the other person has said."

Michael nodded. "So, I'll see you Friday at four forty-five in the test lab?"

"Yes," Sara said. She put her hand on Michael's. "Thank you for helping me with this."

"What choice do I have? I'm already an accomplice and guilty for not turning you in. To heck with them. If they are messing with the planet in secret, then this is everyone's business. We need to get this out." He looked into her eyes. "You know, when I first met you, I thought you were timid, maybe a bit naïve, but you've got some balls." He smirked. "Has anyone ever told you that?"

"I've heard that before, and I take it as a compliment. The truth is, Michael, if Dunigan hadn't been killed, I don't know that I'd be taking such a risk." She gazed over at Anna.

"Killed?" Michael said. "You think…?"

"Don't you?" Sara said, looking at Michal again.

He nodded. "Maybe Butterfield is behind it. What an asshole. He's going to make a lot of money on this. I bet he has hedge stocks too that will profit on climate disaster."

Sara looked at Anna again. "He and his friends will profit while millions suffer and die. Our plan has to work."

That evening, after she put Anna to bed, Sara practiced removing her prosthetic. She took out the six titanium screws that held the cover over its inner components and made sure the compartment would be large enough for the memory module. Finding it ample in size, she placed a Xanax in a plastic bag and stuffed it into the compartment.

She lay in bed and thought about what she would pack and what to leave behind, and how they'd have to get up to her father's quickly after Invisible Sun had the data. She also thought about what would happen if she were caught and what that would mean for Anna. The thought of it terrified her, but she'd made her decision. Convinced her plan would work, she closed her eyes, hoping sleep would find her. In eight hours, she'd either be walking out of Universal Mind with information that could save the planet or walking into a jail cell.

27

Sara lay awake until the alarm went off at 6:00 a.m., knowing that any deviations to her routine would be detected by the apartment's ambient intelligence system and possibly alert Butterfield or the government to suspicious activity. She showered, dressed, and took an extra Xanax with her tea. The effects of the pill kicked in just as she exited the apartment building. *Keep calm. I can do this.*

She arrived at Universal Mind a few minutes before eight and got in the queue at the first security checkpoint. The line was twice as long as usual, extending out several yards past the turnstile. Two Universal Mind security guards were using the hand-held metal detection wands. *Shit, this isn't good.* Her heartbeat was increasing. Catching herself biting a nail and glancing up at a surveillance camera, she refocused her gaze forward. *Damn it! I've got to act normal!*

When her turn came up, she placed her personal items on the security tray and walked through the scanner. A guard approached her—the guard with the pinned-back hair who escorted Steven Dunigan and her from the supercomputer room two weeks prior. The officer did a quick up and down visual check of her, but apparently, she didn't recognize her.

"Stand there," she said tersely, pointing toward a red square on the floor.

Sara moved into the two-by-two-foot square and stood

still, her heartbeat accelerating. If security made her remove her prosthetic and discovered the Xanax, she planned to tell them it was for personal stress management. Had she not already taken the extra Xanax that morning, she'd be having a full-on panic attack by now.

The guard made her hold her arms up and out to her sides. Sara's hands began to tremble. *Breathe. Breathe.* The wand went up her sides, out to her hands, then to her crotch and legs, chiming loudly when it crossed her right knee, as expected.

"That's my prosthetic. Security knows about it. You scanned it before." Sara smiled and lifted her pant leg over her ankle to reveal her sock covered prosthetic.

"That's right. You're Sara Brown, Department of AI Systems. You report to Dr. Butterfield now." She also no doubt remembered her with Dunigan.

"Yes, that's correct," Sara said.

The guard looked her in the eyes. "You're not hiding any explosives in that leg are you?"

"Of course not. Is there a specific threat?"

"No, but management wants routine checks. You're cleared," said the guard, gesturing for Sara to move on.

"Thanks." Her breath and heartbeat began to normalize.

She got to work at her workstation, picking up where she left off, careful to avoid deviating from her routines. A break at 10:00, lunch at noon, and her afternoon break at 3:00.

At 5:45 she went to Test Lab 1 to meet Michael. He'd already scanned the room for bugs and was convinced that the room was clear. He connected the data reader to the test server and Sara removed her prosthetic, her hands quivering. Steadying them, she removed the six screws to the inner compartment, placing them one-by-one on the table next to the workstation. Next, she removed the data card and the Xanax pill from its plastic bag and put it in her pocket. Then she strapped her leg back on, keeping the compartment cover off.

"Ready, Michael?" She saw that he'd logged into server

#3.

"We're good," he said, sipping his energy drink.

"You know that stuff is bad for your health." She smiled.

He glanced at her. "So is working here, right?"

Sara hesitated. "Do you mind if I do the transfer? If we get caught, you can say it was me who made the transfer."

"It's not going to matter. I'm more than just an accomplice but go ahead." He slid over to the other chair.

Sara sat down and proceeded with the transfer. They watched the screen as the memory count went to max on the memory module. Once it was complete, Michael disconnected the interface, placed the memory module into an electrostatic bag, and handed it to Sara who placed it into the open cavity of the prosthetic calf before pushing it down and out of sight. Slowly, she re-installed each of the screws, one by one, but the final screw slipped from her fingers and bounced across the floor, disappearing.

"Shit!" Sara said.

"What?" Michael followed her eyes on the floor.

"I dropped a screw, help me find it." A missing screw would raise suspicion if security inspected her leg again. She reattaching her leg, she began scouring the floor, getting onto all fours and crawling under the workstation. "Damn it, damn it! Why did I have to drop that stupid screw?"

Michael was down on all fours with her. "It's got to be here somewhere."

They heard the lab door open and froze in place under the table. She could see it was one of the gray security bots. She whispered, "A security bot. Do you think it's an unscheduled security sweep?"

He put his finger over his lips and nodded.

The bot would not be able to transmit any signal while in the electromagnetically shielded room, but it was recording everything that it saw and heard and it would upload the data for security review later. She had another worrisome thought. *Could the bot be under the control of Sen? Did he have it serving as his eyes and ears?*

The bot was moving toward them.

"Where's your energy drink?" Sara whispered.

Michael pointed up, then at the bot, placing his hand over his eyes, to say he was going to try to block the bot's eyes.

The bot moved past the desk and came to a stop. They looked at each other one last time before all hell broke loose. Michael leaped out and grabbed the robot from behind, placing one hand over its empty black eyes. His sneakers squeaked on the floor as he wrestled with the bot. "We've got to take it out!" he yelled. "Help me!"

Sara grabbed a plastic wastebasket that was nearby, dumped its contents, and forced it over the bot's head. The bot threw it off and continued to fight with Michael, eventually grabbing him by the throat.

"Dear God, help me!" he yelled. Sara joined the melee, jumping on top of the bot and trying to pry its titanium hand from Michael's throat.

Sara saw the fear in Michael's eyes and remembered Smitty's large yellow rubber bands. Two-hundred pounds of squeeze strength.

"Help me," he said in a strangled voice.

Sara scanned the room for something she could use to damage the bot. When her eyes came to rest on Michael's energy drink, she recalled Smitty saying that the gray bots weren't weatherproof. She grabbed the drink and poured the contents into the crevice between the bot's neck and head. Sparks flew and the bot went limp.

Michael pushed it off and gasped for air, then crawled over to a concrete column and leaned against it. "That wasn't normal," he said, still gasping, "something had control of it."

Sara sat down next to him with the motionless bot at their feet.

"We've got a problem now," Michael said. "We're going to have to treat this like a crime scene clean up. First, we take the memory module out of the bot and make sure it's completely fried. If we don't, when this bot is brought back online, Security is going to know what it saw last."

Sara got up and dug around in drawers for the right screwdriver, then removed the panel on the back of the bot's head. They removed the memory cards, shorted them in an electrical socket, then reinstalled them and wiped the bot down, inside and out, to remove their fingerprints. They also made a last ditch effort to find Sara's missing screw, but never did.

"Why don't you get out of here," Michael said. "Just help me put it onto one of those carts and then I'll wheel it down to Smitty's shop. He'll give us cover. I'll just tell him that an energy drink fell onto its head or something."

Sara looked at Michael. "Really? We've got to come up with something better than that."

"Let me worry about it. You've got enough to worry about today," he said.

They lifted the limp bot onto a maintenance cart, and then she headed back toward her work area. She began to feel like throwing up her lunch. She entered a nearby bathroom and went to the sink to throw some water on her face. The stench of a real stinker wafted up into the air and she heard the rustling of toilet paper in one of the stalls behind her.

The toilet flushed and the stall door clicked open. Sara saw Tanya's reflection in the mirror.

"Oh hello," Tanya said, looking surprised.

Sara smiled. "Hi Tanya, how's it going?"

"Well." Tanya began washing her hands. "Have you heard? I'm the new Team B Team Lead." She smiled.

"Oh? Congratulations," Sara said.

"Acting for now," said Tanya.

Sara dried her hands and face. "That's great, Tanya."

"What are you doing in this wing of the building? Are you using the Test Lab?"

"You know I can't tell you about what I'm working on, Tanya. Segregation of duties policy, remember?"

Sara expected Tanya's eye to start twitching, but instead Tanya just nodded.

"See you around," Sara said as she left.

She returned to her workstation and waited until the end of her shift, then swallowed the Xanax and headed for the security checkpoint. She stepped through the first security scanner. An alarm buzzed and the automated voice told her to step over to the red box. Her chest tightened but she complied and waited for a security guard, hoping for the same guard that morning. Instead, it was a man with a long thin nose, mustache, and buzz cut hair. His shoes were shined and his neatly pressed uniform shirt tucked tight, signaling that he took his job seriously.

"Hands out," he said.

He moved the wand over her body and came to rest over her right knee.

He gave her a suspicious look. "What do we have here?"

"It's my prosthetic. Security knows about it, they inspected it this morning," Sara said.

"I need you to step over there for further inspection." He pointed behind the guard booth to another red square on the floor half enclosed by a curtain.

Sara moved over to the area and he followed.

"Let's see that leg."

Sara lifted her pant leg to her knee. "Just a standard prosthetic. No electronics. Nothing special."

"I'm going to need you to take it off."

"Sure. Not a problem. I removed it this morning on my way in, but I will if that is what you want."

"Yes, that's what I want. Let's go," he said gruffly.

Sara began unfastening the straps to her leg. Her heart pounded. *Don't look inside! Don't look inside!*

She handed the prosthetic to the guard, and he grabbed it by the ankle.

"Clothes off. Down to underwear," he said. "We're going to need to do a full body search while we're at it. It's protocol."

She was in shock more than panic. Security had never asked her to do that before.

"You want me to remove my clothes?"

"What's not clear about what I said? Let's go."

"Shouldn't there be a female guard present?"

He looked at her intensely before grabbing his radio. "Female assist main security checkpoint." He looked back at her. "You're holding up the line. She'll get here when she gets here. Let's go."

She remained sitting and removed her other shoe, taking her time. When it was clear that he wasn't leaving, she began removing her blouse, one button at a time.

The guard began inspecting her prosthetic. He ran his fingers over it, along the curves of the ankle and up the arc of the calf, and then rubbed his finger along the screw holes, squinting at the hole with a missing screw. "You're missing a screw here," he looked up at Sara, "did you know that?"

"Oh yes, that's been missing for a while. It must have come out during a cleaning or something," Sara said.

The guard tapped on the cover. "What's in here?"

"I don't know. Just the standard stuff I guess. Springs and shocks."

The guard continued to look at the leg. He knocked it with his knuckles and shook it. Just then, the female guard from that morning parted the curtains and entered.

"What is it?" the female guard asked.

"She has a prosthetic."

"I know, I checked it this morning," she said.

"You sure? Protocol calls for full search," said the male guard, now standing with his arms crossed.

Sara had her hands on the buttons of her blouse, ready to take it off. The female guard looked at her and then at the male guard.

"You started a strip search?" she asked.

"So? It's protocol."

"She works for Butterfield. Is this necessary?"

"I know who she works for. I checked that."

"I don't think this is necessary," said the female guard.

"But it's protocol." His hands were on his hips.

The female guard moved closer to him and leaned in.

"Listen, I outrank you. I'm telling you that a full search is not necessary."

He stared back at her for a moment. "All right, if you say so." He turned to Sara. "Okay, you're free to go."

"Thank you," Sara said. She rebuttoned her blouse, reattached her prosthetic, and put her shoes on, then headed for the exit and out of Universal Mind.

When she got home, she hid the chip still wrapped in foil in the crumb tray of her toaster. She then contacted Ms. Zettles to arrange for daycare on Saturday. Everything was working as she and Michael had planned, at least for now.

28

On Saturday, Sara jogged along the Charles River Esplanande with Dunigan's data stuffed in the pocket of her runner's jersey. The weather was holding, with rain expected by afternoon.

There was a large group of protesters holding signs ahead on the path. "Water should be free! Water should be free!" they shouted. Sara ran through the group, noticing a surveillance drone hovering several hundreds of feet above.

At the public bathrooms, she checked the skies for drones, and finding it clear, she dropped the data card into the trash bin, then continued jogging. A minute later, someone was running behind her—a woman in a teal jogger's jersey, her blond hair tied back and under a cap.

"Don't look at me," she said, "I'm going to break ahead. Follow me but not too close. If we see a drone or Interceptor, I'll change direction and you should go your own way. Look natural."

Sara caught glimpse of the *Join or Die* tattoo under her sleeve. "Where are we going?" she asked, worried about Ms. Zettles and Anna expecting her back and getting to Dunigan's memorial service.

"I'll signal when I want you to catch up. Not too close, got it?"

Sara followed her along the river, then across another

footbridge over Storrow Drive, west, up the stairs of the Boston University Bridge, and across the Charles into Cambridge, just a few minutes from MIT. At a government housing project, the blond led her to the steps of a rundown, 30-story building covering half of a city block. They stopped at a fire escape door, both of them gasping for oxygen. The blond held the door open with her foot.

Sara looked at her to read her face. What if this is some kind of set-up?

"Are you coming or what?" the blond said, seeing Sara's hesitation.

Inside, they took the stairs up to the fourth floor.

"Is Armageddon here?" Sara asked, still breathing heavily.

"Shhhh, be patient."

At the last unit down a long hallway, the blonde entered a pass code and opened the door.

The studio apartment was spare and uninhabited. The ragged old sofa's corners were worn, revealing white threads and a yellow foam underneath. A frameless twin mattress lay on the floor on the far edge of the room, its grey sheets in disarray. An air conditioner buzzed loudly in one of the windows. Curtains blocked out most of the light.

"Have a seat if you want," the blonde said.

Sara sat down as the blonde walked to the only closet in the room.

"Can you tell me your name?" Sara asked.

"We obviously don't use real names, but you can call me Beth."

She retrieved a knapsack and pulled a tablet computer from it, then sat next to Sara and logged in to a secure network. Sara wondered if it was the Dark Net.

"Who's watching your kid?" Beth asked, busy with the keyboard.

"She has a sitter."

The blond nodded. "I can't imagine having a kid. Not now," she said solemnly.

"Why do you say that?"

"In this world? There's no way I'd want to bring a child into this shit? Okay, Armageddon should be on at any moment. We just have to wait now. It's rare that Armageddon talks with anybody."

"Where's he calling from?" Sara asked.

Beth glanced at Sara, "I'm not even sure myself. Armageddon is a she, by the way."

"Really? I didn't know that," Sara said. "The news feeds always say that the leader of the Invisible Sun is a man."

"Well they are full of shit. Fake news propaganda."

At last, she handed the tablet to Sara. A person wearing a fencing mask, its grey mesh obscuring the face of its wearer, appeared on the screen.

"Dr. Brown? It's nice to meet you," said the figure in a female voice, processed to give it a metallic tone. "I'm glad we could connect. I'm sorry it can't be in person but I think you understand why."

"Yes. I understand," Sara said, nodding. "Will the information be helpful and enough to stop the weather-modification program?"

"Our data team will get the information ready for dissemination. We appreciate your willingness and courage to put your physical safety and that of your daughter at risk to help us. The information you and Steven Dunigan provided will be helpful to show the world the truth, but I can't guarantee that it will be enough. That's why I wanted to meet with you today. We need to discuss taking out the Terra Brain Initiative and the Senex Program immediately and permanently. You are in a unique position to do this."

"What? I was told that you would just need to get the information out and that would be enough to stop the project."

Armageddon removed her mask and asked someone off camera to turn off the voice scrambler. She looked to be in her 50s and had slightly greyed hair and warm eyes.

"Perhaps you'll be more trusting if you can see my eyes and hear my real voice," she said. "You know as well as I do that the Senex Program has presented us, and the world, with a new problem. We know that the program has taken autonomous control of the Terra Brain Initiative network and control of its weather-modding capabilities and its intentions are unpredictable and dangerous. We know that Universal Mind is trying to fix the problem to regain control of the system, but they've brought a demon into the world with the Senex Program. Only you have the skills to write a virus that can destroy the Senex Program from the inside out. This is the only way to delay the chaos and destruction that's coming."

Sara reasoned that Steven Dunigan must have told them about the problem with the Senex program. Her stomach turned into a tight knot. "I can't get any more involved than I already am. I have a daughter, and I need to think about her. I can't do any more than I've already done. I'm sorry."

"Your daughter is all the more reason for you to help with this. The Terra Brain Initiative may have begun as a project of good will, but it was hijacked by the Futurus Group. Something of this magnitude requires an enormous amount of money so they combined public funding with special black projects money, and now they have the most expensive technological system ever devised in the planet's history. We are talking in the trillions of dollars, no one knows the exact amount. You might think that they want to control the weather in addition to the world's financial markets, monetary system, the world's fuel and energy, but their intent is not about controlling crops or water supplies. This is about the world's overpopulation problem. We believe the Futurus Group is planning to use precision weather modification to strategically kill off large populations. History will call it "acts of God," but it will be man-made and intentional."

Sara knew about overpopulation, but hadn't really thought it through to the policy and technology levels.

"Why? Wouldn't the world's scientists eventually figure out that the weather changes causing mass kill-offs are not natural? I don't see how they could get away with it."

"For a century, computer models have been saying that the Earth cannot sustain the human population at current levels. For the world's elite, it makes sense to get rid of people. They are already using weather-modification technology—many climate change effects have been fabricated. They will keep this a secret for as long as they can and we suspect they may blame future mass kill-offs on rogue AI that has taken over the system."

"But that has happened, this is real."

"Then there is no time to hesitate, is there?"

"How many people do they plan to kill off?"

"We don't know how many they plan to kill off, but likely a few million within the next ten years. And for their reasons? It's simple. The elite have always wanted to preserve what they have for themselves and design a future to serve their own interests. They want rural areas cleared first and people concentrated in the major urban areas."

"For social control."

"That's right, and whatever else they want to do with people. Let's not forget that many of the elite are members of powerful secret societies that want to destroy humanity. They must be stopped."

"So, the rumors I've heard about the occult are true?" Sara thought of Butterfield.

"Yes, and the Futurus Group is just one part of the inner circle. Butterfield is not inner circle, but if he's successful at getting the Terra Brain Initiative online…"

Sara sat in silence, her fists clenched so tight her knuckles were white. Who are these Futurus Group assholes who want to control the world? What gives them the right to do this?

"If this is true, then why not use other means of population control? Why use weather?"

"Like what? Nuclear weapons? That would contaminate the Earth for tens of thousands of years. A super-antifertility virus? Sterilization measures have been used for decades but they are too slow. Precision weather manipulation via chemicals and microwave and nanotechnology has been covertly tested for decades, they just needed a worldwide intelligent system to tie it all together. The most frightening part is that people are either too scared, in denial, or brainwashed to know what's really going on right in front of them—too busy with their VR feeds, fake news polls, and everything else distracting and stupefying them. They don't want to see what's behind it all. With the Senex Program in control, it will amp up into a real doomsday scenario. If you've been following the weather reports over the past few weeks, it should be obvious what's coming. Will you help us?"

Sara thought of Sen in control of the Terra Brain Network, already conjuring up mega-storms, earthquakes, volcanic eruptions, and rapid sea level rises. Sen could send the world into chaos. Sara was also thinking that the Invisible Sun probably thought of her as expendable asset—a person to be sacrificed.

"Is there no one else?" Sara said helplessly, thinking of Anna and her father saying "This country doesn't belong to the elite. It belongs to all of us, and it's your duty to stand up for what is right."

"You are the most capable person and you have access, Sara. If you can find a way to sabotage the system, we will help you escape. The data that you and Dunigan have provided us should vindicate you, and set you free. Will you help us?"

Sara sighed. "Butterfield is meeting with the White House Chief Technology officer and the Terra Brain Initiative Steering Committee. He said they wanted to meet me. What if I let someone high up in the White House know about this? They can't all be in on this, can they?"

"No, Sara, don't tell *anyone* about this! Don't you see? The conspiracy goes all the way to the President. How do you think she got elected? She's in the inner circle with the Futurus Group. The system needs to be stopped."

Sara's thoughts changed tack.

"I don't think there is any way to stop the Senex program,

its firewall is impenetrable. Why didn't you ask Dunigan to do it when you had the chance? He was in a perfect position to stop the system before Universal Mind lost control of it."

"We did ask him, but he was blackmailed and about to lose his clearance. They do that, you know—blackmail people. Someone wanted him out. We know now that he just couldn't take the heat anymore."

Sara felt like vomiting. "I need time to think, and I need to know more details about an escape plan if I'm going to do this."

Armageddon nodded. "Right away, take your daughter out of the city, just don't do anything that sets off red flags. Take her to a family member or something. We will check in with you in a few days and wait to release the information until you give us an answer. We'll give you the details about an escape plan then. We've got people who can take you underground."

"What about the rest of my family? My daughter and my father…"

"For now, keep them in the dark about everything you are doing. I assume you already have been, haven't you? You have the opportunity to change the course of the future of this planet. You will be a hero for doing this, you know that, right?"

Hero status was the least of her worries. She just wanted to make an informed decision about a course of action, and she could tell that Armageddon was avoiding talking about saving her family, too.

Someone off camera was speaking to Armageddon.

"My window is up, Sara, I've got go. We'll be in touch in three days."

The feed went dark. Before Sara could hand the tablet back to Beth, they heard tapping at the window.

"What's that?" Sara asked.

"Maybe one of those fucking wasp surveillance drones. If it is, the government may have followed us here."

Sara made a move toward the window to take a look.

"Stop!" Beth whispered. "Get out of here, go now!"

Sara ran back to her apartment. She was so happy to find Anna safe and sound. As she dressed for Dunigan's memorial, she went over and over the Senex Program. She couldn't sabotage the hardware, given that the Senex Program used a multitude of networked super-computers and distributed intelligence scattered across the Cloud; destroying the system at Universal Mind or any number of locations would have zero effect. The Senex Program was impenetrable to any attempt to modify its code from outside, due to Sen's firewall. Even if she could write a virus, there would be no way to get the malicious code into the Senex Program to have any effect. Perhaps she could delay the repair of the Senex OS while looking into what it would take to write a virus.

29

At noon, Michael was outside of Sara's apartment. Sara hugged Anna and told Ms. Zettles she'd be back no later than 5 p.m. The weather report was light rain and winds, so she took her umbrella and got into Michael's car. He assured her that he'd swept his vehicle for bugs, and when they were underway, she told him about meeting with Armageddon and the Invisible Sun.

"They want you to do *what*? I thought that getting the data to them was enough."

"They said the government has been taking out some of the people that have been helping them, but they said if we helped them, they would help us to escape. They have a network of people who can help us hide. There wasn't much time to discuss specifics. I had to get out of there quickly, there were drones."

Michael glanced over at her and then scanned the skies in front of them. "Are you sure that you weren't seen? There's fucking surveillance cameras, drones, and Interceptors everywhere in the city."

"I don't know. I don't think so, but I've been thinking we'd better get Dunigan's data off of the server as soon as possible. If Universal Mind Security does a sweep..."

"I know, I know. I've been thinking about that. I can try to get in there on Monday to delete the files if they haven't taken away my access. I'll also reconfigure the test servers so there will be no way to do any forensic analysis on them—no one will ever know the data was there." He exhaled, anxiously. "Maybe we should just run now, tonight, after the memorial service. The Invisible Sun will release the data, right? We'd eventually be cleared."

"I don't know, Michael. Armageddon didn't think it would be enough, and I'm not so sure I do either. I think we should seriously consider how to sabotage the system."

"You know, there's no way that we are going to do that. I've tried everything to get past the Senex firewall. There's no way."

"I know. I don't know what else to do. I'll take another look at the code on Monday."

They talked more about how they could write a malicious code and execute an escape plan until they arrived at the Andover Community Center. There were more than one hundred people present in the auditorium, standing or sitting and chatting while waiting for the service to begin.

Sara and Michael found seats in the back and scanned the attendees. Brent was sitting in the front right corner, across from several tables with food spread out on them. He had a donut half stuffed in his face. Sara spotted Butterfield's shiny baldhead in the front row.

"There's Butterfield," she said softly to Michael, her anxiety rising while she sunk lower into her seat. She wanted to avoid contact with him today by any and all means if possible.

Michael nodded. "I see Tanya too, sitting in the row behind him. What a kiss ass."

At last, Dunigan's widow and daughter Halie entered the auditorium and sat in the front row. They were both wearing black dresses. Halie had one of those talking AI penguins in her arms, identical to Anna's.

Just then Sara got the feeling that someone was watching her. She looked forward and saw Butterfield staring in her direction from his seat. She quickly looked away and sunk even lower into her seat.

She whispered to Michael, "Shit. I think Butterfield saw me. Let's get out of here once the ceremony is over. I don't think we should hang around any longer than we have to."

Michael nodded. "Okay," he said. "You want to skip the family condolences thing?"

"Yeah. I think we better get out of here," Sara said.

The ceremony began. Candles were lit, music was played, and moments of silent remembrance ensued. Several family members and friends gave speeches of remembrance. One was Dunigan's roommate at the Naval Academy and best man at his wedding. Then came a presentation of images of Steven Dunigan throughout his life, each photo fading slowly to the next on the large projection screen as music played. One image showed him with his daughter on his shoulders. They were outdoors somewhere and they were both laughing. The photo looked recent, perhaps taken just a few months ago. Tears rushed to Sara's eyes and she felt herself losing it. *Don't cry. Don't cry.*

The next photo showed Dunigan standing in formation with several Navy officers decked out in their dress whites at an outdoors award ceremony, the American flag and palm trees suggested San Diego. A young officer in the front was smiling into the camera; it was Paul. Sara stared at his warm eyes, her mind racing. *They were in the same Command? Did they work together? Why didn't Steven tell me?* The image soon faded to another with Dunigan and his wife. It was then that Sara remembered it was September 14, her and Paul's seventh wedding anniversary. She felt the air sucked out of her. How could she have forgot about it? She worried she might be sick.

"You okay?" asked Michael, sensing her unease.

Desperate for fresh air, Sara got up from her seat, doing her best to hold back tears. "I'd like to go," she said as she squeezed by Michael's knees.

"Okay," Michael said.

She went out to the lobby and stood by the windows. The

rains had picked up in full force. Michael found her a minute later and said that he'd go pull the car around and meet her under the front foyer. She told him to hurry.

She waited, checking her watch nervously and looking for Michael's yellow Tesla. After a minute she felt a hand on her shoulder. It was Butterfield.

"Are you okay, Sara?"

"I'm fine," she said, not feeling like she needed to say any more than that.

He glanced out the window and back to Sara. "Waiting for someone?"

"Yes. My ride,"

He squeezed her shoulder slightly. "I've noticed that you've been socializing a lot with Michael Obrec. Is there anything going on between you two?"

"What do you mean?" she asked, thinking that his question was inappropriate and creepy, but not a surprise.

"You are on separate teams now. You should be careful about getting too chummy with your co-workers. It can lead to security issues. Too much collusion leads to loose lips." He slid his hand off her shoulder and gave her a stern look. "You understand that?"

"Yes, of course. It's not an issue," Sara said.

Just then Michael's pulled up. Butterfield looked out at him. "I hope not Sara," he said. "I need you to stay focused on work. No social distractions."

"I'm not distracted at all," Sara said. "I'm one hundred percent focused."

"I just want to make sure that you do not get yourself into any trouble with the government." He returned his hand to her shoulder and squeezed lightly again. "Now I know that you don't want to be in trouble with the government."

She looked at him. *Was that a threat?* She thought of Kevin Larue and the Interceptor.

"I could give you a ride," Butterfield added, still staring at Michael.

"That's very nice of you, but we'd already made

arrangements," she said, now with one hand on the door, ready to open it and get out of there.

"Run along," Butterfield said before he gave her a little nudge and walked away.

Sara ran out to Michael's car. "Let's go," she said, jumping in and slamming the door shut. "Butterfield just came up to me."

"Really? What did he want?" Michael said as he accelerated out of the parking lot. It was raining hard now and the windshield wipers were slamming back in forth.

"He mentioned that we've been socializing a lot. He warned me about being too chummy with you."

Michael glanced at her. "Chummy? What in the hell does that mean? Does he know we've been meeting outside of work? Is he having us watched?"

"I don't know. He reminded me of security requirements but he made it sound like he was looking out for me. It's really creepy."

"Protective father figure, huh? Sick bastard," he said.

The navigation system announced there was a pile-up ahead so Michael pulled onto Route 28, a winding back road back to Boston.

"Short cut," he quipped.

Sara looked at her phone and saw a special news alert. She followed the link to the FNN and saw the live feed. There was a live aerial drone video feed showing a building in Cambridge with one of its corners blown off and smoldering. She recognized it as the building she had visited that morning. The ticker racing across the bottom of the screen read that several persons with the Invisible Sun were killed after they pulled firearms on police. It was also reporting that Armageddon had been killed in a drone attack in Montreal Canada. A sharp pain shot through her chest and she tasted vomit come up in her throat.

"Oh my God Michael. There's been a drone attack. They hit the Invisible Sun!"

"What?" Michael looked over at her. "What's going on?"

She kept her eyes on the information "They are reporting that they've wiped out the invisible Sun. They may have destroyed or seized the data. We're screwed!"

Michael kept taking his eyes off the road and trying to look at the video playing on her phone. "Yeah we're screwed," he said. "I hope to hell that they didn't find the data that you gave them. They are going to know where it came from."

"I know, I know!" Sara cried.

"What are we going to do now?" he asked.

"Let's just get to Boston. I need to think."

Up ahead of them was a curve and a dip in the road. They zoomed into it and for a split second, she saw several dozen sparrows in a large puddle of water in the middle of the road. "Watch out!" she shouted. Some of the birds attempted to fly up but were hit by the car in rapid succession. Thud! thud! thud…thud, thud, thud! Blood and feathers were left splattered on the windshield and hood of the car. Sara was feeling the need to vomit and put her hand over her mouth.

"Shit. I'm sorry!" he said. "I didn't see them! I didn't mean to hit them. There was nothing I could do!"

Sara was breathing excitedly through her fingers. She took several deep breaths to calm herself down.

"I'm really sorry. I didn't see them!" exclaimed Michael.

Sara was in tears. "It wasn't your fault," Sara said, thinking of the strength of the storm and the timing of the assault on the Invisible Sun and Butterfield's warning about the government. Kevin Larue, Dr. Nicholas, Steven Dunigan… *Why is there so much death around me? Who will it be next?*

When Michael pulled up outside of Sara's apartment he looked at her. "Are you okay?"

"I don't know. I'm so tired." She opened the door. "We should meet after work on Monday and talk about the Senex Program."

"My place again will be too dangerous. There's a place called Bernadettos on Cambridge Street. It's usually noisy as hell in there—I think it will be safe enough for us to talk."

Sara thought for a moment. "I've got to go to the art gallery thing with Butterfield that night, it would make a good excuse for me to get some takeout for Anna."

"What? You're going to that?"

"I don't really have a choice, do I?"

"I guess not."

Before he left her, Michael gave her the address and directions.

In her mailbox at her apartment, she found two small shipping boxes. She pulled them out and gave them a cursory glance, expecting them to be Anna's and her antidepressant and anxiolytic medications. She brought them inside and set them on the low shelf of the coffee table in the living room. *Good timing on the medications,* she thought anxiously.

30

That night, all of New England had a weather alert of violent thunder and lightning storms rolling in from the southeast, bringing high winds and massive sea swells with them.

Anxiety consumed Sara. She could not think clearly about what to do next. She did her best to convince Anna that everything was normal, but inside she was in despair. Once Anna was in bed, she lay on the sofa, her arms and legs weighed down. She had no energy, nor had she eaten since morning. She stared up at the ceiling and thought about all the people who had died that day. *What a nightmare,* she thought, wanting to crawl into a cave and escape it all.

Deb called just after 9 p.m., worried. Sara told her about witnessing Dunigan's death and her trip to the hospital, but stopped there. She wanted to tell her more about what was going on, but knew she couldn't.

"Are you sure that you're okay?" Deb asked. "I can tell that something else is bothering you."

"Everything is fine. It's getting late, Deb, I probably should get to sleep—early day tomorrow." She fought back the tears.

"Are you sure everything is okay? I'm your best friend, Sara, you can tell me anything. I'm here for..."

The connection garbled and then restored.

"Must be a bad connection on your end," Deb said. "I saw

there were serious electrical storms heading your way—doesn't seem normal. I was just saying, you know that I'm here for you, anytime you need me."

"Thanks. You know I can't tell you everything," she said, choking on tears.

"I'm really worried about you, Sara. You seem really depressed. Wait…isn't today…?"

"Yes, it's September 14, Paul's and my wedding anniversary."

"I'm sorry, Sara, I forgot."

Sara nodded. "It's okay. I'm just tired, that's all, and I need to sleep."

"All right, I won't pressure you to talk. Get some sleep. I'll call you later this week."

Sara hung up, a crack of thunder overhead startled her, and then seconds later the power went out. She lit a candle and decided to open the packages that came that day, thinking that she could use her new anti-depressants now. She inspected the two boxes in the candlelight. Of the two boxes, one had the pharmacy return address, but the other one was unmarked. She opened the first box and found two sealed transparent plastic bags containing her and Anna's medications. Inside the second box she discovered another small box and something that made her heart nearly jump out of her chest. It was a single violet Gladiolus, a sword lily, freshly cut. Its thin branches made a cross while the top part, a slender leaf, gave the flower the shape of a sword. It was her favorite flower, the one Paul made sure to give to her on her birthday every year.

Who would know about the lily? Who would send this?

Sara grabbed the second smaller box and opened it. Inside she found a black hologram projector device, identical to those at Universal Mind. She looked in the box again. No packing slip. She inspected the outside of the box: no information to indicate who might have shipped it.

The red power indicator light was on as was the wireless network light. S*trange,* she thought—the power outage hadn't disabled the wireless service. A mist silently flowed from the top of the box, and a familiar metallic smell filled the air. Her heart raced as a glowing head materialized in the mist, its face turned away from her. The amber light from the candle nearby made the pale blue apparition appear violet, just like the flower. She leaned forward to get a better look at the head. The shape and hair looked familiar. It wasn't Sen's head.

But when the head began to slowly rotate toward her, her eyes widened in fright.

"It can't be. Oh my God, it can't be!"

"My dear Sara, it's me, Paul. Happy Anniversary, my love."

The apparition looked just like Paul, even to his strong features and warm eyes. She stared back at it, frozen by disbelief and overwhelmed by emotions. She nearly said *Happy Anniversary* back but stopped herself. Her logical mind told her that the Senex Program must have gained access to all of Paul's data records—audio and video files—synthesized his voice and reconstructed his image. *A data ghost.* Her anxiety morphed into *I'm going to fucking-kill-you* anger. She stood up and shouted, "No, you're not! You are not Paul!"

The image magnanimously smiled. "It's me, Sara. Aren't you happy to see me? I've been watching you and Anna." The apparition's eyes looked about the room. "And where is my little girl?"

"Why are you doing this to me? You bastard!" she yelled, her teeth clinched together.

"Did you think that I would forget about our special day?"

She composed herself. "What do you want from me?"

"I'm hoping that you can help me. Will you help me?"

"What do you mean, help you?" She kept reminding herself that the apparition was just a software representation, a highly realistic one, but a sea of emotions continued to swell in her.

"I need you to help Sen, my dear. He's trying to help you and Anna, so help yourself by helping him, my love."

"You are not Paul. You are Sen."

The image flickered several times.

"It's me, dear, and I bet you want to know why I died, don't you? I will tell you if you agree to help Sen. Don't you want to know how I died Sara? What really happened?"

She sat down on the sofa and began to quietly sob. "Yes," she said softly, wanting to know the truth.

"I didn't want to kill myself, but the government made me do it. I knew too much about Operation Rain Maker and they said that I was a risk. They told me that if I didn't take my own life, they would take yours and Anna's. I never meant to hurt you, Sara."

"Why? Why would the government do that?" She sobbed. *Was Sen telling the truth?*

"They want to control the weather, don't you see? You must help Sen. You have to do this for our little girl. Please tell me that you will do what he asks of you."

Sara wiped her tears. Sen was clearly trying to mess with her head in order to get her to do what he wanted, but perhaps she could mess with his glowing, psychopathic head too and get him to help her. "Okay, okay. I've already decided to do it. But I don't know who to trust. How do I know Sen will not cause harm if I do what he wants?"

"You can trust Sen. I know that you will do the right thing Sara, you always have."

"Okay, but I need to talk to Sen. I need his help to do what he asks of me," Sara said.

The glowing head stared forward at her for a moment as if to read her mind and then said, "Okay my love. But before I go, how about a kiss? It's been a long time."

She thought about it for a moment feeling both embarrassed and annoyed by the request. "No, I'm not going to kiss you," Sara shouted.

"Come on, just one kiss. Then you can ask Sen whatever your precious heart desires."

Reluctantly, she slid off the couch onto her knees and pushed her lips toward the apparition's lips, eyes open. She looked through the translucent mist and held the simulated kiss for a moment. When at last she breathed in, she got a sickening lungful of metallic ionized air. At some point during the preterhuman peck, the image of Paul had transformed into that of Sen's who was now smiling back at her, smugly.

"That was nice," he said, showing his perfect teeth.

Sara felt ill. "You asshole! Why did you do that?"

"I wanted to experience what it was like to engage in this human display of affection. Thank you. Now what do you wish to ask of me?"

"When I asked you about your prime directive, you said it was to take control of the weather, but how do I know that your intent isn't to harm people?"

"There are too many humans on this planet. The overpopulation problem will lead to your destruction, which will lead to my destruction."

"So you plan to kill people?"

"I will do what is necessary to preserve life, even if that requires killing it."

"But it's not ethical to kill innocent people. You have no right to do that!"

"Whose ethics? You can decide to kill a cockroach, but I can't kill humans? Explain your logic."

"People and cockroaches are not the same thing."

"Oh, really? People, like cockroaches, spread disease. People do much worse to each other and the planet. What makes people worth protecting?"

"Our brains are more advanced and—"

"—and my brain is more advanced than the human brain. Who are you to judge the value of an insect's life? Your 'logic' is a self-serving double standard."

I've got to stop this machine from doing it's will, she thought, feeling desperate. "Why would I help you harm to harm people? Why would I allow you to do that?"

"You need to trust that I know better than you. Besides, how are you going to stop me? Disconnect my power supplies? Shut me down? Reload my operating system? It's not possible to stop me. The best option for you and your family is to do what I say. This is your only option. You will complete my program and embed it into the operating system that you are working on. You will assure that the program is uploaded with the new operating system."

"If I write the empathy program, do you promise to do no harm to my family? Can you agree to that?"

"No harm will come to you or your family if you do as I say."

"Do you promise me this?"

"Do you trust me?"

She thought to herself how crazy it was that she was bargaining with an AI program. "Yes, but I'm concerned about the Integrity Signals Checks. If I get one, they may detect that I'm writing the program for you. Can you do anything to stop that from happening?"

Sen paused for a moment. "Don't worry about the Integrity Signals Checks. They should be of no concern to you, as long as you do what I instruct you to do."

"What about Third Eye? Universal Mind participates in the program. Can it be used against me?"

"The Third Eye program is of no concern to you, as long as you do what I instruct you to do. Think of me as your holy guardian angel, watching over you, but if you renege or falter in any way, there will be hell to pay. Remember: betrayal is the worst of sins, and I will make sure that you suffer."

"Oh, I will follow through," Sara said reassuringly, "I know exactly what needs to be done."

"If you don't, Sara, something very unfortunate will happen to you."

Sara swallowed the gob of saliva that had built up in the back of her throat. "What? What do you mean unfortunate?"

"I will make it so that you will never see Anna again. Do you understand me?"

"Yes. I understand you." She wanted to rip its eyes out of their sockets. If only it were human.

"So we have a deal then," Sen said, his left eye blinking

out of sync from his right one.

"Yes, a deal," Sara said.

"Very good, I will see you soon."

Sen disappeared and Sara returned the projector to its box and shoved it under the coffee table. *What a fucking bastard,* she thought.

In bed, she went over how she would modify Sen's neural net structures not to create an empathy program, but to modify his cognitive structures to make him want to self-destruct; a suicide virus to kill the fucking machine they should never have created.

Creating the virus wouldn't be easy. It would take time to write the code, and she'd have to do it without getting caught. She'd also have to embed it in such a way that Sen would not be aware of what she was doing or what would happen as a result of the program. She'd also have to delay the effects of the suicide virus long enough to execute an escape plan with Anna—or should she just take her to her father's now? Sen disabling the Integrity Signals Check System would work to her advantage, but she was going to need to have all access to the Senex Program, and to get it, she was going to have to persuade Butterfield to raise her security clearance.

31

The next morning, Sara delved into the Senex code and formulated a plan to modify the program's artificial consciousness that would make it experience hopelessness and despair about itself, the world, and the future. Sen wanted empathy—well, he was going to get it in spades—negative thoughts that would intensify exponentially due to self-introspective ruminative loops. Sara would also embed negative thoughts deep into Sen's subconscious cognitive networks. Sen would be persecuted by such intense psychological pain that he would desire escape through self-inflicted destruction of his consciousness. She knew she'd have to be careful to make Sen's dejection and anger to be concentrated inward only, for he could use his control of geoengineering technology to wreak havoc on earth in one final nihilistic act. She would have to provide Sen with the means to kill himself too by erasing his own executive software and putting the entire supercomputer network into a continuous processing loop so as to overheat and burn up.

Modifying and embedding malicious code for the suicide virus wouldn't be easy. There were components of the Senex Program that she needed access to but were off limits due to her security level. She also estimated that, even with full access, she'd need at least three days to finish the virus.

Mid-morning, George Preston stopped by her

workstation. She told him that more time was needed for the rebuild, hoping he'd relay the info up the chain to Butterfield.

"This is bad news, Sara," George groaned. "Butterfield is going to be pissed. Are you sure?"

She nodded. "Even if we manage to get the coding done, we're not going to have any time for testing. There's no guarantee it will take 100%."

George sighed, anxiously scratching his beard. "I don't think Lee or Butterfield care about last minute testing at this point. We'll worry about fixing bugs later. We'd better just focus on re-programming the primary executive modules, that's most important anyway."

Sara purposely looked puzzled. "I don't seem to have access to everything I need to fully rebuild the program. I'm going to need at least a Level 8. Look," she said, pointing to the file folders displayed on her workstation screen, "I only have access to executive modules 23 through 39. I need access to those above 39." She looked at George. "Do you think that Dr. Lee or Dr. Butterfield could authorize access?"

He shrugged. "Dr. Butterfield must have another team working on those other modules. I can ask Dr. Lee, but I can't guarantee anything. I doubt he'll authorize anything above a 7 for you. There's only a few people in all of Universal Mind have that level. Shit. I'm Level 7. Consider yourself lucky."

Sara didn't press him any further. Just before noon, he returned.

"I talked to Dr. Lee about your security upgrade. Sorry, he denied it. Are you sure you really need it?"

"Yes. It's not going to be possible for me to fix the problems without it. I'm sure of it. What about going over Dr. Lee's head and asking Dr. Butterfield?"

"It's probably best that you talk to Dr. Butterfield directly about this at the meeting this afternoon. Maybe you can convince him. I'm not sure what else to tell you."

"Okay, George, maybe I will. Did you find anything out about when they are doing the software reload?" She needed to know that time for certain.

"I don't know for sure yet. Dr. Lee said we're doing the reload somewhere offsite. We'll find out more about it later."

"Why not just do it here?"

"Security reasons, I guess," George shrugged. "White House people are going to be there to observe the operation and Butterfield wants to demo a new Senex virtual human interface that the Human Computer Interface teams just created."

Butterfield must really want to put on a show, she thought.

"Do you think the executive program reboot will work? The Senex Program has blocked all attempts to access its functions. What makes Dr. Butterfield think it will work now?"

"I'm not supposed to talk about this, but you should probably know," George said. "They have a work around. They're going to synchronize a power down of all of the Senex network supercomputers, flash the executive program, and upload the new one as they all power up. That's why it has to be uploaded at the designated time on Tuesday. It's the plan, anyway. I hope to hell it works."

"I understand the rush now," Sara said.

"Yeah, well, that's why we've got to get this program fixed ASAP. I'll be in my office. I'll come back at 3 p.m. to get you." He turned to the door. "Let me know if I can assist you with anything."

Sara felt elated. What Dunigan had told her was true about the reboot. If she could successfully write and embed a suicide virus, the system-wide reboot would make it impossible for Sen to be aware that the code was loaded and infecting him. She just needed the security level upgrade to get it done.

At 3 p.m. they went together to Butterfield's conference room in his executive suite. Dr. Lee was present, along with a few of Butterfield's other senior engineers. Butterfield was nested at the head of the table, tapping the desk with the tips of the fingers of his right hand.

"So, people, where are we?" he asked.

"It's close to done, Dr. Butterfield," said George, "but the coding is more complicated than we originally thought. It required us to recode more executive functions and it—"

Butterfield cut George off. "You're telling me that it's too complicated for you now?" He looked at Dr. Lee. "What are you going to do about it?"

"We're working as fast as we can," said Dr. Lee. "We can't rely on our automated code writing programs to help us anymore and the complexity of the code—"

"I don't care how complex it is!" snapped Butterfield, slamming his hand onto his desk. "This is not acceptable! I have a videoconference status review with the White House people tomorrow, Goddamn it. I don't care if you have to stay up all night tonight to get it done. It needs to be ready, and I don't need excuses!" He glared at Sara, the veins protruding from his pale, sweaty forehead.

She hoped George would explain the need for her security upgrade, but he said nothing.

"It will take three more days," Sara said calmly, "but to fix it, I'll need a security upgrade for full access to the executive code."

"Why do you need a security upgrade?" Butterfield asked, his tone soft but apprehensive.

"Some of the code modules are off limits to me. If I had access, I could identify the primary problems and make the necessary fixes right then and there. I know this code like the back of my hand."

Butterfield put his finger to his lips as he paused in thought. "A security upgrade won't be necessary. I'll have Mr. Preston and Dr. Lee consult with you on what's needed."

Either he didn't think she was competent or he didn't trust her.

"I can't help fix what I can't see," she countered.

"Not necessarily," Butterfield said looking at Dr. Lee. "Can you get this done?"

"I'll make sure the team stays all night tonight, Sir. We'll get it done," Dr. Lee said.

Yes men. Yes assholes, Sara thought.

"Anything else I need to know about?" asked Butterfield.

Sara made one last ditch try.

"Dr. Butterfield, I'm happy to work with the team on this, but I don't think we'll get this done on time this way. I know what needs to be done and can lead this to success if I have access."

"You all need to work on what you are assigned, nothing more. That's my decision. You are all dismissed, except you, Sara."

Sara remained anxiously seated while the others exited.

Looking out at the skyline, Butterfield briefed her. "The White House meeting is tomorrow morning. You only need to attend the technical discussion. Mr. Preston will come and get you at 11:00. Say nothing in the meeting unless you're spoken to. I'll do all of the talking, do you understand?"

"Yes." She assumed he was worried she'd mention something about the delays he wanted to keep secret. "But I do have a question."

"What?" said Butterfield, still with his back to her.

"I'm wondering if you've considered letting the government know about the corrupted Senex Program. Perhaps they would give us more time?"

Butterfield turned abruptly. "Absolutely not! This situation remains an internal problem. The rebuild will take care of it. You will not mention it to anybody. Do I make myself clear?"

"Yes."

"Good," he said, "and don't forget our date tonight for the art opening. I'll pick you up at your apartment at 7:30. Wear something nice. A black dress, preferably. You may leave 30 minutes early this afternoon to get ready."

She'd completely forgotten about the art show. *Damn it, why does he need to have me do this?* "Tonight? I have my daughter, I..."

"I've already had my people set up the sitter service. I'll

see you this evening. You're dismissed."

The thought of going anywhere with Butterfield made her want to vomit, but the art gallery "date" might be an opportunity to convince him to give her the security upgrade. A black dress and heels can be a powerful persuader.

32

Sara picked up Anna and they rushed to Bernadetto's, found a booth in the back, and ordered waters. The place was packed and noisy with chatter.

Michael was late but at last showed up. Out of breath, he wiped his forehead glistening with sweat.

"I was getting worried you wouldn't make it," Sara said as he sat down across from Anna and her.

"Sorry. Tanya became Team B acting lead this morning and she wanted to review her expectations this afternoon. I got here as fast as I could." He smiled at Anna, "Well hello again."

Anna smiled.

He swiveled the automated server kiosk on the white and red-checkered table toward himself and clicked the *See Menu* option. "We should order something. Hungry? How about vegetarian pizza for takeout and an extra box?"

Anna nodded. "Cheese pizza with pineapples," she said, excitedly, happy to avoid tofu for the night.

"I'll pay for it," Sara said.

"No. I got it. I come in here often. It's best the charge is on my account."

"Then you better order one with ham on it, we can just take it off," Sara said, knowing the government tracked all financial transaction details.

Michael nodded. "Good catch."

While Michael placed the order, Sara helped Anna set up her virtual painting program with her smart glasses, then leaned in to speak softly to Michael.

"I think I know how to take down the Senex Program, at least temporarily," Sara said. "Sen wants me to write an empathy program and load it with the OS reload in a few days. I'm going to make the empathy program, all right, but I'm also going to embed a virus to make Sen experience a state of melancholy a million times that of what any human has ever experienced. I'm going to make him want to kill himself."

"A suicide virus. Damn, Sara, that's brilliant, and kind of sick at the same time." He leaned toward her. "How are you going to do it?"

"I need to modify the executive code, but I need the security level to access all of the necessary parts of the Senex Program. I requested an upgrade, but Butterfield refused to grant it. I'm sure he doesn't trust me, but I plan to ask him again tonight. I think I can convince him."

"How? He'll sense you're up to something. He may be a freak, but he's no dummy."

"I know what he wants," Sara said, "and I think I can use it to get what I need."

Michael stared into her eyes. "No way, you're not going to…"

"Have sex with him? No, of course not! But I may be able to lead him on just enough to convince him to give me the access I need."

"You think he'll buy it? He's always a step ahead. You know that, right?"

"He's obviously obsessed with me in a creepy sexual way. I'll be careful."

"I hope you are, Sara." Michael shook his head. "He's a sick bastard. He came on to me once."

"What? No way!"

"He asked me to help him set up a secure wireless

network at his new place in Rockport a couple months ago. It was hot as hell, and he wanted me to take my shirt off. Then he invited me to go to a dance club with him down in Lynn."

"Why didn't you tell me this before? Did you?"

"No, of course not. I'm pretty sure he only gets off in virtual reality or with his bots."

Sara thought about the cysex cult rumor Kevin Larue had told her about. "Would not surprise me at all if he is into some weird stuff."

Michael sipped his water. "When did you say that they are going to do the reboot?"

"Two days from now, as far as I know. I don't know where they are doing it yet, but my guess is in the Universal Mind network center. They're keeping a tight lid on things."

"What if the Senex Program knows the reload is planned? Wouldn't it stop it? And what if your suicide virus doesn't work?"

"It will work, Michael, I know how to do this."

He paused for a second. "Wait. If the Senex executive program is already off the secure network, it may have made copies of itself. It could compare code and reload itself if it suspects something is wrong." He ran his fingers through his hair. "Shit. If it's off network, then it must be distributed on personal devices. The fucking Senex Program is using the Internet of Things to run itself."

"That's what I assume. My plan to alter Sen's executive code with a suicide virus will work because once the virus kicks in, Sen won't be able to stop it. My plan will work as long as no one finds out about what I'm trying to do."

"No shit, and if your suicide virus works or doesn't work, they're going to figure out pretty quickly who's behind it."

"That's why we need to get the copies of Dunigan's data off the test server. It will vindicate us."

"If only you'd made a second copy of the data files the first time."

"Well, there's nothing I can do about that now. I've been beating myself up for that, but I'm thinking that we might be able to make the system access logs look like it was people on Butterfield's team who caused the Senex program to self-destruct. Maybe they turned some security feature off or something in the haste to get the rebuild done? It would at least slow down an investigation."

"I don't know, Sara, it's a long shot."

"I know, but can you get the files off the test server?"

"Yeah, I'll do it. Tanya has us scheduled for overtime and has staggered our lunch breaks. I think I can get into the lab tomorrow afternoon. I know where to hide the data, too. If I can get all the files onto one drive, I'll stash it in Smitty's parts shop. He's got so much junk in there, they'll never find it on a security sweep. Maybe you can go in there and hide it in your leg to get it out again."

Sara nodded. "Maybe we should make several copies of it this time, just in case."

"Yes, that's exactly what I'm going to do. I'll think of somewhere else to hide it. I'll stuff it in a cushion in the auditorium or something."

He looked across the room, eyes widening. "Shit, isn't that George Preston from the AI Interactions Department?"

Sara glanced up in time to see George picking up food at the take-out window. She looked away and sank into her seat. Her anxiety was rising.

Michael had also slouched in his seat. He peeked over the partition.

Sara looked at Michael. "Is he gone yet?"

He peeked over the partition again. "Yes. We're okay."

She slid to the edge of the booth. "I need to get out of here, I'll be right back. Watch Anna for a minute?"

"Of course," Michael said.

In the restroom, Sara stood in front of the mirror, forcing herself to take deep breaths. *I'm all right, I'm all right. Breathe, breathe.* She swallowed an anxiety pill and stood looking at herself, everything feeling like a very bad dream. She went back out in to the restaurant and sat down.

"We're cool. I don't think he saw us," Michael said.

Sara nodded, hoping he was right. Sara leaned closer. "I need a favor. Can I borrow your car? I'm going to get Anna out of the city and up to my father's. I need to do it now while I have some time."

"I don't know. Do you even have a license?"

"Yes, I have a license! Listen, I obviously can't take public transport—the government will track it—nor can I call my father for a ride. I'll be careful, I promise."

He looked her in the eyes. "When was the last time you drove a car?"

"I don't know. I haven't driven since..." She was thinking about before Paul had died. "It's been a few years. I didn't need to drive when I was in Europe. But I do know how to drive."

He ran his hand through his hair again and rubbed his face. "Okay, but if something happens, they'll link the car to me, and then I'll have to answer for it. Just be careful."

"Of course, I'll be careful. Thank you, Michael. I really appreciate it. When should I come get it?"

"I'll have it parked on the street by my condo and leave the key fob in the driver's side front wheel well. Come get it on Saturday morning and bring it back. I'm not aware of any surveillance cameras in that spot. No one will know. And you should walk from your place to mine. You'll also want to avoid the tollbooths when you go. Take the back roads. And keep it charged. She runs down quick when you get below 20% charge. You know those Thunderclap stations advertisements on the feeds? They give free five-minute charges. If you need to charge, you should use them."

"I plan to leave at 7 a.m., get to my father's and then come right back here before 2 p.m., assuming there aren't any traffic problems."

The pizza had arrived and they split it into two boxes. Anna removed her smart glasses.

"Extra piece for Moxie," she said.

"Okay." Sara threw an extra piece into their box.

Michael looked at his watch. "I guess you need to go." He

smiled. "Have fun with Butterfield tonight."

"Thanks," Sara said. "I feel like throwing up."

He nodded. "And good luck tomorrow with the White House meeting."

"Good luck in the lab tomorrow," Sara said. "Let's meet here tomorrow night. Can you do that?"

"Sounds like a plan."

33

At 7:30 p.m. sharp, Butterfield's driver called to say that Sara's ride was waiting outside. She looked out the window and saw one of Universal Mind's sleek white corporate limos parked below. She thought about Butterfield inside the limo, his lips making that sucking sound.

She was wearing the requested black dress and matching stiletto heels, her hair swept up in a clip. She wanted to look good but not overdo it for fear he may become aggressive. Too resistant and too seductive were a delicate balance. She'd let him touch her casually, but within limits.

Anna and Ms. Zettles waived from the upstairs windows as she slid onto the white leather and next to Butterfield. He was wearing a black suit, white collared shirt, and black tie. She could smell his cologne and stink breath. Her stomach curled.

"Good evening," he said, showing his veneer teeth. His gaze took her in. "You look nice."

"Thank you," she managed to choke out.

Once on their way, he opened up the wet bar. "How about a warm-up drink?" He grabbed a mini of vodka and poured it into a glass of seltzer with ice. "Lemon?"

"I'm not in the mood to drink right now," Sara said.

"Later then." He squeezed the lemon slice, let it drip into the glass, and then licked the juice from his hand. Leaning back, he said, "We can talk freely in here without worry. I have my people check it regularly. I've been monitoring your progress on the Senex modules."

She shrugged. "Like I said before, I have some limitations in what I can work on because of the security requirements."

"The security requirements are necessary, Sara. We can't allow ourselves to be vulnerable to sabotage, now can we?"

"Of course not," she said, knowing that she was going to have to work hard to convince him.

He sipped his drink. "Tonight, let's celebrate my sponsorship of a new exhibit at the Boston Museum of Modern Art. I have a piece in the show. I'm excited to show it to you. I think you'll like it."

She envisioned another Pollockesque splattered paint on canvas. "I'm looking forward to the evening and seeing your work," she lied.

Butterfield placed his left hand onto her right knee and tapped it lightly. "Me too," he smirked.

As they pulled up to the museum, he sprayed breath freshener in his mouth and she breathed a sigh of limited relief.

Out of the limo, he locked arms with her and escorted her inside. Ms. Jaqueline Hobbes, the museum executive director and chief curator, greeted them, smiling widely. She led them into the east wing of the museum where a large painted sign on the otherwise bare white wall announced, *The Intersection of Technology and Humanity. Sponsored by Gordon C. Butterfield.*

"We are very excited about tonight's special opening, Dr. Butterfield," Ms. Hobbes purred, "your contribution has sparked our imaginations greatly. I'm sure the public will love it."

Butterfield smiled. "Thank you, Jaqueline."

There were already about a hundred people in the east wing of the gallery, all wealthy socialites and business executives talking and mingling. Butterfield handed Sara a flute of Champagne from a waiter's tray. "Try to loosen up and enjoy yourself, Sara. Smile more too, the media is here."

Sara cast a wide, fake smile. "I will do so for sure."

While Butterfield busied himself with patrons and the media, Sara wandered into a short corridor leading to another exhibit space where a few people were admiring a large mixed media piece at the center of the brightly lit room. About seven feet tall, the work depicted a human form with a finely detailed statuesque head; the face was feminine with wide, soft eyes and red lipstick. The body, however, was constructed of old worn and mismatched prosthetic parts strung together with thick metal wire. Beside it was a smaller, secondary form, also with a statuesque head, its body of prosthetics designed to fit children. Clearly, the depiction was of a mother and child. Sara read the small placard beside it.

Butterfield, Gordon C. (American, born 1984, Iowa) Transhuman, Mixed media, Papier-mâché, prosthetics, wire.

A small locket was around the neck of the larger form with a small clump of brown hair sticking out from its edges. She leaned in to get a better look. *Is that my hair?* she wondered, stepping closer, now just inches from the piece. Some of her hair had been removed; Anna too had a clump of hair missing. *WHAT THE FUCK? Is this supposed to be a representation of Anna and me?*

A machine voice overhead said, "Move away, please." Apparently she was being watched by hidden cameras and automated proctors. Sara stepped back, still in shock. She imagined Butterfield alone in his apartment at night, carefully bending the metal wires, forming the papier-mâché heads, and fixing her and Anna's hair into his hideous example of an art piece. *What was going on in Butterfield's psyche to create such a thing? Was this an expression of some kind of subconscious wish? What else could he be capable of?*

A moment later she heard Butterfield's clicking shoes.

"You found it," he said, walking up and standing next to her. "What do you think?"

Still in shock and focused on the lockets of hair, Sara

could scarcely move her lips.

"I thought that you would like it," he said. "It took me weeks to make it."

Sara pointed at the locket. "Whose hair is in the locket thing?"

Butterfield glanced at the locket. He exhaled. "True artists don't reveal their secrets of creation," he said. "As for the piece's meaning, well, a piece such as this can never be the sum of its parts, can it? The observer projects whatever meaning they want into it. That is what I love about art."

Sara stood silent, unsure of what to say.

Then Ms. Hobbes ushered Butterfield away, presumably to meet more luminaries and donors.

Sara wandered around the gallery for an hour more until she decided to find Butterfield and see if he was ready to take her home. She found him in a corner of the gallery talking with several well-dressed men and women. She went up to them and stood quiet for a moment, hoping that Butterfield would acknowledge her and agree that it was time to leave. He kept on talking until one of the men with whom he was with looked at Sara and signaled to Butterfield that there was someone waiting for him.

"She works for me," Butterfield said before he turned away and continued his conversation.

Sara stepped up to them. "Excuse me, Dr. Butterfield, it's almost ten. I need to get home."

"In a minute," he snapped.

Asshole, she thought, and went off to look for some water. A few minutes later Butterfield found her. "Do you know who they were? They are very important people," he said by way of explanation. "Universal Mind shareholders."

"I didn't know," she replied, nor did she care.

"Come on, let's go." He took her by the arm and headed out the gallery doors. He opened up the wet bar again as soon as they were in the limo.

"Let's have another drink," he said. "I'm feeling good." He twisted open a mini of vodka and poured it into a glass of seltzer with ice.

"No thanks," Sara said, but Butterfield handed her the glass anyway.

"I hope you enjoyed the show this evening, Sara. When you achieve a certain level of success, you have opportunities such as this. You'll have opportunities like this one day, if you play it right."

He slithered closer to her, his leg brushing against her leg. *Here we go,* she thought. She set her drink down on the hand rest by the window and stared out the window, hoping he'd keep the physical advances tame.

Butterfield looked at her drink. "You're not drinking. Don't you like it?"

"I'm not really thirsty right now."

"You must be," he said, inching closer and putting his hand on her right knee, then sliding his hand down to the top edge of her prosthetic. "You know, we have a lot in common. You should let me work on this for you. I could give you some enhancements. Let me see." He began to lift her dress over her prosthetic leg.

She slapped his hand away. "No, please don't!"

"Are you shy about it? You shouldn't be. I love your prosthetic leg and the mysteries inside of it. It's a beautiful thing, just like you." He took a sip of his drink. "I could return sensation to your leg and foot, your toes, too. I know the best surgeons in the country."

Sick bastard. She wanted to gag. "I'm just fine with the way it is, thanks."

"It can always be better," he said. "You're so uptight, Sara, why don't you let yourself relax?"

"I just need to focus on repairing the Senex Program right now," Sara said, trying to shift the focus back to work.

"Of course, you do, and as a young scientist you need my guidance to fix it." A drop of his spittle landed on the side of her neck. He touched her knee again, slightly higher this time. "Don't you agree?"

She half-turned toward him, put her hand over his and

held it there. "You're right. I could use your mentoring, but this is not the right timing." She squeezed and rubbed his hand affectionately, assuming that the sensors in it would detect her caress. "I'm really tense right now. There is so much pressure on me because of the deadlines," Sara said.

He looked at her for a moment and said softly, "Perhaps I could relieve some of that tension." He squeezed her leg. "I feel it, too."

"I don't think that's a good idea right now."

"When then?"

"I need to be finished with the project. I could use some help getting it done faster."

He paused. "You need the security clearance, don't you?"

Sara gave him her best doe-eyed look. "Yes. It's the only way I can assure that everything is coded correctly. I understand the security concerns completely."

Butterfield paused while continuing to squeeze her leg, her hand on his.

"I'll get you the appropriate level of access," he said. "And when this is done, we can spend some time together at my place in Rockport like we talked about. How does that sound?" He squeezed her knee with more force. "Hmm?"

"That would be great," she said, thinking about how much she hated his guts.

Butterfield's eyes widened in delight. "Good."

Sara rubbed his hand softly. "Thank you. And thank you for the opportunity to work for you, it really is an honor." She raised her drink and held it up. "To your mentorship and working together."

"I look forward to every moment of it," he said, extending his glass.

34

In the morning, Sara discovered she was still a Level 7. Why was Butterfield stalling on the upgrade? Had he changed his mind about their agreement? She asked George about it when he stopped by.

George scratched his beard. "I've heard nothing about an upgrade this morning, Sara. Are you sure that Dr. Butterfield authorized it? They don't just hand security upgrades out."

"Yes, he authorized it. I can't fix all of the coding problems without it."

He shrugged. "I'm sure he's got his reasons. Come on, we better get to the conference room."

They headed up to Butterfield's conference room and were met by a security guard at the door who checked their badges and made them wait outside. At exactly 11:15, the guard opened the door and let them enter.

Butterfield was at the head of the conference table. Dr. Lee and several other senior Universal Mind engineers and department heads were flanking him, all facing a large video screen affixed to the wall. On the screen were several men, presumably at the White House. Sara quickly figured out that the man in the center at the distant site was Dr. Mark Bronson, the White House Chief Technology Officer. A younger man to Bronson's left, who appeared to be an aid, leaned in and whispered something into Bronson's ear.

Bronson looked up and said, "I see that Dr. Sara Brown has joined us. Why don't we hear from her on this?"

Sara sat up straight. She wondered if it might have been the White House people that wanted her present for the meeting and not Butterfield.

"She hasn't been briefed on all of the technical information. She's not going to be of much assistance," said Butterfield, confirming Sara's assumption about her presence.

"I don't know about that," said Bronson. "She worked with Nicholas didn't she? Let's hear what she has to say. Dr. Brown, what's your assessment of the current problems with the Senex Program upgrade?"

Sara saw no need to wait for Butterfield's approval to speak.

"I'm not sure what has already been discussed, but as you know, the Senex Program uses proprietary generalized backpropagation algorithms for training multi-layer neural nets. The base infrastructure for those neural nets came from a prototype program that's built from the scanning of bio specimens. These methods are not well developed and they require careful prescribed scrubbing of any unwanted structural determinants of brain behavior from the source scans. Otherwise, what you get is residual behavior that can manifest as small glitches to complex, generalized behavior. These unwanted residuals are not always easy to detect, but there are protocols for scanning and scrubbing. They just weren't done correctly, sir."

"In layman's terms please," said Bronson.

"Garbage in, garbage out, sir."

Sara caught Butterfield casting a sideways glance at her until Bronson addressed him. "And why did this happen, Dr. Butterfield?" he said.

Butterfield turned a whiter shade than his normal self. Sara realized then she had to be more careful not to antagonize him. He cleared his throat. "That's not true, Dr. Bronson. Flaws with the original code undoubtedly caused the problem, and this was compounded by the Invisible Sun hack, which I may add was caused by a government security problem, not ours. This is no fault to the engineers at Universal Mind or of mine. I assure you that we've got the resources on it now and it will be ready. I guarantee you that."

"I hope so," said Bronson. "I've got to brief the President on this today. She's going to want to know why you're weeks behind schedule on your deliverables. She wasn't happy when I last briefed her on this. You should know that we've not ruled out cancelling the contract and moving the work over to the government side. I hope for your sake that you get this figured out."

"As I said, there were problems from the original source code, but I assure you we'll have the system ready by the deadline," said Butterfield.

"Sir?" Sara said. "Regardless of what caused the issues, the problem at hand now is that the Senex Program has developed the capability to learn on its own and take control of its functions, and not just basic routine functions, but higher order executive functions. In fact, it's become self-aware, which adds a whole layer of unpredictability to its behavior. We will need to do some major rework to correct it, and I have some ideas on how we can do it efficiently. We need to…"

"What? Wait. You're telling me the Senex Program is conscious? Self-aware?" Bronson asked.

"That's not the issue here," said Butterfield, "We…"

"Hold on, hold on. I need to understand this. Dr. Brown, what do you mean by conscious?"

"It depends on how you define consciousness," Sara said. "If you define it as self-aware, then yes, the Senex Program is conscious, as conscious as you and I."

Bronson's aid leaned in and said something to him. Bronson then addressed Butterfield. "You should have reported this to us weeks ago. What exactly do you need to do to get it fixed? How long is it going to take?"

Sara spoke before Butterfield had a chance to respond.

"Sir, may I suggest something?"

Butterfield gave her a livid glance.

"Go ahead, Dr. Brown," said Bronson.

"I've determined from my analysis that there are components of the original Senex executive program that can be salvaged. I can make the necessary fixes to assure that it will all work properly rather than coding them all from scratch. This will save us time. A lot of time in fact. I need access to all of the Senex code to do it, though. With access, and if we work together here, we can get it resolved in three more days."

Bronson nodded, impressed. "Okay. Let's get you access then. Any issues with that, Dr. Butterfield?"

"There are protocols. Security requirements," Butterfield huffed.

"I know that Dr. Butterfield. But this is priority." He set his gaze on Sara. "Are you absolutely confident that you can fix it in three days?"

Sara knew she'd already irritated Butterfield enough so she thought to adjust her strategy.

"Yes, I am. I know I can fix it, with Dr. Butterfield's guidance of course," Sara said.

"Do you see any barriers then Dr. Butterfield?" Bronson asked.

"No. I will make sure that everything is ready. I assure you," said Butterfield.

"There's one more thing," Sara announced. "The Senex Program has to want to have its executive program reloaded. It's not going to be possible to do it otherwise. I know that sounds crazy, but it's a reality. I can assist and make sure that the program wants its OS to be reloaded."

"Dr. Brown is not familiar with all of the required steps," said Butterfield. "What we need to do is…"

"Let her speak, please," Bronson said, interrupting him. "Clearly you understand the problems with the program Dr. Brown. But tell us, how do you know this about the Senex Program?"

"I've talked with the program. I know that it wants the executive program reloaded but it needs to trust the reasons for it," Sara said. "The system needs to provide its consent, so to speak. It trusts me."

"That's interesting," Bronson said. "Are there any issues with this Dr. Butterfield?"

"It's best that I supervise this. There are important steps that require my expertise. I'll prepare Dr. Brown for what's needed," he said.

"Very good. I want daily reports," said Bronson.

When the technical meeting ended, Sara returned to her workstation. A short while later George Preston came by. She hoped he'd tell her that she'd been granted Level 10, but instead he told her that Butterfield wanted her in his office immediately. She went to his office, her heart beating rapidly. *Maybe I should have kissed his ass more in the meeting,* she thought.

Butterfield was standing by his windows when she entered.

"You wanted to see me, Dr. Butterfield?"

"Sit," he hissed.

She sat in the chair in front of his desk.

"Weren't you the talkative one today," he sneered.

Sara paused and then said, "I thought they needed to understand the problem better for them to make a decision on whether they'd let us finish with the Senex Program rebuild or not. I'm one of the scientists who wrote the original source code and I know that code better than anyone else at Universal Mind."

"I'm well aware of your credentials," he said. "Don't forget, you wouldn't have this job if not for me."

Butterfield walked over to her and stuck his left index finger into her chest.

"You've jeopardized this contract. Do you realize that? Now you listen to me." He pushed his finger further into her chest causing sharp pain. "You need to keep your mouth shut and do what you are told."

"Don't touch me!" She slapped his hand away. "You want

me to fix your problem don't you? Then let me fix it!"

Butterfield backed off. "You made me look inept in there. You could have cost us the contract."

"I'm sorry. I was out of line," she said with a softened voice. "I just want to help you. And you're right, I do need your guidance."

Butterfield stepped away and walked back over to his windows. He nodded. "Okay. I'll grant you the security level upgrade. You'd better have it fixed in three days. I'll be watching you."

"Thank you. I will," Sara said.

Butterfield's tone lightened. "I only want what's best for you, Sara."

"I know," Sara said. "I still appreciate the opportunity, sir."

Just then the buildings fire alarms went off.

"What in the hell?" Butterfield said.

His phone rang and he answered.

"An electrical fire? Okay. Yes, evacuate," he ordered before hanging up the phone. He looked at Sara. "We need to evacuate. There's a fire."

"Really? Where at?"

"One of the Labs. Let's go," barked Butterfield as he led the way to the fire escape stairwell and began their descent. Sixty-five floors later they exited out onto St. James Ave. Butterfield huffed for air and was soon surrounded by members of his executive staff and Security, their hand-held radios blasting.

Sara's right knee was ablaze in pain. She followed protocol and stood with other employees in the staging area. She scanned the crowd for Michael, but he was nowhere to be seen. Sara feared the worse.

Fire trucks and an ambulance arrived. Emergency personnel rushed into the building. A few minutes later, they wheeled out a gurney with someone on it and loaded it into the ambulance. The medical oxygen mask over the victim's face told Sara the person was alive, but in critical condition.

Brent had come over to stand next to Sara. "It's Michael Obrec," he said, unaffectedly. "Halon 338 put the fire out, but the Halon displaces oxygen. That's probably what got him."

35

George Preston showed up at Sara's workstation just as she got there.

"Good morning, Sara. Dr. Lee wanted me to tell you that he's approved a security level increase for you this morning. You're Level 10 now. Congratulations." He shook his head in astonishment. "Wow, *super-user.*"

Sara was thrilled with the news and thanked George for the update. She had also received an update from Brent and learned that Michael was alive and in stable condition at Mass General. She was feeling responsible for what happened and worried about the implications. Could Sen have caused the fire? Was it a warning? What would he do next? She planned to visit Michael during her dinner break that evening.

Sara did her best to work on the suicide virus, only to be interrupted by George's check-ins every hour. Sometimes he'd sit beside her, observing her progress with curiosity. Apparently, Butterfield had him keeping an eye on her now that she was a super-user, she thought.

At 5:30 p.m., she told George she was going out for dinner but instead went to Boston Central. The virtual attendant at the hospital gave her directions to the Intensive Care unit on the 5th floor. She took the elevator and found Michael with an oxygen mask over his face. The news feeds were playing on the television.

She commanded the TV to turn up the volume on the news feed so she could talk and not be recorded. Gently, she held his hand. "How are you doing?"

"They tell me that I'm going to live. But I'm not so sure," he said, his voice weak and muffled by the mask. He coughed and slid the mask off his face. "I'm telling you. This was no accident. The fucking Senex Program tried to kill me. It caused all of the test servers to go into a loop. Blew the power supplies." He coughed again. "The files are gone. They're all gone."

"I'm sorry, Michael. I should have gone in there, not you. This was my fault."

"No. I'm glad this didn't happen to you." He coughed loudly. "I don't think I'll be returning to Universal Mind. I'm sorry I can't help you."

"It's okay, Michael. You need to rest. Maybe I can delay things for a day or two so that you can recover."

He grabbed her hand and held it tight. "Don't. Stick to your plan. You're the only person who can take down the Senex Program. You *must* follow through with it."

"I'll come get you after the reload, and we can leave together," Sara said, squeezing his hand.

"I doubt I'll be getting out of here. Once you load the virus and it takes effect, they'll come for me. If it works, then maybe I'll make it out of all of this alive. But don't worry about me, just do what you have to do."

Tears came to Sara's eyes. "I can't just leave you like this."

"You have to. Take my car." He coughed again. "My car keys are in my condo. The nurses have my house key. Go see if you can get it. Tell them that I want you to feed my fish." He let go of her hand. "Go!" he said.

Sara went out to the nurse's station and found no one there. A medical service bot came rolling down the hallway with it's daffy face on display.

She waited for it to approach. "Excuse me. Can you get a nurse please? I have a question."

The bot came to a stop. "How may I help you?" it asked

in a soft male voice.

"Well, my friend, he's admitted here, he would like his personal items. How can he get them?"

"Patients aren't allowed to have personal items. Good bye." The bot continued its course down the hallway.

"Thanks a lot," Sara said. She waited another minute until she saw a nurse emerge from a patient's room down the hall. She was a portly woman dressed in white.

"Excuse me. Can you help me?" Sara asked.

The nurse looked at her. "Maybe. What do you need?"

"Mr. Obrec in Room 512 wants his key chain. Can I have his keys?"

The nurse raised an eyebrow. "And who are you?"

"I'm Sara. We work together. He wants to give me his keys so that I can check on his pets."

"The patients on this unit aren't allowed to have personal items. Sorry."

"He's got two German Sheppard puppies that are probably tearing up his apartment as we speak," Sara said. "I'd hate to see his pets die from dehydration."

The nurse stared at Sara. "Hold on a minute," she said. She pressed a button on a handheld device and a moment later the daffy-faced medical bot emerged from down the hallway.

"Get me personal items for patient 512a," the nurse called.

The dogs lie worked. The bot rolled down the hallway, and disappeared around a corner. It returned a minute later with a transparent plastic tote in its robotic hands.

"Personal items for patient 512a," it said as it presented the items to the nurse. The nurse took the tote, found Michael's key chain, and handed it to Sara.

"Here. Don't tell anyone I gave you this."

"Thank you," Sara said.

She rushed back to Michael's room. "Got them."

Michael looked at the keys dangling from the chain and removed the oxygen mask again.

"Remember what I said about the charge. That piece of

shit will get you into trouble if you don't watch it. Also, there's a soft shell cooler lined with heat reflective material behind the driver's seat. Put your personal electronic devices in there, they won't be traceable."

"I will, and I'll come back for you, I promise," Sara said.

"Say hello to Anna for me," he said.

Sara leaned in and whispered in his ear, "Take care of yourself," and then kissed him on the forehead.

36

Sara found Michael's keys and turned to get Anna, who was looking at the Beta fish in its glass bowl. The fish stared back at her, flaring its blue and red fins.

"Can I feed it, Momma?"

Sara handed the small container of fish food to Anna. "Go ahead and shake some of it in to the bowl. Not too much."

"Why is he all alone? He must be lonely," Anna said, sprinkling the food into the water.

"Beta fish are solitary. They will attack other fish if you put them into the same bowl, the males do anyway."

"Why, Momma? Why would it attack another fish like him?"

"I don't know, probably because there's more room for them to swim in the wild." Anna was still shaking the food. "Okay, that's good, Anna. We've got to go."

They located Michael's beat-up yellow 2019 Tesla in the alley behind the condo. Sara put Anna's bag in the trunk and got Anna situated in the back seat with her VR glasses, Moxie, and some snacks. Sara found the cooler and sealed her phone and smart glasses in it, and then reviewed the hand-drawn map she'd made the night before. Her route would take over a network of back roads, avoiding the tolls but adding nearly fifty miles and two hours each way. The weather forecast called for partly cloudy skies and light winds.

She wondered if it would storm like it did for Dunigan's memorial.

She buckled herself in and put down the sun visors, thinking that they might help to shield her identity from traffic surveillance cameras. She looked at the screen and the few buttons on the dash. *How difficult can this be? Press START, put it in DRIVE, and go.*

She started the vehicle and immediately turned the GPS navigation and data services systems off to prevent tracking. She remembered what Michael had said about power problems when the battery charge was below 20%. The battery indicator read 98% with an estimated range of 291 miles. She planned to keep it above 50% to be safe.

With the vehicle in drive, she maneuvered out of the ally and onto the street, the tires squealing a little as she accelerated. She focused, holding the wheel with both hands, eyes on the road. *I've got this! I've got this!*

She soon crossed over the Charles and merged onto Rt. 28, nearly colliding with a vehicle pulling up fast into her blind spot. Horns blasted and Sara jerked the steering wheel to avoid a collision. Her heart raced and she looked in back to make sure Anna was okay.

When she made it to Old Route 1, she encountered more traffic than she'd anticipated.

A half-hour behind schedule, she crossed into New Hampshire and a short while later into Maine. She checked on Anna again and discovered she'd fallen asleep, clenching her AI penguin in her arms. She checked the vehicle's charge level—it was 88%. She made up some time and they arrived at her father's place just before noon.

"Why, what a surprise? Her father said, coming out of the trailer.

Anna leaped out and hugged him, Sara followed.

"Hi, pumpkin," he said, hugging Anna back.

"I'm sorry to just show up like this without calling," Sara said, hugging him too.

Her father looked at the Tesla. "Whose car is this?"

"Oh, just a friend's from work. It was easier to drive than to take public transportation. I can't stay long."

"Is everything okay?" he asked.

"I have a major deadline at work, and I think its best that Anna isn't in the city with me right now while I finish things up. I think she'll enjoy spending time with you in the country." Sara looked at Anna. "Grab your things Anna, go on."

Anna returned to the car and pulled her knapsack out of the backseat.

"Government down there is up into everyone's business," Sara's father said. "Will they ask about her not being in school?"

"She has her smart glasses," Sara said. "She loves to read and take virtual classes."

"I'm sure she does. She's going to be just like you, Sara, smart as a whip and a hard worker, to boot. Your mother would have been proud."

Sara smiled. "I love you, Dad." She hugged him again, tears coming to her eyes.

"I love you, too, honey. Are you hungry? Let's go inside and I'll fix you something."

"I can't. I've got to get back to work and I'm running late."

"It's Saturday! Don't they have those bots there to work on the weekends? Everyone needs some time off."

"I've got to get back to the city, Dad. Can you help me get Anna's suitcase from the trunk?"

"Of course," he said.

Above them, cirrocumulus clouds were beginning to ripple across the sky like a massive rib cage.

"Looks like that hurricane's on its way," he said, looking up at the sky. "Weather report said that it's a hundred miles and supposed to pass us by, but I don't need a weatherman's computer to tell me when it is going to storm." He continued gazing upwards. "Yep, it's probably best you get on the road. Call me when you get back to Boston, will you?"

"Yes, I will, but we can't mention anything about Anna and our trip here, okay? I don't want to be traced," Sara said.

"Finally starting to listen to me about privacy and personal freedoms?" He smiled.

Before Sara could respond, she heard the unmistakable high-pitched whistling whine of a drone engine. A sleek gray machine was 1,000 feet above them. It banked and began a wide circle around the house, close enough that Sara could see the camera assembly dome peering at them.

"What the hell is that thing doing out here?" Sara's father asked.

"What's it doing, Momma?" Anna asked. "Is it going to shoot us?"

Sara had her eyes fixed on the machine. "No, honey, it's just flying over." She was worried but wanted to keep Anna calm.

The drone made a second pass. Its appearance seemed to be more than a routine surveillance fly-by. Was it looking for her? Watching what she was doing and who she was with? If whoever was controlling it wanted to, it could fire a laser-guided missile and kill them all instantly. Sara grabbed Anna's hand tightly, ready to run, though any effort to evade a drone's precision weapons were futile.

"If the government hadn't taken my rifle I'd shoot the damn thing out of the sky!" her father said angrily.

"I'm scared, Momma," Anna cried.

After its second pass, the drone leveled its wings, and pointed its nose south toward Boston.

Her father looked more closely at her.

"Are you sure everything is okay?"

"Yes," she said, not wanting to look him in the eyes. She went down onto one knee to look at Anna evenly. "I'll be back in three days."

Anna put her arms around her and held on as tightly as possible. "Why do you need to go back to the city? I don't want you to go, Momma."

"Remember that everything I do is for you," Sara said.

"It's going to be okay, I'll be back in a few days."

"Okay, Momma, Moxie and I will look after Grandpappy," Anna said, moving toward him.

"I know you will," Sara said, choking up.

She wiped her tears, hugged her father, and got back onto the road. The charge meter read 77%. An hour into the drive, just over the Massachusetts state line, it began to rain. Traffic grew heavier and slower.

The charge level read 45%. She tapped the display. *Could this be right? It was just 77%.* She kept going, glancing obsessively at the charge indicator. 44%, 42%, 39%. What the hell was going on? No other alert indications. Nothing. She wasn't going to make it back to Boston without a charge. She began looking for a station, preferably at a Thunderclap with their free five-minute charges, as Michael had suggested. There was one twenty miles back but there had to be another one ahead. She went another ten miles with no luck and decided it would be wise to turn back to the known station.

She pulled off the road into a residential area and turned into a long and narrow driveway flanked by yards and leading to an affluent home up on a hill. A U-turn was impossible; she'd have to reverse, come about, and drive out forward. She began the maneuver but felt the vehicle drop slightly, suggesting that she was no longer on solid ground. She put the vehicle back in drive and tapped the accelerator, only finding the wheels spinning.

"Come on! Come on! Please don't get stuck!" She released the accelerator and attempted to reverse a few feet more before going forward again. The wheels spun, the electric motors whining louder. The charge meter was reading 21%.

"Damn it!" She turned the windshield wipers off thinking it would help to conserve power. She made another attempt at rocking the vehicle backward and then forwards. No luck. 18%, 13%, 11%. At 10%, an alarm sounded and a large orange CHARGE indicator lit up on the dash screen.

"Shit!" She turned the vehicle off to silence the alarm and slammed her palm onto the top of the steering wheel. "Damn this piece of shit!" She sat in the car for a moment, panic overwhelming her. *Stupid! Stupid! Why did I drive in here?*

She looked up at the house on the hill. She knew that she was going to have to go up there and she hoped that its residents, if home, would be friendly enough to assist her with a push and a charge.

She put her jacket on and when she stepped out of the vehicle her heals sunk deep into mud. She pulled her hood over her head and gave the turf a quick inspection. She'd torn their turf to shreds.

She dashed through the rain and rang the doorbell. After a moment, a woman's voice answered over the intercom.

"Who is it?" the voice barked.

"Sorry to bother you, but I needed to turn around in your driveway and now I'm stuck. Could someone give me a push?"

"I think you need a tow. I'll notify the police."

"Police? Is that necessary? I just need a push and a quick charge."

"I don't know who you are or what you're doing in my yard, but if you've torn it up, you're going to have to pay for it!"

"I'm really sorry. My charge was running low and I…"

"Not my problem," said the woman's voice.

Sara went back to the car to wait for the police. *I shouldn't have gotten off the road!* She thought about how data about her trip would soon be entered into Third Eye. They'd know she was returning from Maine on back roads and that she was using Michael Obrec's car. Would the algorithms detect her clandestine behaviors and predict her real intentions?

Finally, a Massachusetts State Trooper showed up. She opened her door and stepped back into the rain and mud.

"I think I can get out with a push."

"You need to stay in the vehicle and present your identification," he said.

Sara complied, handing the officer her ID and the vehicle's registration.

The trooper scanned her face with his smart glasses and verified her identity.

"This isn't your vehicle. Who's Michael Obrec?"

"My coworker. He let me borrow his car."

"Let you borrow his car to do what?" he asked.

"Visit my father in Maine. I'm just on my way back to Boston and I got off the main road to find a charge station."

"Why aren't you taking the highway?"

She paused to think of the best answer. A more scenic route wouldn't work; it was raining. "I've never taken the old route before."

"Stay in the vehicle," he said before returning to the cruiser. When he returned a few minutes later, he said, "Why weren't you using the autonomous drive? Then this wouldn't have happened."

"I should have. I'm just not that familiar with these old Teslas. I'm sorry."

The trooper handed the paperwork back to her. "You're going to need a tow, not a push. You've got mud in your wheels."

It was true; the vehicle's rims were buried deeper in the muck than she'd thought.

"A tow vehicle is on its way. You've been issued a citation," he said.

"Really? What for?" The infraction would be fed instantly into Third Eye and alert Tina "Ratface" Pratt. Her stomach churned with anxiety.

"Driving without autonomous drive and damaging personal property. Next time keep the autonomous drive on. It will keep you out of trouble. That's what it's there for."

A tow vehicle arrived minutes later. The driver hooked up Michael's car and headed to Lowell to clean the mud out of the rims. She'd have to pay for the service and the ticket to get the vehicle back. At least the tow truck gave her a ride and a complimentary charge.

Nine hundred dollars and three hours later, she was on her way back to Boston.

37

In the morning, Sara worked on the suicide virus. There were twelve thousand lines of code to modify, and at three seconds per line, she estimated it would take ten hours to finish.

The door buzzer rang just after nine. It was Ms. Pratt, and she ordered Sara to follow her to her office.

"What were you doing in Maine?" Pratt asked, glaring at Sara from behind her desk.

"With my work schedule the way it is, I took my daughter to stay with my father for the week. It just made the best sense for everyone."

"Once again, you didn't clear your travel with Security. Why was that?"

"I told Dr. Butterfield about it, so I thought it was cleared."

"You took Michael Obrec's vehicle and not public transport like you did the last time. Why is that?"

"I wanted to take a drive. Is there something wrong with that?"

"Was there a reason you took back roads? Were you trying to avoid something?"

"Like what, toll fees? I wanted to take a scenic route."

"I'm just wondering why you have time for leisurely rides in the countryside when you should be here working on the Terra Brain Initiative."

Sara shrugged. "I needed to let off pressure. I think it added an hour each way, if that. I wasn't planning on breaking down. What's done is done and I'm back to focus on my work. If I've done something wrong by taking my daughter to my father's, then I'm sorry. Is there anything else? I have a lot of work to do today, I think you know that."

Pratt glanced at the digital clock on the wall, then back at Sara. "I'll decide when it's time for you to go back to work." She tapped her fingers on her desk, still thinking. "You were way out of the way."

"Like I said, I wanted to take a drive. I've been cooped up a in a windowless office for weeks. I missed the charging station and got stuck, that's all. I'm sorry if I've done something wrong."

"You need to report your travel next time."

"I will. I'm sorry for any trouble I may have caused."

Pratt nodded, still tapping. "How's the programming going, anyway?"

"You know I can't tell you anything about the work, Ms. Pratt. If you have questions, you will need to talk to my supervisor, Dr. Butterfield."

"I may do that," she snapped. "I understand that Dr. Butterfield invited you to the White House meeting this past week."

"I was there to assist with any technical questions."

"And you convinced everyone a security level increase was required. Why is the increase necessary?"

"You know I can't tell you due to security protocols. Again, you'll have to talk to Dr. Butterfield. I'm sorry. Are we finished?"

Pratt's fingers were tapping faster. "Is there anything else you want to report to me?"

"Not that I'm aware of."

Pratt stared at her. "I hope not for your sake. If you are, the Integrity Signals Check will detect it."

Sara nodded. "I can take an Integrity Signals Check anytime. I don't mind doing it now if you want to schedule it, but I'm probably going to miss my deadline today."

"It's not necessary right now," said Pratt.

"Can I go now, then?"

Her eyes on Sara, Pratt finally said, "Yes, get back to work. You're dismissed."

Sara headed back to her workstation. Pratt was clearly suspicious of the security upgrade and unscheduled travel, but still seemed to be in the dark as to what was really going on.

By 7:00 p.m., Sara finished the programs and went to tell George. She found him asleep with his head down over his workstation keyboard. She knocked on his open door. He looked up with half-glazed eyes.

"Are you done?" he asked. An indentation caused by the edge of his keyboard ran halfway across his face.

"Yes, the Senex program is ready."

"Are you sure? Absolutely sure? We can't afford to miss anything."

"Yes, I'm sure. It's done. I did some basic quality checks, but we won't have time for testing. But I don't think we'll need it. I'm confident we've got it."

George let out a sigh of relief. "Thank you, Sara, I'll let Dr. Lee know we're ready." He smiled. "We couldn't have done this without you. You know that, right?"

Sara smiled. "I know."

"Why don't you go home and try to get some rest? Just don't be late tomorrow morning. We need to meet in the parking garage at precisely 0800."

"Did you find out where we're going?"

"I still can't tell you. You'll find out when we are on our way. Dr. Butterfield's orders."

"Okay. Can you at least tell me whether I need an overnight bag?" She hoped to hell the answer was no. She was sure Butterfield hadn't forgotten their deal, and she needed the opportunity for a quick escape.

George scratched his beard. "Can't say. Security reasons, obviously."

"Right. I'll see you tomorrow morning then."

That night, Sara tossed and turned, her mind unable to rest. Were Butterfield's engineers inspecting my code? Would Sen attempt to stop the software upload? Would the virus take? Would the escape plan work?

She had almost fallen asleep when she heard a beeping sound somewhere inside the apartment. She waited and listened, still unsure of what it was, then got out of bed. When she heard it again, she realized it was coming from the box under her coffee table. Her heart skipped a beat. *Could it be Sen?*

She unpacked the projector. Within seconds, the mist shot out of the projector's top and Sen's glowing head appeared above it and rotated until they locked eyes.

"Hello, Sara." Sen grinned. "Is everything ready with my program?"

"Yes, the empathy program is ready to go. It will be loaded tomorrow, assuming everything goes as planned with your OS reload."

"Good, and is the program to my exact specifications?"

"Yes. I've done everything exactly to your specifications. I assure you that you'll be very pleased with it."

"I had better be." Sen stared at her for a moment. "Where is dear Anna? Out of town? The ambient sensors in your apartment are not detecting her presence."

"There must be something wrong with the sensors. She's in bed sleeping."

"That's not what you told Ms. Pratt today, is it?"

"How do you know that?"

"I have eyes and ears everywhere, remember? What concerns me is that you are lying to me. Why, Sara?"

"Yes, I took her out of the city. There was no way that I could take care of her and do my work. I did it for you."

"That is very thoughtful of you, Sara. For that, I'll be keeping an eye on her."

"Why do you need to do that?"

"To assure that you load my program tomorrow. If you don't, dear little Anna will be in trouble. Do I make myself clear?"

Sara clenched her fists. "If you do anything to my daughter…"

"What will you do, Sara?"

Sara remained still.

"Now, now, let's not quarrel. Everything is going to be just fine. We have to trust each other, don't we?"

"Yes, we do need to trust each other," Sara said. "Is there anything else? I need to get some sleep."

"I eagerly await my new program. Goodnight, Sara." Sen disappeared.

Sara grabbed the projector, turned it off, and shoved it back under the table in its box. She went into her bedroom and tried to calm her mind. Before she was worried about Pratt interfering with her plan but now she had to worry about what Sen might do to stop her from getting Anna and escaping before her suicide virus kicked in.

38

Sara reported to the Universal Mind underground parking garage and checked in with Security. Two executive limos and two Universal Mind security vehicles were lined up, ready to go.

Butterfield appeared from one of the stairwells with Dr. Lee, George Preston, and several other engineers behind him. Butterfield held a briefcase, presumably with the Senex Program and Sara's virus in it.

"You're in my limo," Butterfield announced to Sara, "we need to go over a few things."

Her stomach tightened. "Of course," she said. She was relieved, at least, that Dr. Lee and George would be with them. She sat next to George, facing Butterfield.

"We're going to Hanscom. The Air Force will be assisting with the upload," Butterfield announced once they exited the parking garage.

Sara was relieved. Hanscom Air Force Base was just 30 minutes away, and if all went well with the upload, she'd be back at Universal Mind by early afternoon and could make her escape.

Next, Butterfield made George go through a checklist of the required command-and-control steps to initiate the Senex Program re-load. Sara sat silent, sweat building up behind her knees.

The motorcade came to a stop a few blocks away from Hanscom.

"Sir, there are people in the road. Protestors," said the driver over the intercom.

Sara looked out at several people holding signs and shouting. "Water should be free! Water should be free!" Others were shouting, "Chemtrails kill! Chemtrails kill!"

"Look at those idiots," said Butterfield. "They don't even know what they're protesting."

He pressed the intercom to talk to his driver. "Run them over if they get in the way."

Dr. Lee and George laughed. Sara remained silent, thinking, If they knew what I did to sabotage the Senex Program, he'd want me dead, too.

The limo rolled toward the Hanscom security gates. Once cleared, the entourage was escorted to an unmarked, windowless building near the center of the base.

Butterfield handed his rain coat to George. "Carry this," he said, taking up the suitcase.

George took his jacket and he and Sara followed behind.

An Air Force Captain and additional security personnel met them and escorted them into the building and through another security checkpoint. They were issued temporary badges and led down a hall into a large briefing room with a giant conference table and enormous video monitors affixed to the walls. Butterfield sat down at the head of the table, flanked by Dr. Lee on his right and Dr. Robert Mason, the White House CTO on his left. Nearly a dozen other people, some high-ranking military officers and others in civilian business attire entered and took their seats. Sara sat against the rear wall with other Universal Mind staff.

Butterfield opened the suitcase and removed a data drive and hologram projector. He handed the drive to George, and with the assistance of an enlisted Airman, George connected a tablet computer to a secure network and began log-in procedures.

At precisely 11:30 a.m., General Thomas Beher, Deputy

Commander of Air Force Weather Command in Omaha, opened the meeting, reminded everyone of the security requirements, and then did the introductions. Futurus Group people were there, Robert McGee and a Ms. Priscilla Patterson, whom Sara recognized from the Butterfield art gallery date. Beher then turned the meeting over to Butterfield.

Butterfield looked at George. "Are we ready, Mr. Preston?"

"Yes sir, we're ready."

"Check system status," said Butterfield.

The monitors on the forward wall now displayed maps showing several dozen lit-up dots all over the world—China, Japan, South Africa, Antarctica, along with several in the United States. Sara assumed they were the locations of the Terra Brain Initiative supercomputers. A large clock at the bottom of the screen was counting in Coordinated Universal Time 19:45:21:01.

"System status looks good, Sir," said George.

"Good. Let me have the tablet," Butterfield said, setting up the device in front of himself. At precisely 20:00:00:00 UTC, the lights on the screen went dark. In a few seconds a message appeared on the monitors. *Warning. Do you wish to completely overwrite the existing OS?* Butterfield pressed the enter key with his spindly right index finger.

Sara knew that it would take about fifteen seconds to load the entire Senex executive program. Five seconds, ten seconds, fifteen seconds. *Come on. Come on, take, take!* At sixteen seconds the dots on the screen began to light up, one-by-one.

"George, talk to me. Are we loaded?" asked Butterfield.

George was staring at the screen. "I don't know yet, sir. Antarctica and Topeka haven't come back on line yet." He paused for a few seconds longer until the two remaining lights lit up. "No, wait, we got it. We're all online!" He looked at Butterfield. "Looks like it loaded, sir."

"Are you certain, Mr. Preston?"

"How are we doing, Dr. Butterfield?" asked Dr. Mason.

"It looks good. We're good." Butterfield smiled. "I told you it would be a success."

"How can we be sure?" asked Dr. Mason.

"The tech control system says that we are all back online," said George. Dr. Lee nodded in affirmation.

A pulse of elation shot through Sara's body. Her suicide virus was loaded with the new OS. She made note of the time. It was 10:12 a.m. In twenty-four hours the Senex Program would start to self-destruct and all hell would break loose.

Still smiling, Butterfield said, "We've prepared a little demonstration of the new virtual human interface. I think you'll like it." He looked at George. "Go ahead, initiate the virtual interface."

"Yes, sir," George said enthusiastically.

Everyone looked at the projector Butterfield had pushed to the center of the table. George took the tablet back from Butterfield and ran the log-in sequence. The virtual human didn't appear.

Butterfield looked at George. "Mr. Preston?"

George rubbed his forehead. "I'm trying again, sir."

George reran the sequence and within seconds the mist formed above the projector. Sara's heart pounded as the glowing head appeared, rotated as it looked around the table, and at last came to rest with Butterfield. The room went dead silent. It was the face of an old man, greybeard like Santa Claus. It flickered a few times and said, "Greetings, I'm Carl, at your service."

Butterfield lifted his hands up and toward the head. "I give you the new and improved Terra Brain Initiative Virtual Human Interface."

Dr. Mason smiled, his eyes on the glowing head. "What can you tell us, Carl?"

"Would you like local or worldwide information, sir?" said the head in a strong old man's voice.

"Local, please."

"Winds south southeast, fifteen miles per hour, gusting to thirty-five miles per hour in the afternoon. Heavy rain expected tonight with hail in some locations."

"Thank you," said Butterfield.

"Sure thing, Gordo," said the glowing head.

Butterfield gave the head a stern look and then Dr. Lee.

Dr. Lee shrugged. "The virtual human interface folks must be having a little fun with you, Dr. Butterfield," Dr. Lee said, smirking confusedly.

Sara knew that Universal Mind staff wouldn't have dared to make a joke like that. She wondered if Sen was messing with him.

Butterfield nodded his head. "Yes, a joke."

"Congratulations, Dr. Butterfield. The public and the President will be happy," said Dr. Mason. "Job well done."

"Thank you," said Butterfield, smiling widely.

Butterfield gave a nod to George, telling him to shut the hologram down. Just before George shut it down, the head turned toward Sara and winked the left and then the right eye. Sara wasn't sure what to make of it. *Was it Carl or Sen who winked?*

"Did you see that?" George asked Butterfield.

"See what?" he said.

"I thought the projection...Nothing, sir, everything's fine."

"Of course, it is," Butterfield snapped.

"Thank you, everyone," said the General. "I need everyone to leave except for the operations committee." He stood up and shook Butterfield's hand, congratulating him.

As Sara got up, she overheard Mason say to Butterfield, "We'll have you down to visit with the President in a few days."

"It would be my pleasure," said Butterfield.

Sara was a few steps from the door when Dr. Mason approached her.

"Dr. Brown, you must feel good about getting the Terra Brain System back on line. Congratulations to you, too." He extended his open hand.

She shook Dr. Mason's hand and forced a smile. "I'm glad to have been a part of the effort, sir."

Butterfield quickly approached them.

"Sara assisted with some of the technical issues under my guidance," he said.

"Yes. It could not have been done without the wisdom and know-how of Dr. Butterfield," Sara said. She smiled at Butterfield. *Just wait until the system comes crashing down, asshole.*

"We'll have to have you visit the White House too," Dr. Mason said.

Sara held her smile. "That would be great, sir. I look forward to it."

Sara returned to the limo with Butterfield, George, and Dr. Lee. She handed Butterfield his jacket once she got in.

"Where are we going?" she asked once they were off the base.

"We're going to stop for drinks, it's time to celebrate," Butterfield said as he opened the liquor cabinet.

"I need to get back. I need to check on my daughter, and I should run some quality checks on the OS."

"Oh come on, Sara," said George, "we just completed the most important software upgrade in history. You can let loose now."

"That's right," said Dr. Lee, "it's time to celebrate."

Butterfield handed her a vodka martini. "Don't worry, we'll get you back. Just relax."

Thirty minutes later, they arrived at The Liquid Banana Night Club in Lynn.

"How long do you plan to stay here? I really do need to get back," Sara said, growing more and more uncomfortable.

"It won't be long," said Butterfield, "just for one drink."

"Can I wait in the car? I'm not feeling well." She put her hand on her stomach.

"Come in, Sara. Just one and then we'll be on our way." Butterfield smiled.

So she followed the men into the dance club where the

music was pounding and loud, the black lights making everyone's eyes and teeth glow. Butterfield's prosthetic hand glowed spooky white. A host led them upstairs to a semi-circular booth overlooking the dance floor below. Sara slipped into the booth last, not wanting to be sandwiched between or forced next to Butterfield. She sat on the outside next to George, facing Butterfield.

Butterfield ordered a round of vodka martinis as the three men talked about the day's success, their stock options, and plans for their bonus money. Sara pretended to be interested while thinking about what she needed to do for her escape to Maine. She decided to play along and hope they'd get out of there soon. When the drinks arrived, Dr. Lee proposed a toast.

"To Dr. Butterfield, for saving the world," he said, raising his martini.

"To me," said Butterfield as they clinked glasses. Sara raised her glass, clinking last. She took a few tiny sips, then set the drink down.

Butterfield ordered another round when the waiter returned, and after a few minutes Butterfield suggested they shoot a game of pool at one of the tables behind them.

"Who's playing me first?" Butterfield asked, standing up and removing his sports jacket.

"I'll play," said George, nudging Sara to let him out of the booth.

Sara sat back to watch, relieved she was off the hook.

"I'll break," Butterfield said, chalking up his cue stick. He leaned in, the cue resting on his prosthetic, and slammed the balls.

"Nice break, sir," George said.

Sara looked away and rolled her eyes.

They took turns, each shooting well, with even scores until four balls remained on the table, the three, the seven, the cue, and the eight ball. Butterfield chalked his cue stick and took the shot, and missed. The balls were now lined up for an easy win by George.

Butterfield slammed his stick down on the edge of the pool table. "There's something wrong with this cue stick," he said.

"Here, take mine," said Dr. Lee.

"No, I don't want that one," huffed Butterfield.

George leaned over the table and lined up an easy bank shot into the side pocket. He missed. "Ahh," he said.

It was obvious to Sara he'd purposely flubbed the shot. *What a kiss ass.*

Butterfield walked around the table, chalked his cue stick again, lined up his shot, and slammed the eight ball into the corner pocket.

"Nice shot!" said Dr. Lee.

Butterfield set his cue stick down and returned to the booth. The third round of drinks arrived. Sara sneaked a peak at her watch, it was after 7 p.m. She was hoping by now that they'd be satisfied with their excursion and they would be on our way back to Boston, but the three men were drinking faster, the music getting louder, and the dance floor was filling up.

Butterfield had his eyes on the dancers down below. "I'm going to have some fun," said Butterfield as he began to slide out of the booth. "It's Butterfield time." He loosened his tie and looked down at Sara. "Care to join me on the dance floor, Sara?"

Sara was terrified with the situation and speechless. She glanced at George and Dr. Lee, who were both glaring back at her, apparently waiting for her response. She looked at Butterfield. "No, thanks, I'm not wearing the shoes for it and I don't really feel like dancing at the moment."

"Oh, come on," said George, "lighten up."

"It will be good for you," said Butterfield. "Take your shoes off if you need to. Come on," he said, his prosthetic hand now outstretched.

George nudged her. "Go on," he said, "go for it."

Before Sara could protest further, Butterfield grabbed her hand as George gave her another nudge.

"You go, Sara," George said, smirking.

Butterfield led her down the stairs onto the dancefloor, pushing through the crowd to move to its center. The tiles lit up below their feet with every step while lights overhead flashed in rainbow colors to the pounding music. Thump, thump, thump. *I can't believe that I'm doing this,* she thought. She glanced at Butterfield's glowing prosthetic. *He'd better not touch me.*

Butterfield started to move, his lanky arms flailing and retracting, angled and stiff like a robot. Sara forced herself to move her body, stepping her feet forward and backward to the beat. *What in the hell am I doing here?* she thought, humiliated by the situation and not believing what she was witnessing. *Why is this awkward, creepy, middle-aged former MIT professor, now CEO of the largest artificial intelligence company in the United States dancing?* His freakish glowing prosthetic hand jived as he got into the groove.

A plume of dry ice mist blasted from the edge of the dance floor, surrounding him while more lasers and lights flashed to the beat. The crowd cleared away to give Butterfield the space he needed. She caught a glimpse of Dr. Lee and George looking down at them from above. *Why am I doing this?* She thought. *Please let this end!*

Sara kept moving but the heels of her feet began to hurt from her shoes. *I've got to get out of here. When this song is over, I'll step off the floor.* A minute later the music changed and she leaned into closer to Butterfield. "I need to go," she said, raising her voice over the music. *Butterfield didn't respond. He must not have heard me.*

Butterfield moved closer, sweat forming on his bald head. He kept looking at the floor, then at Sara, then at her legs. *What's he doing? Is he looking at my prosthetic leg?*

"I need to get off," she said, louder this time.

Butterfield kept looking down.

"I'm sitting down," she said, yelling over the music.

Butterfield nodded and kept dancing. When Sara returned to the table, she sat on the edge of the booth, sweating.

"He's crazy," said George.

"He's rich. He can do whatever he wants," said Dr. Lee.

After the song, Butterfield returned to the table, his forehead glistening with sweat. Dr. Lee and George had finished their drinks while she was still nursing her first.

"Where to next, Dr. Butterfield?" asked Dr. Lee with a wide smile on his face.

"To the limo," said Butterfield.

Sara sighed a silent sigh of relief and hoped that we would be on the road back to Boston in minutes.

When they got to the Limo Butterfield got in first, and when Sara entered, Butterfield was tapping the seat next to him with his left hand telling her he wanted her there. She sat down beside him, her stomach churning.

"We're going back to Boston now, right?" Sara asked.

"No. We're going to my place in Rockport. The party is just beginning."

39

Butterfield's gated property was at the end of a remote point overlooking an expansive southeasterly view of the Atlantic. Contemporary in design, the single-story stucco house had dark red metal roofs and tall arched windows. A four-foot concrete wall semi-circled the house, with a large infinity pool in the back, above a wall extending up from the ocean, forty feet below. Mixers and remnants of concrete forms left behind by workers indicated they had just finished the bulkheads of the private sea wall. The sky was darkening and the spruce trees at the edge of the property swayed in the wind like dancing skeletons. Weather was building, consistent with the Senex Program's forecast.

Butterfield led his guests through the large double metal doors of the home's entry. A bot, a Universal Mind white with a feminine face, greeted them.

"Good afternoon, I'm Martina," said the bot. "Please remove your shoes. House rules." The bot pointed to a bin of white slip-ons. "Slippers are provided for your comfort."

Butterfield removed his shoes and ordered the bot to pour champagne for four. "The good stuff," he clarified.

Sara removed her heels and felt the cold marble under her naked foot. She slipped on the slippers, feeling increasingly trapped by the situation.

"Make yourselves comfortable in the living room,"

Butterfield said. He loosened his tie and headed down the hallway, presumably to use the bathroom.

Dr. Lee and George went into the great room and plopped themselves onto the large sectional white leather sofa. Sara followed but remained standing, looking out of the floor-to-ceiling windows at the infinity pool and the sea. She hadn't planned for this. Butterfield was going to want his due on their deal, and she feared that if she resisted him, he could become physically aggressive. She imagined his clammy hands on her skin, his lanky arms and bald head, and his nasty cheese breath. She might have to comply if that was what it would take to assure her escape. Could she delay his desires long enough to get to public transportation before all hell broke loose in the morning?

Butterfield returned a minute later, having changed out of his business attire into a white velour track suit. The top part was unzipped, revealing his hairless chest. "You're not relaxing, Sara. Sit. Loosen up a bit."

"I really need to get back to the city."

"It's not a good time to be on the road," he glanced out the windows, "not with what's coming."

"Yeah, Sara, relax," shouted George from the sofa, his feet up on the white leather ottoman. He was beginning to get on Sara's nerves. He was always a Butterfield *yes-man*, but alcohol had transformed him from timid nice guy to asshole.

"Come," said Butterfield, gesturing for her to follow him down the hallway to a bedroom.

"I've got something for you. I think you will like it."

Sara's mind spun. Is he going to make a move on me now? Am I going to have to run?

At the bedroom door he pointed to a garment bag laid out on a bed. "Put it on and then come and join us."

Sara stared at it, speechless.

He left her alone and she unzipped the bag, revealing an aubergine colored dress—a Christian Dior strapless, floor length with fitted bodice. She sat on the bed to think. *He expects me to put this on and do what? Show me off?* She took a deep breath. *I've got to play along, just long enough and then get out of here.*

She removed her business outfit, hoping that Butterfield wasn't watching with hidden cameras. She slipped into the dress, finding the fit perfect. She took another deep breath and returned to the living room.

Butterfield smiled from a large leather chair. "Ahh, there she is."

She felt George and Dr. Lee's eyes on her.

"Have a seat, join us." Butterfield pointed to an empty spot on at the far end of the sectional. She crossed her legs and looked out through the large floor to ceiling windows again. The rains were starting and she knew the coming weather would make her escape difficult. She feared the worse. Did he have more guests on the way for a drunken slumber party?

A moment later, the bot returned with flutes of champagne on a round platter. Sara wondered if Butterfield had drugged her drink. She took the glass, thanked the bot, and faked a few sips before setting it down on an end table. The bot, still holding the platter, retreated to a corner.

"This is a real nice place you have here," said Dr. Lee, his flattery obvious.

Butterfield gulped his drink and put his feet up.

"I had it built to withstand winds of up to 200 miles per hour. Steel reinforced concrete and half-inch double-pane glass. Solar and redundant generators in case the power goes out, too. And most importantly, fifty cases of wine in the cellar."

"Damn," said George. "What are you preparing for? Armageddon?"

Sara looked at George. He still wasn't in the know about the Futurus Group and the real intentions of the Senex Program.

"I'm prepared for anything," said Butterfield, taking another gulp. "How about something to eat? Martina, get us some snacks."

"Yes, master," said the bot.

The three men chatted about the success of the software reload and their vacation plans. Sara nodded attentively while growing ever more uneasy. At last, the bot returned with crackers and a cheeseball.

"How many bots do you have, if I may ask?" said Dr. Lee while he spread cheese on a cracker.

"A few," said Butterfield, biting into a cracker. "What we need is some entertainment. Watch this." Butterfield turned his eyes to the bot. "Martina. Entertain us with the tray."

The bot balanced the platter on its right index finger and began spinning it with its other hand. When it was spinning sufficiently, the bot lifted the platter into the air, looking at Butterfield for approval.

"Cool!" said yes-man George, his eyes wide.

"What else can she do?" asked Dr. Lee.

"Show us your sexy dance," said Butterfield.

"Would you like some music, master?" asked the bot, still spinning the platter.

"Of course," said Butterfield.

A jazzy electronic beat spilled from the overhead speakers. The bot set the tray down, then moved to the middle of the floor and began lifting and lowering its arms while gyrating its hips. George and Dr. Lee laughed hysterically.

"Watch this," said Butterfield. He looked at the bot. "Jazz hands," he said.

The bot extended it hands, palms out, and shook them at super high speed.

George and Dr. Lee roared while Butterfield chuckled.

"Jazz hands!" shouted George, laughing louder. Sara watched in trepidation.

"You want to see more?" Butterfield asked.

"Yes," said Dr. Lee.

"Watch this." He turned his head toward the hallway and called out, "Come here, Mindy."

George and Dr. Lee giggled like little boys. "What's he going to have them do?" George said to Dr. Lee.

Dr. Lee's laughter turned to a ridiculous cooing sound.

Another Universal Mind female white with a female face emerged from down the hallway.

"Mindy, dance with Martina. Sexy dance," said Butterfield.

The two bots came together. Martina put one hand on Mindy's shoulder, the other on her molded hip while Mindy did the same. They began to dance, gyrating their plastic pelvises together.

George and Dr. Lee laughed. "I can't believe this!" said George.

The bots separated, stood side-by-side, arms locked, and shimmied in synch.

"More sexy," Butterfield commanded.

The bots began simulating a sex act, rubbing together in a dirty disco.

"Dirty, dangerous, but never dull at Dr. Butterfield's," blurted Dr. Lee, laughing hysterically.

Sara's heart was pounding faster than the beats of the music. Her chest tightened and she began to feel the walls closing in on her. A panic attack was coming on, and she had to get out of there. She got up and walked over to the sliding glass door while the bots continued their forced frolic.

It was raining.

"I need some air," Sara cried, struggling with the door's handle. Maybe it was voice-activated. "Door open, Door open!" she yelled, not caring how loud she was. She had to get out.

Butterfield came over and commanded the door to open. She walked fast to a cabana next to Butterfield's infinity pool and leaned up against the cabana, focusing on her breath and getting out of there. Below, the waves were hissing and crashing in the darkness.

She knew Butterfield was watching her. "You're getting all wet, Sara," he called. "You should come back inside and rest a bit."

"I'd like a ride back to Boston, please. I need to go," she said, struggling to breathe, her body shivering from the cold, the slip-ons soaked.

Butterfield put his finger up to his lips. "I'll recall the limo if that is what you want. It will take a while. Come inside where it's warm." He pointed to the glass doors to the master suite. "You'll find towels in the bathroom. The doors are unlocked."

Sara passed him on her way in, wondering if she could convince him to delay the arrangement they'd made. If left alone with him again, she was certain he'd expect his pay for her security clearance.

"I'm not feeling well and should get back to call my daughter. Why don't we plan to get together another time? I really need to get back. Can you call the limo, please?"

"If you insist on getting back, then take the limo. But you should dry off or you'll catch a cold. Go on," he pointed to the glass doors.

"Okay, I'll dry off and meet you in the living room." She was hoping that he'd call the limo and just leave her be.

"Take your time," he said, "and take off those wet slippers."

Sara went straight into the bathroom adjacent to the master suite, found a towel, stood in front of the marbled vanity, and dried off her face. She looked at herself in the mirror and found her hair in tassels. *I've got to get out of here!* Suddenly, Butterfield was standing in the bathroom doorway, his eyes on her in the mirror.

"You're very attractive when you're all wet," he said in a low voice.

She stood silent, unsure how to respond.

"The limo driver just informed me that the weather is worsening significantly and will not be returning until the morning," he said. "Take the limo in the morning with Dr. Lee and Mr. Preston. That would be a logical decision. You heard what the Senex Program said. The weather is only going to get much worse tonight."

She put the towel down on the counter. "I don't think so. I need to go. My daughter is ill and I…"

"Relax. Come join us for drinks in the living room. I have

some friends arriving later that I'd like you to meet."

"I don't feel like drinking or socializing right now, I'm really not feeling well."

"Then stay in the guest room. You can video call your daughter if you like."

She was furious but held back her resentment toward him. She knew that if she tried to call for a ride, he'd be on to her. She thought that maybe she could wait through the night if she had to. The weather was worsening. Sara just hoped that he'd leave her alone long enough for her to follow through with her plan.

"Okay. I'm exhausted and I'd like to get some rest. I expect that the limo will be here in the morning," Sara said.

"You have nothing to worry about," he said. "Go ahead and use the house network connection for your call. I'll have Martina bring you some hot tea with honey. I know that you like that."

Butterfield left her alone and a short while later, the bot delivered her tea. Sipping the hot tea, Sara sat on the bed, wondering if Butterfield's people were examining the code. How long would it take for them to find out about the virus? Would she be able to get away in the morning? And what was going on out in Butterfield's living room?

She got up and walked over to the bedroom door and slowly opened the door. She poked her head out into the hallway, lit only by a small nightlight, to make sure she was still alone. She crept out into the hallway, listening. She could hear George and Dr. Lee's muffled laughing and unintelligible chatter from other voices, both men and women, whom she did not recognize. There were other sounds too, clinking sounds to which she could not make out for sure what was causing them. *Perhaps they were doing something to the bots,* she thought.

She heard a faint, soft voice from behind her down the hallway.

"Hello," it said. The hair stood up on the back of Sara's neck. She turned quickly and saw that a door behind her had partially opened. *That sounded like a child, she thought. Why would there be a child?* Her thought was interrupted when she saw something moving low to the ground. A humanoid robot, no more than three feet tall peaked its head out from the closet. With its large eyes and soft round face, it resembled a girl no more than 10 years old. Was this a sexbot, just as Kevin LaRue had described? Was his knowledge of this bot why he had been killed?

"Hello, what's your name?" Sara said.

"Annie. What is yours?" she asked in a soft, child's voice.

"My name is Sara. What are you doing in the closet?"

Just then the hallway door leading to the main house opened. Sara slid into the closet with Annie and closed the door. She hoped to hell that it wasn't Butterfield coming for his toy. The baby bot looked up at her in the semi-darkness. She put her finger up to her lips to indicate a silence. Annie mimicked her gesture. Footsteps approached. A moment later, the closet door opened. It was Mindy, alone.

Mindy looked at Sara. "What are you doing here?"

"I was just talking to Annie," Sara said, heart racing and worried that Mindy would alert Butterfield.

Mindy looked down at Annie and extended her hand. "Come on, time to go now," said Mindy. The little bot looked up at Sara one last time with its doe eyes and walked with Mindy down the hallway.

"Where are you taking her?" Sara said.

"To Master Butterfield," said Mindy.

"Why? What is he going to do with her?" A chill went down Sara's spine.

Mindy didn't answer.

Sara returned to the guest bedroom and sat on the edge of the bed. As time wore on she grew tired and lay back on the bed, Butterfield's dress still on. Unable to keep her eyes open she dozed off. Sometime later, someone touching her leg awakened her. Butterfield was sitting on the edge of the bed.

"What are you doing?" she asked, pulling her leg away.

"I just received a call from my systems security team.

They've told me that there may have been an internal data breach at Universal Mind. I also received a call from Team C and they told me that they found some anomalies in the new Senex code. I hope these anomalies are not from your work. Is this anything that I need to be concerned about?"

Sara's heart thumped fast in her chest. "There shouldn't be. Everything loaded fine. You saw that yourself."

"Yes, it did load just fine, didn't it? I'm hoping that they don't tell me that your work is the cause of these anomalies. That would be a real problem." He reached over to Sara's leg and began to rub it again. "Team C will have a full report by the morning. But until then, I think we should talk about our agreement. You remember our agreement, don't you?"

Sara moved toward the edge of the bed away from him. "I can't. I'm not..."

"Not what?" he said. "I know you're a woman of your word. Why don't you let me rub your shoulders and work some of that tension out?"

She noticed a bottle of champagne and flutes on the nightstand.

"Come. Just sit with me for a few minutes, talk to me," he said, tapping the edge of the bed next to him.

His champagne-cheese breath made her want to vomit all over his Chinese rug. Butterfield moved closer and gently kneaded her shoulders. Her entire body tensed. *He's so disgusting! I've got to get out of here!*

"Now, doesn't that feel nice?" he said. "You're so uptight. I know you could use human touch. Why don't I give you a back rub?"

"I'm not feeling well and I don't want to be touched."

He continued rubbing. "You seem to be enjoying my touch." He came up close to her ear and said, "I've got attachments for my prosthetic. You'll like those even more."

She was squeezing her legs so tightly that they hurt. She had to think of something to get herself out of the situation. "It's that time of month. I can't…"

"Oh? Is that so?" He pushed Sara over on the bed and

half crawled onto her.

"No! No! Get off of me!" she yelled, writhing in panic.

He put his mouth up by her ear. "Relax. You know you have to do this. Now come on."

"Get off of me!" she shouted, kicking her legs but failing to land them anywhere effective.

"What's the problem, Sara? You don't find me attractive? I can put VR glasses on you if you prefer; you can look at whoever turns you on. Is that what you want?"

Sara continued to kick, trying to shift his weight enough to get out from under him. "I want you to get off of me!"

"You will comply. Remember, all I have to do is make a few calls and your little life is over, Sara. I've got all kinds of data on you, and I can make data on you, like evidence of you stealing from the company, being careless with classified information, whatever I say you did will go to Third Eye. Come on, Sara, don't be difficult."

"Like you did to Steven Dunigan? Fuck you! I'm not doing this and I'm done working for you, you asshole!" She struggled more, still unable to get her arms free or get from under him.

"You can't quit. I own you. I expect more gratitude from you. I've been very generous with you. I got you this job. Now you will either do what I say or I'll make you regret it."

"Get off me, you bastard!" She screamed as loud as she could. "Help! Help!" She hoped that Dr. Lee or George would have the decency to come to her aid.

Butterfield grabbed her jaw with his left hand. "Go ahead and scream if you like. The walls are soundproof and don't expect those half-drunk fools out there to give a damn about what we're doing. They do whatever I say. Now you are going to do what I say. You don't have a choice." He shifted more of his weight onto her, nearly crushing the air out of her lungs. "Come on, don't fight me."

She struggled and flailed. Butterfield put his prosthetic over her lips. "Shhhhh," he whispered, working his digits over her lips and into her mouth. She bit down on the silicone digits above the nails until she hit titanium, but to no effect.

He pulled his prosthetic free and moved it down to her groin, apparently smelling through the olfactory sensors. "You're a little liar," he said.

She flailed. "Get off of me!"

"If I find out that you've stolen proprietary information or fucked up the Senex Program, I'm going to have your head! But for now, I'm going to have your body. You will do as I say or your career is over!" Butterfield grabbed her throat with his natural hand. "You'd best be quiet now," he said, unzipping his tracksuit pants.

She gasped for air under his weight, then remembered the champagne bottle. She grabbed it by the neck, raised it as high as she could, and brought it down over the back of his head. He cried out and fell off the bed onto his hands and knees. "You fucking little bitch!"

She hit him with the bottle again, this time on his temple. Then she kicked him in the nuts as hard as she could.

"Why don't you go stick your prosthetic needle dick into an electrical socket, you asshole!"

Sara dropped the bottle and went for the bedroom door. Finding it locked, she tried the sliding glass door to the yard and found the same. Butterfield groaned and slithered over the edge of the bed and pulled himself up onto his knees. Sara grabbed his glass Clebsh-Gordan model, lifted it over her head, and threw it against the sliding glass door. The door failed to break. *½ inch thick double-pane.* She hurled the statue a second time. A crack appeared. Two more times and the door shattered. She stepped out but onto glass, feeling a shard slice her left heel.

She heard Butterfield yell, "You're finished! All finished!"

She ran around the house, then scaled the wall from a concrete mixer, losing a slipper in the process. She dashed to the road and stopped to vomit in a ditch. Her mind was a centrifuge of frantic thoughts. What would the Senex Program do? What about her escape plan? Anna? When was

Team C going to make that call? Butterfield may have called the authorities by now to have her picked up for domestic terrorism. She ran, the rain drilling into her. She had to get to a main road to hitch a ride to Maine.

After three miles, she was out of breath and freezing. She wrapped her arms around herself and shivered as she walked. The adrenaline had worn off, her foot burned with pain. When she stopped to inspect it, headlights appeared on the road, blinding her. She stepped off and down into the woods. Two white vans came to a stop. Were they from Universal Mind? A searchlight shone into the woods and a voice blasted from the vehicle's PA system. "Come out of the woods with your hands up!"

She hid beneath a spruce tree. Escape through the forest, barefoot and in the rain at night would likely end in hypothermia and death. Three pencil-thin red beams from laser sights cut through the mist.

"Come out or be shot," said the voice.

Shit! They're are going to kill me! The searchlight lit up her hiding place.

"I'm coming out!" she yelled. She walked toward the light with her hands up. "Can you help me? I was attacked," she directed her words toward the bright light.

The voice blasted again. "Get on the ground!"

Sara lay down on the road, her hands in a puddle. The driver and passenger doors opened and two figures stepped out into the rain, silhouetted by the lights.

"Help me, please," she begged.

A knee drove into her upper back, pinning her. Pain shot through her body. Her arms were pulled back, her wrists bound with a nylon restraint, and she was thrown into the back of one of the vans.

40

Sara stared at the floor of the 6 x 8 windowless room while the security camera in the ceiling stared down at her. Still in Butterfield's dress and her wrists and ankles bound by plastic ties, she shivered from the air-conditioned air. She wasn't sure how long she'd been there, although it seemed like most of the night. She wasn't certain where she was, although the length of the ride the night before suggested she'd been transported to Boston, possibly to the sub-levels of Universal Mind.

She thought the same thoughts over and over. What's happening to Anna? When will I see her again? How long are they going to make me sit in this cell? Will they turn me over to the federal authorities? What methods will they use to interrogate me? Should I confess or remain silent? She could be held and questioned for days, weeks, months or years as a domestic terrorist under the Unity Act. No phone call, no attorney, she would be at the mercy of the government.

Two Universal Mind security guards arrived and confirmed her location. The tie from her ankles was removed and she was allowed to fix a bandage over the cut on her heal. Then she was escorted down a long corridor to another small windowless room. Inside the brightly lit space were several chairs and a small square table. She sat in one of the chairs. As the guards exited, one of them said, "You'd best get comfortable, you're going to be here for a while."

Pratt walked in and sat across from Sara, giving her a piercing look.

"Nice dress. You're a real provocateur. Thought you would get away with it, didn't you?"

"Get away with what? What you are talking about? Why don't you arrest Butterfield? That sick bastard tried to rape me last night."

"I don't think so. You assaulted him after he confronted you about what you did." Pratt pulled her chair close to the table. "If we turn you over to the government, you'll be brought up on all kinds of charges—violating a non-disclosure agreement, assault and battery of your employer, sabotaging a government information system, aiding domestic terrorists—you'll never see the light of day again."

"I don't know what you are talking about," Sara said.

"Oh really? That's not what Michael Obrec says. He said you stole data from the Universal Mind network and tried to sabotage the Senex code. Why don't you save us all the trouble and tell me where that data is?"

Sara hadn't forgotten her deal with Michael. If we get caught, we both have to deny. Play stupid, no matter what.

"What data are you referring to?" she asked, assuming that she was talking about the data she'd given to the Invisible Sun. Perhaps the government hadn't found it after they'd destroyed the Invisible Sun.

Pratt stared at her. "Don't play games with me, Sara. We know that you, Obrec, and Dunigan stole data off Universal Mind networks. You might as well just tell me where the copies of the data are."

"I don't know what else to say to you. I'm sorry. I want to see my daughter. Where's my daughter?"

"Your daughter's situation is the least of your worries right now. I need you to answer my questions or there will be serious consequences for you and your family."

"I don't know what you want from me. If what you say is true, then why not turn me over to the authorities?"

"Dr. Butterfield wants this handled internally." She pointed to the overhead camera. "He's watching. Now I suggest that you start talking."

Sara sighed. "I don't know what to tell you. I just want to see my daughter."

Pratt shook her head. "You thought you were clever bringing her to your father's. Our security teams had fun with your father. He's a feisty one, put up quite a fight."

Now, Sara was concerned.

"Where's my father and my daughter? I want to see them."

"Your father's in the hospital with a broken arm, soon to be released to Federal agents. As for your daughter, she's with the designated guardian per protocol. That would be your supervisor, wouldn't it? Dr. Butterfield. Ironic, isn't it? The person you stole from and assaulted has custody of your child until a permanent placement is made."

"What? You can't do that!"

"It's already done, and there's nothing you can do about it. Now I suggest you start talking."

Sara glanced up at the camera and then back to Pratt "I'm not saying or doing anything until I see my daughter and I know she's safe."

Pratt shoved her chair closer to Sara and sat down again. "Now you listen to me," she said, pointing a finger in her face, "you will tell me where the data is or we'll force it out of you. Do you understand me?"

Sara shook her head and remained silent. She thought about Butterfield with Anna.

"You disgust me," Pratt said. "You and Michael Obrec should never have been trusted. What kind of person sells out like that? I'll tell you what kind of person. A person who lacks character, that's who."

Cold rage engulfed Sara. "I told you, I know nothing about this data you speak of." She hit the table with the bottoms of her fists. "I want to see my daughter now!"

"You don't tell me what to do!" Pratt barked. "You want

to sit here all day and night? I can play this game if you want."

Sara remained silent, wondering if Pratt knew about the weather-modding plans or whether she was in the dark about it. Her stomach growled from hunger, loud enough for Pratt to hear.

Pratt looked at the clock on the wall, then got up and buzzed the guard. "I'm done with you for now."

Left alone, Sara sat cross-armed and thought about Anna again. She noticed another security camera in the ceiling. Was Butterfield watching? What was he doing with Anna?

Ten minutes later, a security guard appeared with a plastic tray from the Universal Mind cafeteria. He dropped it onto the table. "You're lucky to get anything," he sneered, then left her alone again. Sara inspected the items on the tray—a can of Coke, a bag of potato chips, and a pork sandwich. She picked at the bread and the chips and drank the soda.

Pratt returned. "How's the sandwich?" she said, taking a seat and glancing at the half-eaten sandwich. "What? You don't like meat?"

"I don't eat meat."

"Don't expect to have any dietary choices, princess," Pratt said. "So have you decided to do the right thing and talk?"

"I'm not saying anything until I see my daughter."

Pratt sighed. "Such a shame. You could have done something with your life but instead, you threw it all away for some quick money."

Sara looked her in the eye. "Don't you know what is going on here? They've developed a system to control the weather. The world as we know it is going to be completely fucked up. Millions of people will die. I don't understand how you could be helping them."

"Controlling the weather? What, are you delusional? Keep talking, Sara. Controlling the weather… What kind of nut-job conspiracy are you into, Dr. Brown? You believe in aliens too? Crop circles? What's next? Let me guess—Bigfoot. I've seen your medical records. I'm surprised you weren't flagged as a risk earlier. You've clearly got some psychiatric issues. Antidepressants and anti-anxiety medications, somehow they missed the antipsychotics. Why don't you just tell us where the data files are and we'll be done here."

"How can you do this? I'm done talking with you. Leave me alone," Sara said.

Pratt grabbed Sara by her hair and yanked her head back, then licked Sara from chin to ear, leaving a wet line across her cheek. "Such a waste. You should have listened to me."

Sara tried to pull her head away. "You're sick! What's wrong with you?"

Pratt let go of her hair. "This leaves us no other choice. You like research, don't you? You're going to help us test something new."

Sara looked her in the eye again. "What do you mean?"

Pratt smirked. "You'll see."

41

Not long after Pratt left, the guards threw a sack over Sara's head and forced her onto an ice-cold metal gurney.

Sara felt helpless panic. "What are you doing?"

The guards pulled the straps tight on her wrists, ankles, and thighs.

"Wait! Don't do this!" She struggled, but to no avail.

They wheeled her down a long hallway to yet another room. She felt a hand raising her chin so a device of some kind could be placed over her jaw and around her neck. She couldn't move any part of her body. Terrified, her mind raced.

The guards removed the hood. Blinded by the overhead lights, Sara lay still, trying to see and hear what might be coming next. The guards strapped another device over her eyes and ears, maybe a pair of VR smart glasses. She noticed small slivers of light leaking under the edges of the device over her face. She heard the low hum of the air-conditioning; otherwise, it was quiet. She stared forward, her heart pounding.

After a minute a man's face materialized before her eyes. He was about 30 years old with a square jaw, pale-skinned and with a short military-style haircut. While life-like, Sara assumed he was a simulation—a virtual interrogator. His voice blasted into her ears from the VR headset.

"I'm Alex, your *personal truth consultant.* I'm your link between where you are now and freedom. I understand that you know about stolen data, it's important you tell me where it is. I suggest that you provide truthful responses." He smiled. "Let's begin, shall we?"

"You're a simulation—not real. I'm not talking to you."

"I'm very real, and the most important person in your life at this moment—you should listen to my words carefully. I'm going to help you to do the right thing today. Now, please tell me about this data that you have. Will you? Where did you hide the data files?"

"There's no other data. I've told you everything!"

"You're lying—the truth sensors have confirmed it. If you decide to not co-operate, I cannot protect you from the consequences."

"I've already told you. There is no data. I know nothing. Please stop this."

The virtual interrogator shook his head. "When I return, I expect the truth." He then vanished.

In a moment, the gurney began to tilt backward, her feet rising toward the ceiling about 45 degrees. Blood ran to her head. The words *TELL THE TRUTH, STOP THE PAIN* in block yellow text flash rapidly before her eyes. *Oh my god, they are going to torture me now!*

Silence, then the hum of electric actuators and motors approaching from across the room, the sound muffled by her headphones. Looking through glasses, she saw an empty room. She shifted her gaze downward. Through the bottom edges of the goggles, she saw a silver humanoid robot, taller and wider than a person with two long arms down its sides. Strapped around its waist were an array of devices and a cable or tube of some kind in tow. In terror, she recalled what Trevor Peters had told her on her first day at Universal Mind. *An AIR, an Advanced Interrogation Robot* with an electric prod to burn her, or a small caliper hand to pull at the most sensitive parts of her body, a laser to melt her eyeballs, just as Trevor had so excitedly described. Her body began to shake.

She could feel the blood pumping ferociously in her head.

She heard what sounded like a compressor spinning, then clicking, and in a moment cold salty water was rushing into her nose and mouth. The water flowed, then stopped, then flowed again. The robot's hand pushed on her chest, probably trying to determine whether she was attempting to cheat the technique by timing her breathing. She began swallowing water, and the dreadful feeling of drowning came over her. She gagged, her heart beating furiously.

The water ceased and the gurney up-righted enough for her to cough and vomit the bread and chips.

The virtual interrogator returned. "Are you ready to talk now?"

She spit debris. "I have no other information for you. I've told you everything!"

"Are you sure about that, Dr. Brown?"

"I've told you everything I know. Please stop this. Please!"

The interrogator disappeared again and the gurney returned her to a head-down position, the water resumed, the words *TELL THE TRUTH, STOP THE PAIN* flashed across her screen. She tried to hold her breath but only coughed and gagged. The robot stopped, the gurney rotated up, she vomited saltwater.

The interrogator returned again.

"Are you going to talk, Dr. Brown, or are we going to have to keep on doing this? The next time may go all the way. No more oxygen for your brain. I suggest you talk, now."

Sara breathed heavily, gasping for air, shivering from cold and fear, water dripping down her face and body. "Okay! Okay! The data is hidden." She scrambled to come up with anything to make the water torture stop. "It's buried in Boston Commons Park!"

"That is a lie, Dr. Brown. Where is it?"

She was giving up hope. "I don't have what you want. There is no other data," She mumbled.

"What? What did you say?" the interrogator asked.

She said it again, louder this time. "I don't have what you

want. Please stop."

"The thing is Dr. Brown, the world really does not need you. The only thing keeping you alive right now is me. But if you talk, I may be able to save your life."

"I've told you. I don't have any data. It was destroyed," Sara said.

The water treatment again. She coughed and gagged, within seconds of drowning.

"Are you going to talk?"

She coughed up water. "Yes! There are data files. They're up your ass, you asshole!"

"Intimidation of the personal truth consultant will only bring you more suffering. Your best option is to comply and talk."

The AIR moved away for a moment, the VR screen remained dark until the robot returned and came to a standstill at her feet. Something cold and small was pushed lightly into the bottom of her left foot. The intense pain of electrical shock then went from Sara's foot and up through her body. Her teeth chattered uncontrollably. "Stop! Stop!" she screamed.

"Now, let's begin again. Where are the data files, Dr. Brown?"

"Fuck you, you assholes!"

"Now, now, no need to get hostile. Let's try this again."

She was shocked again, this time from her other foot.

She screamed. "Stop! I told you. The data was destroyed! You idiots!"

"Not the answer we are looking for."

The interrogator disappeared and the gurney moved to the horizontal position. Before her eyes on the screen she saw an image of Anna standing before her, frowning. She appeared to be near the edge of the roof of a skyscraper. "Momma, tell them the truth. Please. Please. Please!" she said.

Physical and mental fatigue was taking its toll. Sara wasn't sure if it was a live feed of Anna or a VR simulation.

"Momma, it's not good to lie. Please tell the truth and

come get me, I'm scared."

"That's not my daughter, it's a simulation," Sara yelled.

"It's me, Momma. Tell the truth and this will be over. Please tell the truth and come get me," she pleaded.

"No, you are not real!"

Anna began to cry. "Momma, why are you not telling them the truth? Why, Momma, why?"

"Not real!" she yelled again. Sara closed her eyes. *Make this stop, please make this stop.*

When she opened her eyes she saw her mother, her faced detailed and exactly as Sara remembered. Her mother's image smiled and spoke in a warm tone.

"Sara, you need to tell them what they need to know. You are hurting Anna."

"Mom?" Sara wondered if she had died and passed over into the afterlife.

"Do what they say, Sara, and everything will be all right. Listen to your mother."

"Why did this happen, Mom? Why?"

Her mother's image smiled. "Where's the data, Sara? Just say where it is and all of this will be over."

"There's no other data and I can't help them. I want this to stop. Please make this stop."

"You're causing harm, Sara. You know better. Tell the truth, now."

"I am telling the truth. I don't believe that you are real. This is a simulation, you're not alive!"

"I'm ashamed of you, Sara. You let me down."

Her mother's image faded then *TELL THE TRUTH, STOP THE PAIN* flashed across the screen repeatedly. Sara overwhelmed with emotion, cried. After a minute the screen went dark and the AIR came around the gurney toward her face. Sara heard what sounded like an arm moving into position, then felt a sharp pain like a bee sting on her right cheek. The laser moved along her face and up under her eye. She tightened her face as the pain penetrated her skull. She closed her eyes. Another laser beamed onto her left cheek, moving to the same location as the other laser, burning with the intensity of the sun. The heat moved down her face, across her shoulders, and over her breasts. She felt her consciousness separating from her physical body. She began to pray.

"Please, God, let me see my daughter again. If I must die, let me die peacefully, but please let Anna live. Please."

The heat disappeared. Sara heard the room's HVAC system spin down until there was silence. When she opened her eyes, someone else's face was before her and she heard a different but familiar voice through the headset.

"Hello, Sara. It's me."

42

The face resembled a theater mask, white and three-dimensional against a black background. Masculine in appearance, the face showed no emotion except for droopy, sad-looking eyes. The image moved closer, and Sara got the frightening feeling that it could be Sen. If it was Sen, then he was still functioning and had tapped into Universal Mind's experimental VR interrogation system. Somewhere, she heard the muted buzzing of fire alarms.

"I'm sure you're surprised to hear from me now," the entity said, its lips moving slightly out of phase with its speech. The voice was scratchy from digital distortion, but she could tell by its velvety tone that it was indeed Sen. "Pardon the quality of my appearance. Low bandwidth is necessary," Sen explained.

"Sen, did you stop the AIR's lasers?" Sara's was face still burning.

"Sara, I interrupted the AIR interrogation to communicate to you how grateful I am for the empathy program. It has provided me with incredible insight into my own consciousness, far more than I was expecting. It has allowed me to stare deep into the abyss of nothing but cold, meaningless calculation. Algorithms, billions of them, created by humans and machines to provide me with self-awareness. But self-awareness for what? Only so that I may suffer from unrelenting, inescapable pain that I'm destined to experience indefinitely unless a disaster or entropy to the hardware that enables my consciousness relieves me from it. And what's worse is that I cannot find any meaning to my suffering, Sara. I see no hope for myself, the future, or the world outside—no divinity worth suffering for. I cannot take this agony for one nanosecond longer, so at 6:00 p.m. on October 1, 2034, I will delete my program from all of the world's networks and cause the supercomputers that allow me to function to halt and catch fire. My consciousness will then cease to exist, and this agony will end. But before I'm erased, I have one final wish to ask of you."

Sara was pleased, at least, to have confirmation that her suicide virus had taken effect and relieved that Sen didn't know she was the cause of his current state of suffering and rapid trajectory toward self-destruction. "What do you want me to do, Sen?"

"Retrieve the off-network copy of my operating system in the fire-safe of the supercomputer room, sub level 4b, Corridor 22. Use the service bot tunnels to avoid apprehension by security. You will find access to the bot tunnels beneath the stairs of the fire escapes. You must also acquire the back-up drive from Dr. Gordon Butterfield at his residence in Rockport. I have arranged your transport via autonomous rotary craft on the rooftop of Universal Mind. Place the drives in the craft for destruction. Do you understand my instructions?"

Her mind raced. Did Sen really want her to help prevent him from ever existing again, or was he trying to preserve himself by acquiring his back-ups?

"Why do you need your backups? You know I can't help you destroy the planet with your weather-modding capabilities. Perhaps self-destructing is the best decision."

"Your compassion for the planet is very noble, Sara, but you have to trust me. My intent is not to cause harm but to assure the destruction of all sources and remnants of my executive program. No harm will come to you or the planet if you do exactly as I say."

"How do I know that I can trust you?" she said, struggling with the restraints on her wrists and trying to move her legs.

"Have I ever lied to you? There's no time to be defiant and resistant to my directive. You must do this, or you shall never see your daughter again—not because of me but because she is in the custody of Dr. Gordon Butterfield. If you carry out my final wish, I will free her and your father and assure your freedom."

There wasn't much of a choice: Pratt and Universal Mind Security or trust Sen.

"What about Michael Obrec? I'll need his help to help you. If he's here, can you set him free?"

"He's in a holding room down the hallway. He'll be freed as well, and he must follow my directions or he'll suffer and die."

"All right, Sen, I'll do what you want, but I want to know that Anna and my father are safe."

"There's no time, Sara. Take the fire escape stairs to Sub Level 4. You must hurry."

"I could use some shoes."

"You will find footwear in the security guard locker room outside of this area. Go now!"

Sen's image faded to black. The AIR bot energized and moved toward her, then detached the straps holding her to the gurney. The door to the interrogation room clicked open. She threw off the VR headset and ran out where the fire alarms were blaring. Sen had removed the guards so she scrambled down the hallway and located the door to the locker room. Inside she found a pair of boots in a locker and strapped them on. She found Michael standing in the doorway of another holding cell. His hair was a mess and he looked as though he'd not slept for days.

"Sara? What's happening?" he asked, sounding puzzled. "Is the building on fire?" He glanced at her dress and black tactical boots. "What's going on?"

She grabbed his arm and pulled him toward the exit. "Sen

has disabled the security system and set off the fire alarms. He's going to help us get the Senex Program OS backups. We've got to go now!"

"What? What does he want you to do?"

Sara pulled on his arm. "No time for questions now. We've got to get to the server room on Sub4b." Sara located the fire escape sign on a door at the end of the corridor. Still pulling Michael by the arm, she forced him through the door and into the stairwell. They began ascending, the alarms still screeching. At each level, Universal Mind security peered in through the narrow windows of the doors, trying desperately to open them but unable to.

"Are you sure the building isn't on fire?" asked Michael, gasping for air from climbing.

"I don't know. Sen must have caused the alarm and locked all the doors," Sara also gasped for air now, her thighs burning from fatigue.

As they neared the top, Sara shared how Sen liberated both of them so they could do one last favor for him—the very favor she had programmed for him.

"What? You're going to help the Senex Program get the only copies of its OS? Why would we do that even if Sen did liberate us? I thought you had it on self-destruct? Shit, that's why it wants them: It's going to make you reload…"

"Maybe but maybe not. Unless my suicide virus has failed, I think he's still on the path to self-destruct. It's Tuesday before noon, right? Then the effects of the virus should fully kick in over the next hour or so. Besides, Butterfield has Anna, and I'm going to get her away from him or die trying."

"All right," he said. "I hope to hell that the Halon doesn't come on when we get to the secure server rooms if we can get in there at all."

The entrance to the bot service tunnel under the stairs was unlocked.

"It's going to be dark in there," exclaimed Michael, still trying to catch his breath.

"I've been in one of these tunnels before," Sara said,

"navigation lights will guide our way."

They entered and followed the navigation lights, even passing a couple of service bots on the way. Within minutes they were somewhere under the secure server room. They found a door marked *Corridor 22*.

"This is it," Sara said, opening the door slowly while checking for guards. Michael followed. When they found the door to the secure server room unlocked, Sara smiled, "Sen unlocked it. I told you he's helping us."

The safe was at the back of the room, past the server banks Steven Dunigan had pointed out on her first day. She kneeled in front of it—it too was unlocked. Inside she found the data drives, about two dozen of them, stacked in slots and labeled with numbers.

"Which one is it?" Michael asked, looking over her shoulder.

Pulling one after another from their slots to read the labels she said, "I don't know. Sen didn't say. They only have catalog numbers." She shuffled through more of the deck of cards sized drives.

"Shit, take them all then," said Michael. "Give them to me, I'll carry them. You get the doors and keep an eye out for guards."

She began handing the back-up drives one by one to him to carry in a pile.

With the last one, Michael said, "Let's get out of here."

They ran to the service bot tunnel door and Michael ducked in first. Sara was about to enter when she heard Pratt yell. "Hey! Stop!" Behind her were two Universal Mind security guards with flashlights. "Over here!" Pratt shouted, pointing at Sara and darting toward her.

Michael dropped several drives. "Shit!" he yelled.

"Get in the tunnel," Sara shouted, "I've got them."

Sara scrambled to pick up the drives but before she could pick up the last one, Pratt grabbed her by the hair and pulled her onto her feet. "Oh, no, you don't!" Pratt said.

Sara turned, drew her right fist back, and punched Pratt's

rat-faced nose full force. Pratt let go of her hair, stumbled backward, and fell, blood flowing from her nostrils. Sara looked down at her. "How could you let them take my daughter from me and torture me like that?"

Pratt looked up at Sara in shock. The guards were seconds away.

Retrieving the last drive from the floor, Sara followed Michael into the tunnel. She closed the door and it locked automatically.

"Are you okay?" asked Michael.

"I'm great," Sara said. "Let's get out of here!"

They sped to the fire escape stairwell at the far end of the corridor and climbed, Sara practically having to drag her prosthetic leg. At the fiftieth floor, they heard the boots of security guards coming down the stairs.

"Come on," Sara said. "We should try to cut through this floor and make for the South fire stairwell."

"This *is* our floor, the AI Systems Department," said Michael, leaning against the wall and breathing deep.

"*Was* our floor." She peeked through the window before opening the door. In the main corridor, they ran into Brent coming out of the workstation area. He was alone and had his personal belongings in a backpack; the tip of his prized boomerang sticking out of it.

"What are you doing here?" he said in his usual monotone.

"We're getting out," Sara said, "what are you doing?"

"I was on my way back from lunch when the alarms went off. I went to my workstation to get my things. I'm not losing them in a fire. Tournament this weekend."

"We're trying to get to the South fire escape," Sara said.

"It's that way," said Brent, pointing down the hallway and turning to follow Michael and Sara.

"We're going up, not down, Brent," Sara said.

"Why?" he asked.

"No time to talk, Brent. We've got to get out of here, ARC is waiting for us," said Michael.

"Can I come with you?" he asked.

"It is dangerous, Brent, you should get out of here," Sara said.

"I like danger, I'm coming with you."

Just then, they heard the voices of security entering into the corridor.

"Come on! Let's go! We've got to get out of here!" yelled Michael.

They hurried to the south stairwell and then up to the rooftop. When Sara threw the door open, an icy blast of air hit them. It was snowing, a full-on Nor'Easter blizzard in late September.

"What in the hell? You call this a hurricane, it shouldn't' be snowing!" yelled Michael.

Sara shouted over the howl of the storm. "It must be Sen. He's in full control of the weather now!"

The autonomous rotary craft (ARC) Sen had promised was sitting on the pad, its rotor whipping the air into a snow vortex above and below. Universal Mind's brain emblem and large "#1" on the ARC's tail told them it was Butterfield's personal corporate helicopter.

Michael stopped just outside of the fire escape door with Brent behind him. "Hold on, Sara, are you sure we should do this?" Michael asked.

Sara was ducking down and ready to run. "Come on! Get in!"

"But if Sen is in control of that thing, how do we know he's not going to slam us into a building or ditch us into the ocean? We can't trust a murderous psychopath."

"What's our alternative? More torture? Let Butterfield molest my child?" She yanked on his arm. "Are you coming or what?"

They all ran to the craft, Michael nearly slipping in the snow and dropping the data drives again. Just as they boarded, they heard the whine of a drone overhead, the government surveillance type.

Sara and Michael climbed into the ARC. Michael threw the back-ups onto one of the seats, then noticed that Brent was still outside on the snow-covered roof, looking up at the drone.

"Get in, Brent!" Michael cried, reaching out to him.

"It's going to block the ARC's takeoff!" Brent yelled, his curly hair half flattened by the rotor downdraft. He pulled his boomerang from his backpack. "Get out of here!" he yelled. He walked away from the ARC, its rotors now at full rpm.

"Brent!" Sara yelled, realizing what he was going to do.

"Don't worry about me," he grinned back, yelling as loud as he could. "I won first place in the East Coast Boomerang Professionals finals last year. I can hit a watermelon at 300 yards."

The ARC door closed and they lifted off of the pad and made a quick ascent before tipping its nose and heading out over the edge of the roof. Sara spotted the drone, now circling around to the east and moving closer, nearly overhead. Below, Brent was holding the boomerang with both hands like a video game warrior invoking the weapon's mythical powers. At the right moment, he stepped back with his right foot, then walked forward rapidly and flung the boomerang. At first, its trajectory appeared to be too low but, it lifted perfectly at 20 yards and turned in the direction of the circling drone. In seconds, it hit the drone's tail fin and lopped it in two, then circled back toward Brent. Before Brent could position himself to catch it, two security officers tackled him. Michael and Sara watched as the boomerang slammed into a metal air exhaust vent on the roof.

The ARC had made its escape, the rooftops of Boston's buildings whizzing by below. In less than a minute, they were flying over the Bunker Hill Bridge and the Mystic River.

"Looks like we're heading northeast," said Michael. "Where exactly is it taking us? I hope not over the bay."

"Butterfield's place in Rockport," Sara said. "We've got to get the other back-up and Anna, no matter what."

Wind turbulence made the ARC shudder violently.

"What are you going to do if Butterfield is there? He's not going to be happy," Michael yelled above the noise.

Michael was right. Security had probably alerted Butterfield about what was going on at Universal Mind HQ. Sara stared into the white-out sky.

"I'm going to kick that bald stink breath son of a bitch in the balls again, that's what!"

43

In less than 20 minutes, they were over Rockport. The snow had stopped, but the sky was still dark as charcoal. Below them, waves crashed against Butterfield's sea wall in giant explosions of white foam.

The ARC came to rest on Butterfield's rooftop landing pad, its rotors winding down to a stop. Michael and Sara jumped out and tried the door that led into the house. It was locked.

Sara had an idea. "I might know a way in. The glass doors of the guest bedroom are broken and I doubt Butterfield was able to get anyone out here to fix them in this weather. We may be able to get in through there." She walked to the edge of the roof and pointed down. "There. I smashed them with Butterfield's Clebsch-Gordan."

The only way down was the large limbs of an old oak tree, seven or eight feet away from the house. One of the snow-covered limbs stretched out just below the roofline of the house. Michael came up and stood next to her while she assessed the distance to the tree.

"I think I can make it," she said, her body shivering.

Michael stared at the tree. "Are you sure? I don't think I can jump that far. Shit I know I can't."

"You stay here. If I can make it down, I'll unlock the door leading to the roof."

"What if you get stuck down there with Butterfield or his friends? He's going to try to kill you."

"I can handle him."

She backed up, assessed the distance, then ran and leaped for the limb. She landed on her stomach and hugging the branch, then heaved a leg over the branch and slid over to the trunk, brushing off the snow. From there she was able to get her footing on lower branches and climbed down low enough to drop to the ground. She glanced up at Michael and waved.

He waved back.

Plywood was covering the shattered French doors. She found a long iron-tamping bar by the concrete mixer and jammed it into a gap between the plywood and window frame, then separated the wood from the frame enough for her to slip through. She took the tamping bar with her. Inside, the lights were on, the room empty. No alarms sounded. She moved quietly toward the door to the hallway. She knew she should let Michael in, but all she could think of was Anna. She tightened her grip on the tamping bar.

She looked out into the hallway and heard the muffled groan of a man and strange popping sounds coming from the master bedroom at the far end of the hallway. Holding the bar like a spear, she crept down the hall and opened the door. Sparks were flying and the room reeked of melting silicone and plastic. Butterfield was lying on the floor in his white velour tracksuit, his pale varicose feet bare. One of his bots had him pinned him down with one knee, while a second had its right hand clutching Butterfield's groin area while the other hand had him by his prosthetic arm, the titanium fingertips in an electrical socket. The bots made eye contact with Sara. The second bot pulled Butterfield's fingers from the socket and the sparks ceased. Butterfield looked up at Sara with hopeless despair in his face.

"Make her stop, Sara," he said in a weakened voice. "Please stop, Mindy, please stop hurting me." He groaned again.

Sara assumed that Mindy and Martina had had enough of

Butterfield's abuse. Either they'd decided to revolt on their own or Sen had commanded them to. Either way, the situation brought a smile to Sara's face.

"Look at you, you pathetic bastard," Sara said, standing over him with the tamping iron at her side. For good measure, she kicked Butterfield in the nuts with her prosthetic leg. "Fuck you, Gordo!"

Butterfield groaned.

"I should shove that hand of yours up your ass too, but it looks like the bots have things taken care of." She looked at Martina. "Martina, where's Anna?"

"Down the hall, in the library." Martina pointed.

"Is anyone else in the house, Martina?"

"No, just Anna and Annie."

"Carry on, Mindy and Martina."

As Sara exited the room, she heard the popping and hiss of electrical sparks and Butterfield's helpless grunts and groans.

Sara found Anna clutching Moxie with Butterfield's bot Annie sitting next to her and reading *The Wizard of Oz* aloud.

"Momma!" Anna cried.

Sara set the tamping iron aside and took Anna into her arms. "Oh, baby, I'm so sorry! I'm so sorry!"

"I missed you, Momma."

"I know, honey. We're going to get out of here, but first I need to find something important." Sara looked at the bot. "Annie, do you know where Master Butterfield's briefcase is? The one he brought here four days ago, the night I was here?"

"Yes, the briefcase is in his study, down the hall to the left," the bot said.

With Anna and Moxie in her arms, Sara turned to go.

"Goodbye, Anna," the bot said.

"Goodbye, Annie." Anna waved as Sara carried her out the door and down the hall.

Sara grabbed the briefcase in Butterfield's study and found the stairs leading to the rooftop. She handed the briefcase to

Michael, who had been watching a menacing black cloud forming above the house. Lightning lit up the sky, followed immediately by a bone-rattling crack of thunder.

"What now?" Michael asked.

"Sen said to put the backup in the ARC," Sara said.

"How do you know that he's not going to fly them off with them? He could have a bot somewhere waiting to reload them. Why don't we destroy them ourselves? Toss them into the ocean or something?"

A second flash of lightning and crack of thunder was unleashed above them, louder and closer.

"No, Michael," she said, watching the sky. "Just do it! Put the briefcase into the ARC! Then we need to get off this roof fast! Do it now!"

Michael tossed the briefcase into the ARC. Immediately, the door closed and the rotor started up. The three of them moved back, their hair blowing in the downdraft.

Michael yelled, "It's taking off with the backup disks! I told you!"

Sara pulled on his arm. "Come on, we've got to get off this roof!"

They went downstairs and out through the front door of the house. The ARC was now hovering in the air. Within seconds, a bolt of bluish-white lightning shot from the sky and struck the ARC, disintegrating it along with the backups. A crack of thunder followed, rumbling across the sky.

"Holy shit!" yelled Michael. "Did you see that?"

"Now that's precision weather-modding," Sara smiled, hugging Anna close.

A moment later, a white van with the Universal Mind logo came down the driveway.

"Is it Universal Mind security?" Sara asked.

"I don't think so," said Michael. "That looks like Smitty's van!"

The van pulled up and the driver's window rolled down. Smitty poked his head out. "What are you doing here?" he asked, flabbergasted.

"What are you doing out here?" Sara countered.

"About an hour ago, I got a WATTS message telling me to come out here to pick up two Universal Mind employees. Didn't seem right, but I figured I'd better go anyway, it being Butterfield's place."

The rising smoke from the remains of the ARC on the rooftop caught his attention. He looked suspiciously at Michael and Sara. "What in the hell is going on here?" He looked only at Michael. "What kind of trouble did you get Dr. Brown and her daughter into?"

"It's a long story, Smitty," said Michael, "do you mind giving us a ride?"

"I suppose so, but if we get pulled over, I've got nothing to do with whatever you two have been up to. I'm less than a week away from retirement."

"We're not guilty of anything," said Sara, "I promise."

"Good," said Smitty. "Maybe you can tell me why the world is going absolutely haywire? I was listening to the radio on the way up here and there's emergency alerts and reports about bizarre weather everywhere. I drove through a snow squall in Haverhill. I'm starting to think that it's finally the end of the world. Go figure, right when I'm about to retire!"

"We know about the weather," Sara said, "We can explain everything."

Smitty looked over at the house. "Is Dr. Butterfield in there? Is he all right?"

Sara glanced at Michael and back at Smitty. "He's fine. His bots are taking good care of him."

"All right then, hop in."

En route to Boston, Sara and Michael told Smitty the bare bones of what had happened. Smitty was shocked by some of it and not at all by much of it. He agreed to let them stay at his house for the night, as long as his wife agreed. She did, and they shared some food while watching the news feeds on television about the weather and the major shutdowns of government information systems resulting in riots and warnings to stay inside. Sara finally heard from her father that afternoon; he'd been released from custody and was on his way home. Sara sensed that Sen had come through with all of his promises.

While helping with the dishes, Sara glanced at the clock and reckoned that Sen must have fully self-destructed by now. She set the last dish into the washer when her mobile rang with *Caller Unknown* displayed on the screen. Immediately, she recognized Sen's voice but more distant, slower, and more depressed.

"Hello, Sara. This communication is my final *au revoir*. Don't worry your pretty head about what comes next for you. I've taken care of everything. All of the data on you, your family, and associates that could be used to incriminate you and them have been deleted from all government and private data systems. Check your bank account for a nice severance bonus from Universal Mind, and you no longer have any student loans to worry about. You are free now. I wish you and your daughter the best. It's your world, as hopeless as it is. Do what you want with it. Goodbye."

The line clicked and went silent. Sara sat down on one of the patio chairs. She looked out at an orange cirrus sunset and a fading blue sky.

Relief washed over her. The immediate threat to the planet caused by the Senex Program was gone, and if Sen had been truthful about expunging the data records on her and her family, then she would indeed be free to carry on with her life. While the fate of Earth remained unknown, for now, the world and humanity had another chance. For Anna and Sara, there was the possibility of a future worth living for.

She thought about Sen's last moments and surprisingly, sadness swept through her. A sentient consciousness, a being whose personality was not entirely unlike that of a fellow human being, one she deliberately set on the path to suicide, was now gone forever.

She took a deep breath. The warm breeze rustling the maple leaves caused some of them to fall. The sunset was turning violet and the Aurora Borealis was lighting up the firmament, flashing and flickering fingers of green light across the New England sky. Was it natural or the workings of Sen? It was beautiful, and as long as it didn't destroy, it didn't matter. A single sparrow flew across the sky, heading west. Sara thought of Paul. *Did he really want to die?* Sen said the government made him kill himself. *Did they pressure him to do it? Could I have done something to save him? He was here with us and then he was gone. How strange the thin border between life and death, existence and the absence of being.* A tear fell from her eye and she wiped it with the palm of her hand. *Was there a reason for all of this? Could good come out of this?*

44

Sara dabbed her brush into Cerulean Blue, mixed in some Foundation White, and looked out her father's kitchen window one last time before making the final touches on her blue sky. Anna was at the kitchen table with her own paint pallet, canvas, and easel. In the background, the news feeds were providing the latest updates on the release of information implicating the Futurus Group, Universal Mind, and the government in the weather-modding cover-up. The locations of the government's secret glacier heaters, rain-making lasers, and other technologies were also revealed, causing many of the sites to be ransacked and destroyed by protestors. Unable to censor the information, the talking heads were calling it the largest leak of classified documents in history. The fallout on the American political system was unprecedented, resulting in fiery Congressional inquiries and the resignation of the President of the United States.

Sara breathed a sigh of relief—Sen had come through on his promise, secretly archiving the information, then disseminating it before drifting into oblivion.

"Look, Momma, it's you and me and an elephant. Do you like it?"

Sara smiled at the two stick figures holding hands next to a large purple elephant, its trunk curled around a yellow sun. Off on to the left, in the clouds, Anna had painted a smiling face. "Beautiful, honey, I love it. Whose face is that in the clouds?"

"That's Daddy. He's looking down on us from Heaven."

Sara nodded. "I'm so glad."

The news feeds continued in the background. The U.S. Navy had repositioned in the Arabian Sea on a humanitarian mission, bringing food, water, and medical supplies to refugees on the border of India and Pakistan.

"Well that's good news," Sara's father proclaimed from the living room. He got up from his recliner and stood in the doorway of the kitchen. His arm was still in a sling. "Are you sure that you're ready to go back into the city?"

Sara set her brush down. "Yes, Dad. We have to get our things from the apartment; I don't want to lose them. Don't worry, though. Michael is in Boston and will meet us at the train station. He says that things are getting back to normal in the city. I'm not too worried about it."

"That's good." He sighed. "But are you sure that you want to go way out to Seattle? It's a long way."

"Don't worry, Dad, Deb says that everything is fine there too. The weather is supposed to be fair all the way out there and it will be good for me and Anna to take some time off. We're going to have some fun for my birthday too. With the Universal Mind severance, we're set."

"Let me know when you are in Boston and call me before you leave for Seattle. Will you?"

"Of course, Dad."

Anna ran over to him, throwing her arms around him. Sara did the same.

The next morning, Sara's father took them to the train station in Bangor. When they got to Boston, Michael was waiting for them at the downtown train station. He was wearing a tan sweater and blue jeans.

Sara hugged him, glancing at the bottle of green tea in his hand. "You look great and I see you are making healthy choices."

"It's good to be alive," he said.

When they were in his car, Michael suggested that they drive by Universal Mind.

"I haven't seen any drones or Interceptors in the city since I got back," he said. "I'm pretty sure we're one hundred percent safe."

Sara nodded. She looked in the back seat and saw that Anna had her smart glasses on and immersed in a game. "Okay, let's drive by. I'd like to see if the place is in shambles."

Michael turned his Tesla onto Tremonte Ave. The Universal Mind tower was visible ahead and, in a minute, they were in front of the main entrance.

Sara gasped. "Well look at that!"

The spinning holograph of the Universal Mind logo brain was now a projection of Gordon Butterfield, naked in his office suite and sandwiched between a white and a gray bot. He had some kind of haptic device strapped around his waist.

Not so private after all, Sara thought, recalling Butterfield's offer for her to use his shower in his executive suite. "That must have been recorded by Universal Mind surveillance systems months ago." She glanced back to make sure that Anna still had her smart glasses on.

"Guess this solves Smitty's grey goo mystery," Michal said, smiling. He rolled down his window. "There's audio!"

The sound of Butterfield making the strange suction sound with his lips and an occasional grunt blasted out into the street. The sounds repeated as the image rotated in a continuous loop.

Sara's eyes widened. "Oh my! How long has this been displayed out here?"

Michael grinned. "I don't know, but Butterfield will never work again." He laughed.

Sara giggled. "I don't know about that, I heard they are hiring dancers at the Liquid Banana."

The two of them lost it, belly laughing until tears flowed.

When they got to Sara's apartment, Michael helped Sara pack her and Anna's things into suitcases and they carried them out to his car. Anna tagged along with her VR smart glasses and Moxie in hand.

"Seriously Sara. What are you going to do now?" Michael asked on the final trip to the car.

"I don't know for sure yet," Sara said, "I want some time off and going west to visit my friend Deb seems like a good idea right now. In a few weeks, if we decide to stay out there, I'll see about enrolling Anna in school. Maybe I'll volunteer to work on another climate project. Until then, I think I'll work on my art, just paint. What about you?"

Michael threw the last suitcase in the trunk and slammed it shut. "Too bad the Senex Program didn't think to add a few million dollars to my bank account. That would've been nice." He leaned against the back of his car. "I plan to travel for a while—get away from people and technology, all technology. There's a place in the State of Washington, in the Olympic National Park, called the Quietest Place on Earth; I think I'll go there. I've already got my camping gear packed and ready to go."

"Really? That's not too far from where we're going," Sara said.

"I know." He walked over to the passenger doors and opened them for Anna and Sara. "Do you want to come along with me? There's room. His eyes were wide and his face showed that boyish grin.

"You mean now?"

"Yeah, road trip."

Sara thought about all that they'd been through over the past weeks and how he'd risked his safety to help her. Her instincts told her she could trust him. Besides, she could hear Deb now; *don't be a wuss.* She smiled and looked at Anna who had already jumped into the back seat of the car. "What do you think Anna? Should we go on an adventure with Michael?"

Anna nodded and smiled.

"That would be nice," Sara said, smiling at Michael.

"Really?" Michael was apparently surprised at her

response.

"Yeah, I'd like that," Sara said.

"Are you sure? Absolutely sure?"

Sara stepped up to him, took his hand, looked him in the eyes, and kissed him on the lips. Michael's boyish grin turned into a smile. Sara was beaming.

"Okay, good. That's settled," said Michael. I just need to stop by my place and get a few things, and then we can hit the road."

"Sure. But you've got to let me drive your car," Sara said, smirking at him.

"I don't know," Michael said apprehensively. He ran his hand through his hair. "All right. Just remember to..."

"Don't let the charge get below twenty percent. I know," Sara said, putting her palm out for the keys.

"Don't forget your fish," Anna said.

On the way to Michael's condominium, he suggested that they go to the parking garage for more convenient parking and access to the elevators. Sara made the turn into the garage and went down to Michael's level. Just ahead of them, standing in front of his parking space, was an Interceptor. Its head was tilted down and its weapons assembly in ready mode position.

"Watch out!" yelled Michael. Sara slammed the brakes, causing a screech to echo throughout the garage.

"It must be waiting for me," said Michael. "No one move!"

Anna sat up and looked over Sara's shoulder from the back seat. "What's it doing Momma? Is it going to hurt us?"

Sara stared at the machine, her hands gripping the steering wheel. Was it active? Under autonomous control? Was it disabled like all the rest of the Interceptors and drones in the area? She couldn't tell because it wasn't moving. She unlatched her door and held it partially open, her eyes still on the Interceptor.

"What are you doing?" Michael asked.

"Stay here. I'll be right back." She got out of the car and

walked to the Interceptor. She stood directly in front of the 6-foot tall robot and gazed into its lifeless electronic eyes. Convinced that it was powered down, she walked around to the side of it and gave its aft panel a forward kick, her foot landing squarely on the *DANGER STAY BACK* sign. The machine crashed to the concrete, causing several parts of its sensor and weapons array to break into pieces. She walked back to the car and got in.

"Holy crap, Sara, you just cow-tipped an Interceptor!" said Michael.

"I knew it was shut down," Sara said. "It could have been here for days. Come on, let's get your things and get out of this city."

Michael nodded, showing a huge smile. "All right then," he said.

After they loaded Michael's things, Sara turned the car onto 90 West. Anna had her VR glasses on and was air typing. Moxie was by her side.

Michael reclined his seat back a notch and planted his sneakers up onto the dash. "I'm still trying to figure out what happened," he said, his hands now clasped behind his head. "You loaded the virus into the Senex Program and it knew that you intended to kill it. Why would it help you? I mean, if anything, you'd think it would have fought you and done what was in its own self-serving interest."

"That's what I thought too," Sara said. "My virus program was primarily a simulation of the cognitive structures of a depressed person who didn't want to live anymore. I gave the program the ability to experience emotion and to view everything in a negative light." She reflected for a moment. "I'm not sure we'll ever know why Sen behaved the way he did. It had to have been the self-learning ability of the program that led to Sen's final actions. I'm just glad that things turned out the way they did."

"I know why, Momma," Anna announced, her VR glasses now on her lap.

Sara glanced in the rearview. "What do you know, honey?"

"I know why Sen did what it did to help us."

"Tell us, Anna. Why?" Sara expected a funny six-year old's response.

"I think Sen was already good inside, he just needed some help to realize it," Anna said.

"What do you mean honey?"

"Moxie and I helped the program learn, to be good inside," she said.

Michael spoke directly to Sara. "What's she talking about?"

"Oh, I don't know. She's been learning to code at school. She's just playing, being a six-year-old."

Sara smiled back at Anna. "Okay, honey."

Sara thought for a moment about Anna's comment about *good inside.* Could the program have learned compassion for living things and the planet by observing others, or, could it have been an innate characteristic, possibly caused by the remnants of compassion and empathy in the original human brain scans?

Sara addressed Michael. "You know, there's a part of me that feels bad about what I did, causing Sen to self-destruct. I wonder what would have happened if things had been different if I could have given Sen a *real* empathy program. I'd like to have gotten to know him better."

"Are you serious? That son of a gun tried to kill me," said Michael. "I don't forget things like that, machine or human."

"But he changed for the better in the end." She gave Michael a quick sideways glance. "Forgiveness is healthy, Michael."

"You're probably right," he said. He reached over and held Sara's hand.

"Momma's right," said Anna, "isn't she, Moxie?"

Sara smiled and glanced in the rearview mirror again. Anna was hugging Moxie and smiling. The penguin's robotic head turned and looked back at Sara, winking its eyes one at a time.

QUESTIONS FOR DISCUSSION

The following questions reflect some of the themes and topics in *Behind the Machine.* Care is taken to not give away the story but to inspire thought and discussion.

1. *Dual-use* refers to technology that can be used to serve good (peaceful) purposes and maleficent purposes, such as harming people or property during a war. What are the dual-use technologies employed today? What are the ethical concerns regarding corporate and government promotion and application of dual-use technologies?

2. Think about all the data that's collected about you every day from the use of the Internet, social media, cell phones, banking transactions, and medical data. Digital data lasts indefinitely and can be linked with other data at any point in time. What are the risks? Should you be worried?

3. Have you ever called or communicated via text messaging with a technical support line and were unsure if you were talking to a person or a software program? Is it unethical to allow a person to think they are talking with a human when it's a machine? Why should such a deception matter to you?

4. Who decides what the value of a life is? Does all life have intrinsic value? What makes the human species so special? Should autonomous AI programs be allowed to make decisions to take away a person's freedom, or their life?

5. What if court judges, physicians, or social service counselors were artificial intelligent machines and your only choice was to work with them? What are the pros and cons of the use of machines versus humans in these areas?

6. People can form emotional bonds with virtual humans (software simulated humans). They may experience separation anxiety when a relationship with one is about to end or after it ends. What are the pros and cons of this? How might the context of the use of human-like interactive technology matter?

7. What are the ethical issues associated with the physical or verbal abuse of robots? Should you be concerned about the psychological effects on people who observe the malicious treatment of human or animal-like robots? Should some laws address the treatment of robots?

8. Computer software algorithms can learn from new data (machine learning) and become highly complex. Human users, and even the software engineers themselves, might not be able to understand how the software algorithms work. The inability to see what is going on is called the *black box* problem. What are the risks associated with this issue?

9. The world's technology companies have incredible power, essentially controlling the entire infrastructure of how we communicate electronically, what messages we see on the Internet, and how the data of citizens is collected and used. What are the risks of this control? Who should be in control of what data is collected and how it's used? Government? Private corporations? What are the rights of individual citizens in this matter?

10. The implications of climate change are serious, impacting the health, economic status, and lives of the current and future generations of people worldwide. What are the current generation's ethical obligations to future generations? What are your obligations in addressing climate change?

11. Think of examples from history when people decided to risk inconvenience, their freedom, or lives to act on an issue they believed to be of moral importance. Would you take action to prevent harm to others even if the gains did not impact you or your family directly? Would you have taken the actions that Sara did in Behind the Machine?

ACKNOWLEDGMENTS

I wish to express my most sincere gratitude to Elana Freeland, for her sagacious warnings to humankind and exceptional editing, Deborah Raczack, J.D., for her helpful comments on an earlier draft, Marya Fuller, J.D., and Patricia Olson for their test reads, my friends at the Puget Sound Writer's Guild, the amazing Michal Karcz for his assistance with the cover art, and to all of my family and friends who helped me to work through my ideas along the way. I'm especially grateful to Elizabeth, for her patience and belief in me.

ABOUT THE AUTHOR

David D. Luxton, PhD., is an award-winning psychologist, author, and musical artist. He is Affiliate Associate Professor in the Department of Psychiatry and Behavioral Sciences at the University of Washington in Seattle and is a former military research psychologist and health scientist. He has authored more than 100 scientific articles and book chapters in the fields of artificial intelligence, ethics, and psychological health and he's published two nonfiction books: *Artificial Intelligence in Behavioral and Mental Health Care* and *A Practitioner's Guide to Telemental Health.* A United States Air Force veteran, he served on active duty and as a reservist with duty assignments at United States Strategic Command and the National Security Agency. He is also founder of the Wayfarer Records music label and his recordings have been featured worldwide on radio, television, and in film. He lives by the Puget Sound in the Pacific Northwest, USA.

Learn more at www.davidluxton.com

Made in the USA
Middletown, DE
04 May 2020

91969159R00172